THE UNRESTRAINED

THE UNRESTRAINED

SKHARR DEATHEATER™ SERIES BOOK 02

MICHAEL ANDERLE

LMBPN Publishing
PMB 196, 2540 South Maryland Pkwy
Las Vegas, NV 89109

First US edition, November 2020
ebook ISBN: 978-1-64971-322-3
Paperback ISBN: 978-1-64971-323-0

THE UNRESTRAINED TEAM

Thanks to our JIT Team:

Jeff Goode
Rachel Beckford
Dorothy Lloyd
Kelly O'Donnell
Chris Changala
John Ashmore
Jackey Hankard-Brodie
Diane L. Smith
Larry Omans
Angel LaVey
Paul Westman
Peter Manis
Jeff Eaton

If I've missed anyone, please let me know!

Editor
SkyHunter Editing Team

To Family, Friends and
Those Who Love
To Read.
May We All Enjoy Grace
To Live The Life We Are
Called.

*— **Michael***

CHAPTER ONE

On days like this one, he felt like he would never be able to show his face in public ever again.

The engagement had done a great deal to restore his reputation. Those who had once whispered that he was still hurting from a beating delivered at his bride's behest had mostly ceased to speak of it. Many seemed to have decided that he would not marry a woman who would do such a thing—either to his person or his reputation—yet rumors persisted.

Lord Tulius feared that these would hound him until the day he died, or at least until the bruises healed. He felt that was taking forever, so it provided little encouragement.

He still winced when he moved his arms, and his physician had told him that the broken bones would take some time to heal. Salves and even face paints had done little to conceal the damage.

"Toad-fucking barbarians," he whispered under his breath and sipped the hot tisane that had been poured for him. Few establishments could make his preferred beverages perfectly in the city. Only one, in fact, did not disappoint. Even his servants struggled to heat the water to the correct temperature to avoid burning the delicate dragon flower petals.

But the small shop, appropriately named the Dragon Flower, was one of the few that catered specifically to the tastes of those in the city who were selective about what they put in their bodies.

It was also known for other things, such as staff who were known to not wag their tongues about what was said and heard inside the establishment. Such a reputation was sorely underrated in this city.

"More tea, sir?"

The demure voice belonged to a woman who clearly didn't work at the Dragon Flower, mostly since she referred to it as tea and not by the proper name of tisane. He wasn't entirely sure what the significance was, but there was still relevance to it for some reason.

She was at least dressed like the other serving women who worked in the establishment. The long, flowing robes seemed to emphasize a curvaceous form rather than hide it, but unlike the employees, her face and her hair were hidden behind a veil.

He had a feeling that her choice of attire was meant to distract from her features so all who saw her—whether they were men or women—focused on the body that was fully covered but in such a way that one's imagination ran rampant.

Even so, he was a newly engaged man and needed to hold his appetite in check. Not only that, if what he'd heard about this woman was true, there was no point in risking his life by disrespecting her boundaries.

"No, thank you," he said finally, having determined that she was the woman he had come to meet. "But if you would like to share mine, I would be more than happy to oblige."

She had insisted that he speak a predetermined phrase to enable her to identify him correctly.

It had the desired effect and she sat on the other side of the table and studied him closely. Her crystal-blue eyes could barely be seen behind the gauzy veil, but it felt like they dug into the back of his mind to divine all his thoughts and discover everything there was to know about him.

It was an uncomfortable sensation, and Tulius shifted in his seat and looked away after only a few seconds, unable to return her gaze.

"You summoned me here for a reason, Lord Tulius."

"No names."

"Of course."

"And yes, I did summon you for a reason. The whispers have spoken of your connections to those who might be willing to take care of a troublesome character."

He could see her smirk, even behind the mask. "Do you have difficulty spelling out your true intent?"

His eyebrows raised. "I—"

"Do not respond. I know that lords and ladies find it uncomfortable to openly discuss that which you find overly commonplace. We shall consider dealing with this difficult character who plagues you so much—for the right price, of course."

"We?"

"Those I speak to. I would never engage in such a delicate matter myself, after all."

Tulius nodded. "Indeed. I assumed those capable of such acts would want as much distance between themselves and those who would require their services. What kind of price would they charge for those services?"

The woman tilted her head. "That would depend on who you would like taken care of."

It was odd how the way she said it stripped away all the distance he wanted to put between himself and the actual action. It annoyed him, which he supposed was the intention of her pointed use of the term.

"A mercenary." He sipped his tisane and tried to calm himself. The situation was unfamiliar and set him on edge. He had never done this before, although he had heard of those who had, including members of his family. But acting for himself felt wondrously dangerous, even though he knew he wouldn't put himself in any personal danger.

"There are many mercenaries in this town," the woman replied smoothly and regarded him steadily. "There are even guilds—guilds that protect their members."

"Will that be a problem?"

She leaned forward. "That would depend on which mercenary you had in mind."

He ran his fingers over his clean-shaven cheek, took a deep breath, and shook his head. "Skharr is his name. A piece of dung-eating barbarian shit."

The woman paused, leaned back in her seat, and looked at the table. Her long, delicate fingers traced the marble tabletop as she considered his statement.

"Skharr?" she asked finally. "Skharr DeathEater?"

"I assume so." Tulius waved his hand dismissively. "The surnames of the dead do not interest me."

"They should," she replied. "You do know of the DeathEater Clan, yes?"

"Barbarian legends, easily dismissed."

"Barbarians? Yes. Legends? No. You remember what he did to you and your men. Unarmed and on his own. If you're interested in legends, you should hear the one in which he delved a dungeon on his own and came back alive—and wealthy. And there's the legend of how those who tried to stop him never returned."

His expression scrunched into a scowl. "Do not speak to me as if I were a child."

"Then stop acting like one."

He took a deep breath and tried to ignore the insult. "Well then, if legends prove true, you have more of a reason to kill him. Avenge the fallen and enrich yourself, whichever you happen to choose. Perhaps even I can find a way to profit from this little arrangement if you're willing to share what you find."

The woman sighed and shook her head. "I'm not sure you understand. The man has become something of a legend during his short time in our city. Those who would choose to kill him would either be incredibly stupid or incredibly expensive."

"Why the stupid? Are they cheap?"

"Yes, and for good reason. You might find one who is lucky enough to stumble into a kill, but the likeliest scenario sees them giving the DeathEater your name instead. I assume you wouldn't want him to discover your involvement in his assassination, yes? Although I suppose the cheap ones might not want to know who is hiring them or even make assumptions, but are you willing to take the chance that the barbarian might retaliate?"

"That is assuming he survives the attempt, of course."

"Yes. Assuming he lives."

"What are you, his contract issuer?"

"It is in my interest that all who know about my involvement survive their involvement. Explaining the options as clearly as possible helps to ensure that, but you are the one who must decide what path you wish to take."

She made a good point. Skharr had made an impression in their first encounter and Tulius did want to avoid any future impressions that might be made.

He ran his fingers lightly over the still-tender bruises on his face. "Mercenaries are not the choice for me. They have honor codes that might prevent them from killing one of their own. A single assassin, I feel, would be the cheaper and more secure route. One who would not choose to engage the barbarian directly. Poison, I think, would be best, although nothing that acts quickly. I want him to suffer a great deal."

"As you wish. I will make the arrangements and you will hear from me when I have a price."

She bowed her head slightly and studied him closely as he

focused on his tisane. The rich were all the same—arrogant, entitled shits she needed to live with if she wanted to make a living in Verenvan. That didn't mean that she had to like it.

As she exited the tea house, her gaze shifted to either side to make sure no one was following her.

Very few in the city could track her without her being aware of them, and fewer still could keep up with her once she was on the streets.

The flowing dress was discarded, along with her hood and veil, and she tossed them aside as quickly as she could without drawing attention to herself. Beggars and thieves would jump at the chance of the free clothes and successfully hide her tracks.

Her long, rich curls came free as she slipped into a nearby alley and climbed a series of outcroppings that allowed her to reach the top of the building. There, she maintained her balance with each step across the roof with impressive dexterity.

"If I had any investments with Tulius' business, I'd sell them now," she muttered, although she had no one to listen to her except the pigeons that fluttered over the rooftops. "An arrogant prick like that isn't likely to live past the next planting moon."

She stood securely on the edges of the rooftops for a moment before she jumped to the next building, almost as light on her feet as the birds. Still, there was a job to be done and she would ensure that she was paid her percentage for it.

And she would make sure it was one hell of a high percentage.

The Guild Hall was open to visitors from all walks of life, from urchins and thieves to the most elevated in the city. He had even seen the count step into the hall a few times in search of those who would do his will.

Those occurrences were rare, however—rare enough to draw the attention of those who frequented the Hall more often.

The old, bearded man watched as a horse walked through the massive doors. It was white with all the indications of a fine ancestry, mounted by a woman with a similar look about her. Rich red hair flowed over her shoulders, a pleasing contrast to her pale, milky skin, and delicate hands held the reins.

She was followed by a retinue of servants, one of whom guided the beast directly toward him.

Intrigued, he raised his hands from his work and watched as she approached, aware that all the others in the hall were also focused on her progress.

"Guildmaster Pennar?" the servant asked and brought the horse to a halt.

He tugged his beard gently before he folded his massive arms across his chest. "Who wants to know?"

"Are you or not?"

"Fuck off, housemaid."

"Enough!"

The woman's shrill voice carried easily over the din of the hall as she nudged the horse forward until its nose butted the papers on Pennar's desk.

"My name is Lady Tamisen," she continued, her voice now pitched low. "Once you understand why I am here, you will understand why I wish to keep my presence here as discreet as possible."

"You could have done better than to ride in here on a white fucking horse."

"My coming and going anywhere without a retinue would have attracted far more attention, believe me. Now, am I to understand that you are the one to speak to on the matter of arranging a contract?"

Pennar's brows lowered skeptically. "Aye, but too many in the city could do the same."

"Not with the precision I need from you. I wish for work to be passed to a certain barbarian who is a member of the Theros

Guild. He is a recent arrival and one who has made a significant impression since he arrived in the city."

Understanding dawned on the man. "You have work for Skharr?"

"Is there another barbarian in the Theros Guild here?"

Her sharp tone wasn't appreciated but he could at least understand it.

He cleared his throat. "No…no, my lady, there is not."

"So it should be little problem for you to find the correct man, then?"

"I still don't know what you want him to do. Many have sought his services and he's not been the easiest to find of late."

She nodded. "You can tell him I wish to hire him for the same price as Lady Svana did."

"Well, I'll have to consult the archives—"

"No," she interrupted firmly. "Listen to my words and repeat them to him exactly. I wish to pay the same price as Lady Svana did."

Pennar nodded, although he shook his head and hoped his expression was more confused than understanding. He recalled how Skharr had described his encounter with the woman and how he had taken enough coin to pay his tribute to the guild and collected his payment through alternate means.

He doubted that the explanation was common knowledge, or that the woman wanted it to be.

"The same price." He nodded again and cleared his throat. "Understood. But I cannot promise that he will accept the work, only to deliver the message."

The lady reached into a purse at her hip and drew two silver coins from it. "I will undertake the final negotiations with him once we meet, but I believe coin is owed for the guild's cut from his work. Two silvers should cover that, and I'll pay more if that is necessary."

"I still cannot promise that he will accept the work."

"The two coins will be paid to him should he agree to see me at my villa—with no expectations. He can choose to not accept the coins, of course, but should that be the case, I assume they will be returned?"

"Do you find yourself short of silver coins, my lady?"

She sneered. "I have made a habit of not spending any I do not need to. Take heed, I will expect those to be returned to me should Skharr not make an appearance at my villa, yes?"

"Of course, Lady Tamisen."

"I appreciate your cooperation, Master Pennar. As well as your willingness to not tell anyone but Skharr about my intentions." She took three more silver coins from her purse and dropped them onto the table along with the original two.

"Of course, my lady."

The woman smiled, cleared her throat, and adjusted her seat on the saddle. The servants immediately took that as her indication that she wished to leave, and the one at the front turned her horse to start toward the massive doors.

One of the other Theros mercenaries approached his desk. Dozens of gazes followed the entourage through the doors.

It was a rare occurrence but none would pretend that it never happened. Lords and ladies needed the help of mercenaries from time to time, and once it was done, they would either find out once the contract was posted or they wouldn't.

Life moved on, and when the lady was clear of the Hall, they turned their attention to their business.

"Not many ladies around here like that, wouldn't you say?" the Theros mercenary asked, transparently searching for any information on the contract. "What brought her to our doors?"

"A contract. What else?" Pennar collected the coins from the table.

"Not an expensive one. Only five silvers?"

"Folk have killed for less," the guildmaster explained and tugged his beard.

"Will you tell us what it's about?"

"You'll have to see it if it makes it to the contract board, Felix. Exactly like everyone else."

The man snorted. "Ass."

He seemed cheerful enough with the outcome of his probing, however, and Pennar watched him walk away before he took three of the coins—those paid to him for his silence—and slipped them into his pocket before he picked up the other two.

"Fucking barbarians. Never thought I would hope to have more of his like around, but having ten of them would certainly put a dent in the jobs in our particular market, and at a better price too. Oi, boy, get off your ass. You have work to do!"

The boy in question jumped from the barrel he was seated on. He was one of the squires for the Guild Hall and more than useful for running errands around the city.

"You need me, sir?"

"I need you to find Skharr. I doubt he has moved away from the Swilling Mermaid but if he has, the innkeeper will know where more than likely. When you find the fucker, tell him I have work for which he has been specifically requested, got it?"

"Man'll want some coin in his purse to loosen his tongue, you think?"

"It's not likely that I'll give you any coin. Not again. Tell him that if he wants a bribe, he can send someone to me for it. Away with you!"

The boy darted away like he had been stung. It wasn't like the youths to not take what coin they could when they could. Most were drawn from the streets of the city and knew only to take what they could, honor be damned, but he tried to teach them a different way.

Not all would reach the end of the path to be mercenaries themselves, but those who did would make all his efforts worthwhile.

CHAPTER TWO

G odsbedammed, it was morning already.

There were a handful of reasons why he shouldn't have situated himself at an inn so close to the docks. One was the ever-present smell of fish that hung over the establishment that would not leave even if the owner washed it down with lye.

A second was the fact that every morning—even those on which he had no intention to rise with the sun—there was the sound of movement outside. Humanity made so much noise and together with that of beasts of burden that helped their owners, created a cacophony called business. He wouldn't tell anyone they couldn't ply their trade, but there were a few times when he wished he could move to the mountains where silence was prevalent.

Or maybe one of the villas deeper inside the city. The one night spent there had been in complete silence from the outside, although not much of it from the inside.

It hadn't been the most restful night, but he had at least managed some sleep.

The woman in the bed with him moaned softly and muttered

something before she sighed, shifted slightly, and slipped back into a deep sleep.

She was still clothed—something anyone who knew him wouldn't believe. He'd had no intention to force himself on her, even though she had joined him in his room for the past few nights.

Skharr had even offered to sleep on the floor on the first evening when he'd rescued the frightened young woman from the street. A group of men had followed her late at night, their nefarious intentions clear. His presence with her had driven them off, and she'd asked him if she could sleep in his room for the night. A few more nights followed, and he'd woken every morning with her in his bed.

He had a feeling she was surprised that their involvement hadn't ended in sex but despite the few nights spent together, he still knew almost nothing about her, let alone what she thought or felt. The dark hair and tanned skin suggested any number of locations of origin, none of which he could pinpoint, even with her accent.

All he knew was that she was not local, and that was only from what the innkeeper had told him. That and her name —Ingaret.

The young woman had insisted that he join her in bed, and he woke a few times to find her nestled against his chest. It wasn't for warmth since the nights seldom got too cold in this part of the world. Maybe she was simply used to sleeping with someone else.

The barbarian was not, and he disentangled himself gently from her before he sat on the edge of the bed.

A life of peace did not suit him. Odd, that.

She mumbled again and as a cock crowed outside their window, she sat immediately, her eyes wide and mouth open, and a small gasp escaped her lips as she woke.

Bad dreams plagued her—one thing he did know about her. Like him, he supposed, but perhaps not quite as visual as his.

"Lord Skharr?" she asked and looked around, her eyes still not adjusted to the darkness.

Even so, he was not easy to miss. A hulking mass of a human seated on the bed not two feet away from her was easily discernible.

"Not a lord," he grunted softly, stood, and stretched until his knuckles scraped across the ceiling.

"Ah...yes, I remember. I didn't mean to wake you."

"You didn't. I offered to sleep on the floor if I disturbed you."

"You didn't. I like having the company."

Ingaret had mentioned that before. He wasn't sure what it meant and he wasn't the type to question it.

"Hmm," he grunted.

She smiled and ran her fingers through her tangled hair. "You don't appear to enjoy my company, not the way most men would. Why would you take someone into your room if you don't like to be around them?"

Her literacy was certainly something to note. An educated woman wandering the streets of the city late at night was curious, to say the least.

"We protect each other," he stated finally and rolled his stiff neck.

"And how do I protect the feared Barbarian of Theros?"

"The...what?"

"It's... Well, talk of you has spread. You are known as the Barbarian of Theros, your chosen guild."

"Oh."

"How do you believe I protect you?"

"With you in my bed each night, I have no fear that a young whore might tempt me. There is always the risk that she gives me something that needs curing—through fucking or by knifing me in my sleep for my coin."

Ingaret nodded, tilted her head, and drew her slip a little tighter around herself. The gesture wasn't one of discomfort or even a sign that she was cold. To his mind, it was reflexive.

The lie was a passable one and she appeared to accept it without question.

Finally, she appeared to relax, shook her head, and pushed away the nightmares that haunted her. She stood as well and searched for where she had placed her clothes the night before.

"Can I come back tonight?"

"Yes."

She smiled, approached him, and wrapped her arms around his waist. He returned the embrace. She craved closeness and if he said he didn't appreciate it, he would be lying.

Her hair somehow smelled of fresh apples.

After a long moment, she untangled from him and pulled the rest of her clothes on.

"I'll be up later," Skharr grumbled and returned to the bed. "Set the latch when you leave."

"Of course, my lo—" She paused before she completed the offending word, smiled, and pushed a few strands of her hair away from her face. "Of course, Skharr."

Ingaret moved to the door and set the latch to lock before she closed it behind her.

The barbarian shook his head and took a deep breath as his fingers traced the scars on his arm.

"I need a fucking cold bath," he muttered, rolled his shoulders, and grimaced when his muscles pulled stiffly, the result of remaining motionless for the whole night. "Maybe a whore if this must go on too much longer." A nod and a sigh followed that gloomy disclaimer of his words to Ingaret. Horse couldn't offer any insight given that he couldn't hear him from the stable, but it helped to hear his voice. "Or I could become a eunuch."

He shuddered at the thought, pushed from the bed again, and took a deep breath.

"Whore it is."

The docks were busy, even this early in the morning. Wagons drawn by teams of horses or oxen carried heavy loads. New ships sailed in once the chain was lowered at the entrance to the port and sailors shouted orders, sang foreign songs, and worked in unison.

There was enough noise and enough people to cover those who weren't necessarily working. It was calming to watch them. Carel had learned that seeing others work was quite relaxing, especially when he didn't need to do so himself.

The Swilling Mermaid was one of the few places where they could find the space to loiter without having the city guard harass them, and he was not in the mood to move yet. He was waiting for someone in particular and he would not leave until he saw them.

"What will we do today, Carel?"

He turned to look at the young man seated beside him—barely out of his teens with only a hint of a beard visible on his young face. The older man liked to think that Yurunn was a little simple, but the truth was that he had followed him since they were children and it seemed the habit was unlikely to change now that they were grown.

Still, it wasn't a hardship and certainly had advantages. His companion had grown considerably larger since their younger years and had become quite the fighter in his own right. He was well able to keep his friend safe while Carel managed the various schemes that kept them in business.

They both earned well from it, which meant theirs was an equal partnership.

"We are waiting for that cock-sucking whore to leave the

Mermaid. According to the innkeeper, she spends the night there but leaves every morning without an escort."

"We going to jump her, then?"

"No. He says she has no escort but we can't be sure of it. If he's wrong, we'll need to murder them before we can attend to the bitch."

He folded his arms in front of his chest. It was still early morning and he assumed both the bitch and her possible escort had some kind of employment. They had to leave sometime—or perhaps eventually was more appropriate.

The door to the inn opened and he forced himself to not react when he saw who was leaving.

She wasn't the tallest, but her voluptuous form was difficult to miss as well as the mess of brown curls that poured from her head.

"We going to jump her?"

"For the last time, no—and stop staring, you dolt," Carel snapped and averted his gaze.

"I'm not a dolt."

"I know. I didn't mean that. But I want her back and I can't take her if the big fucker is waiting in the shadows like last time."

Yurunn nodded, looked away quickly, and seemed entirely too shifty about it. Thankfully, the woman paid no attention to the people around her as she drew a shawl over her shoulders, shook her head at two young boys who bolted across her path, and continued with a smile.

"When we going to jump her?"

He managed to not snap at the man again. Perhaps he was a little thick in the head after all, although he seemed a little too in love with Ingaret to care about it.

Nothing would stop them from taking her back as long as the younger man played his part.

"We'll get the slut," he muttered and patted his companion on the shoulder. "But first, we need to take care of her protector.

Once he has been eliminated, we can take as long as we want to punish her for trying to leave us, do you understand that? We'll drag her back into our arms."

Yurunn nodded and drew a deep breath. Seeing her again was painful for the large, dull man and Carel intended to use that. The idiot who had protected her would require skill and strength to defeat him, but he had no doubt that his friend would be able to fulfill that part of the task.

"Come on, now. The big one is still inside and we'll pay him a visit. Hopefully, he'll be asleep in bed, which will give us more time to deal with him and the element of surprise. Lessons must be learned."

"Lessons," Yurunn rumbled menacingly.

"And you'll be the teacher. Come on, then. We have someone to beat and possibly kill. But you let me know first if you have a mind to kill him."

"Not sure yet."

The man had a simple mind and one that was easily focused as they moved inside the Swilling Mermaid. A few coins in the right hands had revealed where the barbarian laid his head, and the innkeeper was too busy to stop them from slipping away from the main room. The stairs that led to the rooms above the inn had no guard this early in the morning.

Nothing hindered their cautious but determined advance up the steps and toward the room where they would find their quarry.

Yurunn pushed tentatively on the door. "Latch is down."

"I guess we'll have to break it." Carel didn't bother to lower his voice to a whisper as the thin walls wouldn't prevent the man inside from hearing them. "Any time you feel comfortable, my f—"

His voice cut off when wood splintered. A massive hand extended through the hole, grasped him by the collar, and dragged him into the door.

He struggled to free himself but the sound of wood breaking again preceded a pain that erupted across his head and neck. Somewhat dazed, he looked around and realized that he was now inside the room instead of in the hallway outside.

With a groan of pain, he grimaced and tried to focus. It seemed impossible to see anything but flashes of movement despite the illumination provided by the streak of light that seeped through the hole in the door. He wondered if being dragged through had addled his brain somewhat.

Yurunn remained outside. The dimwit had no idea what was happening and peered into the hole with a bewildered expression.

"Get in here, you fucking moron!" Carel shouted and scowled when blood seeped from a wound on his forehead and trickled down his face.

"Yes," a deep voice ordered and the hand tightened on his collar. "Get in here!"

Wood splintered again and there wasn't much left of the door once the young man entered. Light now streamed in and the two men stared at the hulking mass of a barbarian who stood over them.

The younger man recovered quickly—although he did have the advantage of not being hauled bodily through a door. He wasn't a small man and he uttered a roar of anger as he lunged into their foe. His fist lashed out, caught the warrior by surprise, and thrust him back a couple of steps and into one of the walls hard enough to make it feel like the whole building shook.

Yurunn threw more punches and built himself into a berserker rage. He roared with each strike but oddly, another sound ruined the effect.

Unbelievably, the barbarian was laughing. Blood trickled from wounds across his cheek and over his eyes, but he continued to laugh.

Finally, he pushed his attacker back a few steps. The

simpleton needed a moment to catch his breath, surprised that the larger man was still on his feet.

"Been too long in civilized company," the barbarian rumbled, still chuckling. "I missed it. I thank you for that!"

Yurunn screamed something that Carel couldn't understand and surged into another assault, but he was stopped in his tracks and forced back a step. His opponent moved faster than his size should have permitted and his whole body jerked forward and his fist swung powerfully.

The blow caught the man across the jaw and he careened into the bed before he flipped over it.

He regained his feet quickly, but the room's occupant had followed-through immediately. A knee crunched into his nose to break it easily, and another punch cracked his jaw again and broke it as well.

The young man fell heavily, spitting blood and teeth.

"You finished, you bottom-crawling pit-grubber?" the barbarian asked and touched the cut over his eye lightly. "I am sure I can break a few ribs to slow you again if you have a mind for it."

Yurunn looked like he was about to try to stand again, but after a few attempts, he simply sagged and moaned softly in pain.

Carel had remained huddled safely against the wall—and hopefully out of the way—where he'd been pushed when the fight began. He struggled to find his feet, but the warrior reached him before he could stand fully, twisted a meaty fist into his shirt, and hoisted him almost effortlessly using only one hand.

"I won't kill the two of you this time," the large man rumbled. "Although I feel you might deserve it. Your markings appear to connect you to some of the criminal families that rule the underworld of this city. I have a feeling that a certain amount of violence is required to have those seared onto your body, would that be correct?"

He considered not answering but a swift, hard slap to the side of his head made him reconsider.

"Yes! Yes."

"What did you have to do?"

"I killed a man."

"And have you killed since?"

"Yes."

"So, you think I shouldn't let you live."

Carel looked into the man's eyes, unable to tell if he was joking or not.

"But I have a habit of not killing folk unless I'm protecting my own life—or for coin—and since neither of you weak-spined swill-suckers pose a threat to me and I don't see any coin in it for me, I won't kill either of you. But if you happen to intrude on Ingaret's life—if you so happen to even cast a shadow on her doorstep—I'll snap the big one's neck and smother you to death by shoving your godsbedamned head up his maggot-riddled ass. Now, while that might be a hilarious image, I want you to know that I am in no way less willing to kill either of you. Do you understand?"

He nodded. The cold look in the warrior's eyes wasn't an unfamiliar sight in his business. The hard glare told him clearly that this was the kind of a man who would deliver on threats of violence without so much as a hint of hesitation or guilt.

"I do."

The barbarian smiled. "Excellent. Now then, will you gentlemen exit by the window or the stairs?"

"The…the stairs?"

"A fine choice, I have to admit. Let's go."

He didn't bother to put Carel down before he picked Yurunn up, groaned somewhat with the weight, and carried them both.

It seemed logical that they'd simply be thrown down the steps, but the man carried them to the bottom.

"Troubles, Master Skharr?" the innkeeper asked when they arrived at the foot of the stairs.

"A pest problem. Nothing to worry about. I already cleared the turd-eating vermin for you."

The door opened and Carel was hurled out to land face-down on the dusty cobbles outside. Before he'd even registered what had happened, Yurunn followed and his full weight sprawled on top of him. Both men groaned and tried to disentangle themselves without drawing too much attention.

Skharr smirked as the two rose slowly to their feet and struggled a little with their balance. The smaller man helped the larger, who was more dazed and beaten than his friend, and they staggered away from the inn.

He turned his attention to one of the pickpockets who saw a chance at an easy score and immediately caught the youth by the shoulder.

"They are not worth your time, believe me. But if you have a mind to earn some steady coin, follow them and report their movements to me every day. You'll be rewarded with a gold for every day that you have a report for me."

"A…a gold coin?"

"No, a golden fucking elephant. What the hells do you think?"

"What's an…ephelant?"

"Never mind. A gold coin a day for you. Does that seem reasonable?"

"Aye, sir."

"Good." He placed a coin in the boy's hand. "Now, run along."

CHAPTER THREE

Too many places like it existed in the city. Slums had made certain people too much money for them to want to give their luxuries up. Despite this, others felt more at home in the ramshackle side of the city than they would have in villas on the other side and farther away from the docks.

But there was much that coin could purchase, no matter where the location. From the outside, it looked like merely another building set into the marshes that began to creep in from the delta of the river leading into the sea. Stilts kept most of the houses up, although they barely did their work well once the tides came in.

This house was elevated above the rest. It had taken work and more than a few bodies, but the end result kept the water away from the luxuries contained within.

She had long since put her thoughts on how disastrous the location appeared on the outside away. Lessons were learned and she had arrived at the conclusion that not all was as it appeared. Guards stood watch disguised as beggars outside and studied her closely as she approached.

The roofs offered her enough cover, of course, but the crossbows those men carried would be used if she tried anything stealthy.

All gazes were fixed on her as she moved closer, which left her no way in but through the front door. She could see the signs of urum root addiction in the eyes of the guards, which would only make them that much more aggressive if she tried to circle them.

With a smile, she stepped through the front door as it was pulled open by someone who was waiting for her. Her expression a mask of civility, she removed her cloak and handed it to the man who stood nearby without so much a look in his direction.

After a moment while she waited for the doors to close again behind her, she moved to a large painting of a man in full plate armor astride a white horse. This was supposedly the count, although the man had been unable to ride a horse for years now.

A small click emitted as her hands explored the edges of the painting, and it moved away to reveal a hidden staircase that led into a bedroom.

Folk knew that approaching this building meant the possibility of not leaving it again, but she wondered how many knew that many of those who entered were her in her various disguises.

Micah removed her clothes, starting with her shirt, which revealed an armored corset beneath it. She pulled that off as well, along with the small mechanism around her forearm that would release a poisoned dagger into her palm if she jerked her hand in a specific way.

A belt of darts followed and was hung quickly on the wall for her man to clean, oil, and have the poisons reapplied.

All other trappings that would have made her look like a courtesan were similarly discarded—the earrings, necklaces, and bracelets had been chosen to be shiny enough to keep eyes distracted from the weapons she was hiding. Here, however, she did not need to hide who she was.

A light leather vest fitted comfortably over a brown shirt with similarly light and comfortable trousers and boots. She shook her hair loose and a few beads and gold strands came free as she finally retrieved a leather strap to tie her hair back. With more time, she would have braided it neatly but for the moment, a simple tie would do.

Once fully dressed, she stepped out of the bedroom in the attire that would be more familiar to the people who worked for her and moved directly to the office she had arranged for herself. A large, overstuffed chair was set behind a heavy oak desk. It had been made to look a little more impressive than she knew was necessary, but it did make her feel more comfortable to have something that large and solid between herself and anyone who might come through the door.

A shelf was positioned between her and the secret passage leading in as an additional precaution. There were those in the city who wanted her dead, and they would soon find that killing her would be difficult even if they did manage to catch her off-guard.

A handful of papers already waited on the desk but she ignored those, retrieved a fresh sheet, and quickly noted the details of a new contract. It was a simple enough missive and one that was meant to remain confidential, so she applied the wax seal to ensure that no eyes would see it but those for which it was intended.

A knock on the door drew her attention and she locked the stamp and wax away and picked up the letter she had written.

"Come."

The door opened to reveal a distinguished man who appeared to have passed his fiftieth year judging by the gray that had crept into his thick beard and full head of hair. He was slim with angular features and wore simple purple robes that made him seem to glide as he stepped slowly into the room.

"Denir, good." She stood from behind the desk. "I'll need this letter delivered to the guildmaster—for his eyes only—and as quickly as possible. I won't have folk complaining that I'm withholding information about work from them. Not again."

"Of course, Dame Ferat." The man collected the sealed letter and slipped it into his coat pocket without so much as a second glance. "If it is not an intrusion, the dame should know that her sister has called upon her. I have directed her to the atrium to await her and instructed that she be provided with refreshments while she waited."

"How long has she been here?"

"The dame's sister arrived mere minutes prior to the dame's arrival."

The man's insistence on speaking like that to her was annoying. She knew it came from him wanting to respect her as much as possible but at the same time, it was odd to be spoken of in the third person.

"Send the letter. I'll see what my sister wants. Thank you, Denir."

He bowed stiffly at the hips and never once met her gaze as he spun and padded silently out of the room to send the letter. She didn't know if he did it personally or if he placed it in the hands of those whom he trusted to deliver it. All that mattered was that the missive was sent without delay.

She had other business to tend to.

Unlike the villas, her house was not that large despite the work she had put into making it as comfortable and luxurious as possible. The advantage was that she didn't need to spend hours walking along pathways in gardens to reach any one point of the property. The atrium wasn't far from her office, and when she arrived, she noted that the servants were still delivering platters of fruits, sweetmeats, and other delicacies along with a selection of drinks for her sister to choose from.

The woman looked very uncomfortable in her surroundings. Light-brown hair was tied back somewhat messily, and the look of her clothes made it appear as though she had taken armor off moments before the visit. Her pale skin was darkened by the sun, and everything about her screamed soldier.

Her discomfort fell away, however, when she saw her sister. Both women smiled and hurried forward to wrap their arms around each other in a warm embrace.

"It is nice to see you again, Sera."

"And you, Micah." The mercenary stepped back and grinned. "Or should I call you Dame Ferat? What—with a little bow or a curtsey?"

"Fuck that." Micah moved to one of the tables, selected a silver goblet, and filled it with what looked like honeyed wine. "The guild thought they would reward me with a title, and it's now taken root in everyone's head that they need to address me by it. If you start calling me Dame too, I'll slit your throat and toss your body into the swamp."

"You'll try," Sera retorted and held her goblet out to her.

Micah acquiesced and tapped hers to her sister's once both were full. "What should we toast to?"

"The end of you building this bloody house? At long last?"

"Possibly, although I might have a few alterations for the outside."

"Of course you do."

Sera was still making a name for herself in the guild, of course. She was captain of a peloton and earned well escorting those who needed it to and from Verenvan. Some who didn't know better thought they might have been twins, although Micah was three years her sister's senior.

Not that she would let anyone think that.

They sat and the visitor served herself a platter of the food that had been provided for them. She knew that trying to steal from Sera's plate might be a good way to lose some fingers, but Micah didn't feel hungry enough to even try.

"What brings you here? I happen to know that you hate the swamps I call home."

The other woman smirked. "That hate has a good reason behind it, although it might be explained as simply that I lack your obsession with the area we called home as children. But I do like to see you and talk to you between missions. Neither of us spends enough time in this city for us to wish to spend all our time in it apart."

Micah couldn't help a small smile. "Tell me, what adventures have you engaged in over these past few months?"

"I think you're well aware of what I've been up to, given that you've asked questions around the guild. I have asked you to not concern yourself with my business."

"You're the only family I have in the world, Sera. I'll never not worry."

"Well, if you must know, I was involved in a rather interesting enterprise. The business itself was not quite so interesting, although we did run into a group of bandits who tried to steal all our possessions. We had a man with us, though, who dealt with them rather well—one of those who came to me for an escort. A barbarian."

Her sister nodded and inclined her head like she hadn't learned all the details a few hours earlier. "A barbarian?"

"Aye. Skharr is his name. The man's instincts are difficult to question, as well as his fighting abilities. We returned to civilization while he continued with his mission."

"What can you tell me about him?"

Sera's eyes narrowed. "He's a better fighter than you would think and pretends to be dull-witted when he isn't. Oh, and he's an expert marksman with a bow that I'm not sure anyone else would be able to draw. Why do you ask?"

"I was merely curious." Micah shrugged and nibbled one of the pastries.

"Curious enough to ask around the guild about him, yes?"

She paused in mid-bite and glared at the woman seated across from her.

"He saved many of our lives, Mic," her sister continued, her voice a little lower now. "If you involve yourself in his business, you may find yourself in over your head."

"I can't involve you in my business dealings, you know that, Sera." She shook her head. It was an excuse and she knew it. She had entertained the hope that her sister would help her to discover a weakness in the man's defenses, but it was clear that she had come with her guard up and would not lower it. At least not enough to be helpful.

"I know," Sera replied and smiled. "Now that we've put that subject to rest, can we talk about why the hell you have servants? Can you not clean up after yourself?"

Micah smirked. "Why do it myself when I can pay others to do it for me?"

———

Try as he might, he constantly returned to the idea that humans were the middlemen of the world.

It was an idea that had come to Skharr during his travels, and he had never been able to shake it. Humans were worse at living and surviving in the mountains than goblins and dwarves. Elves of all types survived in the wooded areas far better than them. Orcs loved their deserts, and trolls of various species enjoyed living in and near swamps, rivers, and other wetlands. Humans could not match any of them in any of their preferred landscapes.

His kind, on the other hand, were hardy enough to survive in these various locations better than the others could, which made them able to live almost everywhere.

Ultimately, it meant that humans were the only ones who genuinely thrived in locations that allowed for all their kind to coalesce. Ports at the mouths of rivers were a case in point, where everyone of all species and origins could gather and share everything they had learned and created.

Skharr knew for a fact that the other races weren't as interested in gathering in large numbers, but they did nonetheless.

Not quite in the same numbers as the humans, of course. This was why most non-human workers had been consigned to live near the walls and away from the gates and the port, where they were allowed to ply their trade. Most of them managed to live well—better than they would have in their homelands—but they made no secret of the fact that they would prefer to live where their hearts and families resided.

Still, if he needed a blacksmith, he always elected to find a dwarf. That was a lesson learned from his time training in the mountains. Every elder had chosen to have their weapons made and repaired by the dwarf clans that lived beneath the mountains they lived on.

Under the shadow of the walls above, he followed the sounds of metal clanging on metal. He could even feel the heat of the furnaces, which made the air warmer than it needed to be as he stepped through the doorway under the low-hanging sign that read *AnvilForged Blacksmith*. He held a small chest but the size gave no indication of the weight. It was too heavy to be roped to his belt and needed to be carried in hand.

"Good morning to ye, good sir!" a deep voice shouted from inside. The thick, robust build of the man who barely reached his waist told him he was in the right place.

Even his voice was a little odd. Human languages were difficult for their kind, which meant their accents all sounded the same when they spoke a human tongue.

"And good morning to you, fair master," he replied. "Is Ser AnvilForged present?"

The younger dwarf studied him curiously. "If you needs weapons, I'll be glad to help. Or needs them repaired too."

He nodded. "All the same."

"Fuck off, boy," shouted a voice from inside the shop. "Get back to the furnaces and put your back into it this time. If I catch you mucking about with that *che-nor-cul* across the street again, I'll use your blood to cool them next."

The youth scowled and shook his head. Even so, he did as he was told and returned to the furnaces while another man approached the front desk. He peeled layers of protective equipment from his body with every step and finally revealed a wispy white beard that almost reached his toes, even when braided. It had been coiled inside his protective helm, although Skharr wasn't sure where he had found the space for it.

"Sorry for the lad's lack of manners." The dwarf growled with annoyance. "He's been away from the mountains since he was a boy and has forgotten our dealings with the DeathEaters in the Silver Mountains."

The barbarian's eyebrows rose in surprise. "That obvious?"

"Hard to miss one of the Clan, especially when they approach my homestead. The *Nor-ra-weith* would say you were all born with mountain giant blood."

"Unkind of her to say, even as a clan leader."

"Aye. Do you feel as though she was wrong to say it, however?"

"No, merely unkind."

That drew a grin from the dwarf. "Ah, well. How may we be of service to ye, Master…"

"Skharr. I've lost my bow, Master…"

"Throkrag, although you may call me Throk. Most humans misname me anyway so I might as well make it simple for you dumb fucks. I can also tell you that your skills are likely finer than mine when it comes to crafting bows."

"Aye, but until I have the materials I require, I'll need something to fill the void."

"Then follow me. I am sure we can find something to your taste."

The dwarf stepped away from the desk and motioned for Skharr to follow him.

He assumed that the establishment had been built with few humans in mind when he immediately had to lower his head to step inside with him.

More than a dozen dwarves worked at the furnaces, all wearing appropriate protection against the heat as they expertly handled the tools they had likely built for themselves. Each looked up from their work and raised their hands in greeting to the man who entered their shop.

There would have been no point in trying to speak over the clanging of metal on metal inside.

"Tugerlun, you *dre-no-cul-safte!*" Throk shouted. "Get this beam up to where it needs to be or I'll use your useless *srod*-infested corpse to feed the furnaces. And I wager you'll be shit at that too."

Two dwarves hurried to comply. Sure enough, the beam that was being used to lift and lower their heavier tools was off-kilter and the chains had begun to lean to the side.

Skharr had seen them working in the past and instantly stepped beside them and helped them to push the bar up. It was slow work as another man needed to be in place to adjust the screws and tighten them as they continued to push. Throk did none of the work but he smirked to see his massive customer helping them when the bar rose a little higher than the other dwarves were comfortable reaching to.

"You weak shits need to feel ashamed that a human knows your work better than you do!" he roared once they finally settled it into place.

"My first year away from the clan was living among your kin," Skharr told him. "And there were only so many goblins to kill before I was needed to help in the furnaces. While I was never much good at the metalworking, I could be used for a task that most would relegate to mules."

The proprietor laughed and shook his head. "Now, tell me what brought you to our fine establishment."

"I need a battle-ax made for the Clan—the finest work that can be delivered by the name of AnvilForge. Something legendary, you understand."

"Aye." Throk motioned for them to enter his office away from those working. "You must know that this is no small feat. Importing the metal directly from the mountains will require some time and no small amount of coin on your part."

"I understand." Skharr took a heavy purse from his belt and made no effort to count the coins inside before he placed it on the desk between them, quickly followed by the small chest he had brought with him. "Some three hundred and fifty gold coins."

He could almost see the avarice appear in the dwarf's eyes as he opened both the purse and the chest. The treasure within would have given him at least a year—probably two—of luxurious living in Verenvan.

"A generous start but far from what would be required," he stated finally once he'd made a hasty estimate of the coins.

"I know. This is merely to secure the materials and equipment required, as I understand you lack the tools for a finely forged AnvilForge ax of legend. Once you begin work, more coin will come. More still will be provided once the ax is finished."

Throk nodded and folded his arms in front of his stout chest. "Aye. This is agreeable. How would we know that you can provide the rest?"

"I have paid for the materials and even if I cannot pay the rest, you have what is needed for something remarkable on my coin. Once you begin work, more will ensure that you will have a legendary weapon to sell if I do not pay the final price. It seems, rather, that my trust in you is what will be tested."

The dwarf smirked. "Your knowledge of our work is appreciated. And it has been many years since I have had the opportunity to put my back into something that requires consummate skill. In the meantime…a gift, I think. From us, to secure your trust."

He looked around the office and cursed a few times in his native tongue before he located a heavy item sheathed in leather. He opened the flap and drew out two axes. Both were smaller and easy to wield with one hand, but their appearance was different and more stream-lined than the weapons Skharr had used previously.

"Good for cleaving heads, 'tis true." Throk held both weapons out for display and the barbarian took one. "But you will find that they fly as true as any of your arrows and deliver as much force on arrival."

When he hefted it in his hand, he immediately noted its perfect balance. He wouldn't be able to test it in the office, of course, but the weight of it as well as how thin the steel of the blade was showed that expert craftsmanship had gone into making it.

"My trust is earned," he muttered and sheathed them again. "And rest assured that both will likely see a great deal of use."

"I had hoped so. They have languished here since the man who ordered them died before he could collect, and… Well, the concept that weapons wish to battle as much as their owners might seem unfamiliar to some, but…" He shrugged.

"Not to me," Skharr replied and held both weapons against his chest in their leather sheath. "And there will be no shortage of work for them to do."

CHAPTER FOUR

The new axes hadn't been expected but he was thankful to have them anyway.

His people had no lack of trust in the dwarves and he knew their work would be prompt and worth the king's ransom that was demanded. Their legendary smithing was mostly ignored by humans, and Skharr couldn't think why. Although humans had decent smiths of their own, they failed to reach the elevated standards he had grown used to.

Or aspired to, at least. It wasn't often that he could afford their kind of work, and while he had spent a good portion of what he'd collected from the dungeon he'd cleared, he knew it would be worth every copper, silver, or gold piece spent.

As the sun continued to climb, the heat made the whole city slower and more sluggish. Midday was approaching, when most of the folk would turn their attention to food and rest until the worst of it passed but for the moment, the slow pace made the streets harder to travel through.

Still, he cared less about what the other folk were doing with their lives. He still had a goodly amount of coin at his disposal, even with what had been promised to the dwarves. That meant he didn't need to work, and he considered taking time out of his day to enjoy lunch in cool shade, perhaps closer to the villas where the heat wouldn't be quite so irksome.

Whether he decided to linger or not, he needed to return to the Mermaid eventually. All his possessions were still there and Horse would sulk if he didn't stop in with a few treats to cheer him up.

The animal was getting old, and it would soon be time to see him to finer pastures. Some farms would take older horses in—not for work but to care for them in their last years—and it seemed only right to let him retire there once his time in the battlefields came to an end.

Still, while it was something that demanded thought, that decision would hopefully only have to be made in a few years.

"Master Skharr!"

A small, shrill voice drew him from his reverie and he looked around him quickly to identify who had called him. It sounded like a child, although he knew of no children who would know his name.

"Over here, sir!"

Skharr turned to where a slim youth sprinted after him on the street, slipped smoothly between a handful of men arguing around an ox, and finally reached the massive barbarian.

"Erron, that was your name, yes?" he asked and shifted the weight of the axes over his shoulder.

"Aye, that's my name." The youth grinned and revealed that one of his teeth was missing, although there was no way to tell if it was because he was at that age or if it had been knocked out prematurely. "I was sent to find you, sir. Guildmaster Pennar asked me to seek you out. I went to the inn first and the keeper there said that you had beaten two men senseless and left to parts unknown. Been searching all over the city for you, sir."

"Most would have simply remained at the inn until I returned," he pointed out and gestured for the boy to follow him.

Erron needed to jog to keep up with the larger man. "Well then, not many would have found you, but your tracks were rather easy to follow. Most folk remember seeing you walking by, and I was able to follow at least part of the way to the non-human sectors. I thought you might seek to replace your bow with the work of some elves. Is that what's on your back then? A bow?"

"No." Skharr scowled. He wasn't particularly happy about being so easily tracked through the city. "I'll make the bow myself when I can."

"What's that you have on your back then?"

"The blood of thirteen virgin whores."

"How's they whores if they's virgins?"

"Impossibly rare and hard to find as well. What did you need to find me for, boy?"

"Oh, right! The guildmaster sent me. Did I not tell you that already?"

"Yes, but not why Pennar wanted you to find me."

"Well, he didn't mention it to me either, sir, but if I had to put coin on finding a reason, I would say it had something to do with the fancy miss who visited the Guild Hall not long before he sent me after you."

"Fancy miss?"

"Aye, sir. Rich miss rode in on a horse with a fleet of servants paving her way with flowers and shit."

"Truly?"

"Well, no, but that was how it felt. Had her some right fancy robes on as well—not the kind of miss who would usually find her way into the Guild Hall. Many folk watched her while she talked to Guildmaster Pennar but she didn't say what she wanted loud enough for anyone to hear. A second after she was gone, he shouted at me to go off and find you."

Skharr scowled and shook his head. He hadn't been looking for work. The best part of having enough coin to live on was the fact that he could be selective about which jobs he wanted to take.

Of course, he hadn't taken any since he returned from the dungeon, but he doubted anyone would hold that against him. His back still felt sore from where it had been thrashed with steel and fire, and dull aches lingered across his body despite the healing potions he had taken after the beating he'd received from the lich.

It was enough to make any man want to pause and reassess his life.

His inclinations notwithstanding, it was best to not make the guildmaster wait too long. If it turned out to be work he had no need for, he could simply refuse it.

"All right, boy, I'll go to the hall as directly as possible. I assume you'll earn more if you rush about with those chicken legs of yours, so off with you."

Erron smirked. "Thank you!"

And with that, he raced down the street again and nimbly navigated the crowds that continued to hinder others.

He remembered when he was that small, although there had been no crowds to slip through. His youth had been mountains to climb and caves to explore, both of which were far easier when there were less weight and size to carry around.

It took him longer than he would have liked to negotiate the crowds to the Guild Hall, but he finally moved through the impossibly large doors and rubbed elbows with the other mercenaries. Most were leaving to find their midday meals, but Skharr told himself that he would give the guildmaster time to have his say before he ate.

Sure enough, Pennar was waiting for him when he stopped in front of the stall.

"Took your fucking time," the man noted and an annoyed frown seemed to have been affixed to his face.

"I had business to attend to." The barbarian made a mental

note to not involve Erron in his tardiness. "Urgent business that could not wait."

"Well... I suppose that's in order, then. I don't like to hold a contract for a single person for too long, however. I'd appreciate it if you kept that in mind."

"I will. What is it that could not wait?"

"A contract came in—a young woman of means came to the hall in person, asking for you specifically. Said to give you... these," Pennar paused, took two silver coins from his pouch, and placed them on the table, "To reserve your services to call on her. She said she would pay you for work—the same amount the Lady Svana paid you for your services. Oh, and she was most insistent that it was important to tell you it would be the same payment for your services."

Skharr inclined his head thoughtfully. "The coin is only mine should I meet with her."

"Aye. Now, I remember that the payment for the work was a single gold coin that you handed to the guild. I don't suppose you would care to share what other payment would be involved?"

"It was more than one gold coin," he stated, his face expressionless. "The single coin was all that was owed to the guild."

"And nothing else?"

"Nothing of note. I'll take the silver and attend the meeting. Did she mention where I would find her?"

"No, but I know where you can. Lady Tamisen is her name, and I'll make a note of her residence. I assume that if she didn't want to meet anywhere specific, she wants you to meet her at her home."

"Seems reasonable," he agreed.

Pennar handed him a scroll. "It's written into the contract. Have a care, though. You wouldn't want to get in too deep in noble business. They tend to not appreciate it."

Skharr nodded. "Duly noted."

As he turned, the hair on the back of his neck began to prickle. The odd feeling told him that not all was as it seemed.

A hint of movement to his left caught his attention but when he turned, he saw no one who seemed to show any interest in him. It confirmed his instincts that whoever was watching him did not wish to be seen to do so.

If someone was following him, he knew it had something to do with what the Lady Tamisen wanted. There was no other reason for anyone to trail his steps.

Still, it mattered little. If they meant him harm, he would deal with them soon enough. Until then, it was best to give them a show and get himself some lunch.

"I honestly didn't think I would see you in Verenvan."

The mage looked up from his inspection and raised an eyebrow. "I come to the city often to collect supplies and confer with my brothers to acquire or share any recent knowledge. Those who know this also know I am always in need of more coin. Everything in Verenvan is so costly these days."

Skharr shrugged. "There aren't many mages I trust—or at least know to be worthy of the coin paid to you."

"You wound me to the quick, sir. But yes, it is difficult to find a trustworthy mage outside the guilds, and those work too slowly for it to be worth any coin you might have for them. They never put guild work under any priority. Where did you say you found this?"

The barbarian leaned closer to see what the man was inspecting. "It was at the bottom of the chests I collected from the dungeon. A few jewels were there with them too, and it looked like a charm of some kind. I thought you would know what it was and would likely have a mind to purchase it."

"I didn't think someone like you would have run out of coin

so quickly, especially given the amount you were in possession of after your trip through that dungeon near the mountains."

"There are a few expenses that will require most, if not all, of my coin. I would like to have as much as possible on hand. Are you interested?"

The mage nodded slowly. "I'll be honest, I have no idea what this is—although every charm I have tells me there is magic to it, and a great deal too. I would like to study it. I think…thirty gold coins should be enough for it."

"Forty," Skharr countered smoothly.

"Thirty-three," the man replied, the bartering entirely expected.

"Thirty-five."

"Done." The mage opened his coin purse and counted the coins out in front of him quickly before he took the charm. "A pleasure doing business, as always. And do call on me next time you are near my home."

"Of course."

The warrior had a feeling he had been cheated. The offer had immediately been much higher than any magic-user would entertain for something he knew nothing about.

Then again, there was no way for him to challenge him on it, and in the end, he did need the coin. If he knew the AnvilForges, their price would be well in excess of the coin he had gathered at the dungeon.

Still, the negotiations had left him with something of a foul taste in his mouth. Of course, the only reason why the mage would be interested in buying what he had to sell was if he knew how to turn it into a profit for himself, but the sense that he'd been cheated remained. It would pass, he knew, but it put him in a negative mood as he turned his steps to the Swilling Mermaid.

The feeling persisted and was only made worse by the fact that he knew someone was following him.

Whoever it was knew their spycraft. Skharr had caught little more than a passing glance of what could have been his watcher's shoulder as they blended into the people in the streets. There were no furtive glances and no bystanders who moved quickly away when they thought they had been detected.

He still didn't know if it was a man or a woman. The lack of knowledge soured his mood even further, especially since it seemed there was nothing he could do but watch and wait.

Patience had never been his strong suit.

As he approached the Mermaid again, however, it seemed there would be something for him to occupy his mind with. The boy he had sent to keep track of the two idiots who had tried to ambush him in his room lingered in the yard.

It was odd, but the people in this city had an interesting kind of loyalty when it came to bribes. He had even seen thieves turn down offers of more coin simply because someone had paid them first.

"You're back?"

"Aye, sir," the lad said and straightened from his slouch. "Followed the two muck-suckers out to the swamps of the city. They disappeared into one of the local hideouts for the Orc Skulls. Not enough gold in the world you could pay me to go in there."

Skharr doubted that was true but he wouldn't push the boy into a place where he was likely to be killed for snooping—and painfully and slowly, no doubt.

"Does a coin every day mean you will watch for them and follow when they leave again?"

The boy grinned and nodded. "We are amenable to that."

The barbarian shook his head, a little startled by that pronouncement. Since when did urchins know a word that long?

"Go on, then. Get yourself something to eat."

He put one of the silver coins he'd been paid by Pennar in his informant's hand and gestured for him to go inside. His stomach grumbled and reminded him that it was time for him to have something to eat as well.

Lunch was already being served and unlike most days, he shared his meal with most of the other sailors and dock workers who came in for a meal. At least in a crowded place like this, whoever was following him might feel comfortable enough to reveal themselves.

Or so he thought, but only the regulars frequented the tables and he shrugged and turned his attention to his food. He was determined to not let the presence of someone following him ruin his meal, although it would have to be dealt with eventually. A trap would have to be set or something of the kind, at least.

"Enjoy your meal?" the innkeeper asked and circled toward him.

Skharr shrugged. "Good as any other day, I suppose."

"I wish to apologize for the incident earlier. Allowing others to bother my guests is unacceptable. I will move you to a room with a…well, a door. And if there be anything else I can do for you—"

"Apples."

"Pardon?"

"Do you have any apples?"

The man nodded. "Apples? Yes. You…wish for some apples?"

"For Horse."

"Oh, yes. I'll have the hands in the stable give him apples."

"No, I will feed."

"Of course. Give me a moment."

A few moments later, one of the cooks came out of the kitchen with a barrel full of bright red apples for him.

"Appreciated."

His meal finished, the barbarian stepped out of the main room of the inn, alert for anyone who might follow him into the stables, but no one caught his attention. With a grim smile, he acknowledged that he had little hope of identifying who the person was for now. They would be stupid to follow him when he entered the stables alone with a bucket of apples.

The stable hands were already used to seeing him in their place of business, and he moved to the stall they held for Horse in the back.

The stallion showed no sign of surprise at seeing him, although his interest seemed to be held exclusively by the apples in his barrel.

"I don't suppose you missed me at all, old friend," Skharr muttered, took one of the apples out, and let the beast take it from his hand. "Well, the feeling is not mutual. Having you at my side all these...what has it been? Thirteen years now? Too many battles for either of us to have walked away from, I think."

Horse snorted, lowered his head into the barrel, and helped himself to another apple.

"True, I am the one who involves myself in the battles, but I have weapons and training for it. Either way, I thought the time will soon come for you to settle on a farm that will require you to travel less. Perhaps we can find somewhere with mares for you to stud. I can't speak for you, but I've always assumed that the dream of every warrior who does not die in battle is to fuck himself to death, wouldn't you say?"

Another crunchy fruit was taken from the bucket.

"I didn't say now. I said soon. When you're longer in the tooth and less willing and capable of following me into whatever idiocy I happen to fall into. I always assumed that a life of danger and travel through the world was not something you would have chosen for yourself."

Horse snorted and shook his mane as he chewed the fruit in his mouth.

"Well, it is something to think on. I would never push you into anything you don't want to do, of course. It's not as though any barn or pasture could contain you if you didn't want it to."

A simple shake of the head indicated that he was speaking the truth.

"I'm not sure that the peaceful life will ever be for me. Even if it did include copious amounts of fucking and eating every day. A part of me will always hunger for battle, and I know there will be one out there that will take me to my grave. But that will not be the end of it for me, I'm afraid. Claims to my soul have been made all across the world, and if any of those mages can do what they promise, I am not sure my time in the afterlife will be a peaceful one."

Horse nudged him in the shoulder, and he selected another apple for him.

"I know, I'm a depressing sod of late. My zest for life is as shriveled as Janus' sweaty balls. I've needed to put my fist through something for the past few days, which is a sure sign that the inactivity is wearing me down. Two idiots came to my room, looking to catch me by surprise and deliver a beating, but only one of them put up a reasonable fight. The other was weeping for mercy before I even laid a hand on him. I do have work inside the city that is promising, however. I assume it's another lady who wants a choice as to which lord she'll be tied to. If so, it should provide some measure of entertainment."

A snort from the horse brought a laugh from him.

"I doubt any lord will take kindly to a hell-raised barbarian like me telling him who he can and cannot court. Indeed yes. It promises to deliver good sport in an otherwise mediocre day."

CHAPTER FIVE

The apples were finally finished. Horse could eat through hundreds without so much as a pause. If he intended to find a place for the beast to spend his twilight years, it would have to be somewhere near an apple orchard.

Skharr moved away from the stables and brushed a few pieces of hay from his clothes. It was time for him to find Lady Tamisen, whoever she was, and see what she wanted him to do. The assumption was that she would need him to deliver a particularly painful message to someone, and the fact that she offered the precise payment as Lady Svana had left him a little worried.

If the lady he'd first worked for was talking, husbands out there—potential and otherwise—as well as fathers and brothers would hear of it and be none too pleased.

He would need to have a word with the woman when he had a chance and make sure his name didn't come up in casual gossip among the rich and powerful of the city. It wouldn't be long before someone decided it was time for him to leave—forcefully.

"Barbarian!"

Skharr stopped in his tracks and turned as the innkeeper approached him.

"Is there a problem?"

"Of course not." The man raised his hands placatingly. "I merely wondered if you intended to leave your quarters for a while and if you wanted me to keep your room saved for the duration."

The barbarian scowled and studied the man a little suspiciously. "Work here in the city. Not leaving. Why would I leave?"

"I heard...I'm sorry. I thought you were going on another dungeon run."

"Still recovering from my last. Which dungeon run?"

"It is— Well, one of the more dangerous ones and arranged every year. The Ivehnshaw Tower only appears once for less than an hour on the first full moon of winter and this is the time when the guilds generally recruit adventurers to head in there. I'm not sure how many that would appeal to. Every year, a team makes an attempt—sometimes numbering well above two dozen men, all told. All those who return have eternal glory and riches beyond their wildest dreams. That said, in however many years it has been since this they initiated the challenge, only two have returned."

Skharr looked around casually in the hope that he might see the person following him.

Once again, it proved a fruitless effort. Whoever it was, they were both careful and skillful.

"Two have returned."

"Out of hundreds. Their group left with almost two dozen members."

"How do you know they didn't kill their party members?"

"I don't. But the fact that they were the only ones to ever return from there did make me feel as though at least a few had passed while still inside."

"Does it mean they would be inside all year? If the opening is only available for that short a window, I imagine there is no way out once they are in. At least if all the rules for the other dungeons still apply."

"I don't think they do. Most aren't only available for certain times in the year. All I know is that they returned and it wasn't a full year later."

Skharr let his face turn emotionless and shook his head. "I've never heard of Ivehnshaw Tower."

"It's said that the most powerful of the Ancients set it up as a joke. Another mage said it was impossible to create a tower that was there one minute and gone the next."

"Not entirely unfamiliar. Mages in our time are similarly juvenile."

"Yes, well, it should interest you that those two who returned laden with more treasure than they could spend in a dozen lifetimes also have no memory of how they escaped. That is the tale, anyway, and it's the reason why nothing of the inside of the tower is known. In seven years, not a single detail was shared."

The innkeeper narrowed his eyes and studied the warrior before he shook his head. "Well, I hear they are putting a group together again for this year's Tower Hunt. Should you feel the need to join them, let them know they have a veteran of the dungeons on their side and know that your possessions will be safe in my care."

He nodded. "I am…unsure. But I will decide later. Work now."

A treasure like that was certainly what he needed, assuming he didn't die like the others had. Even so, he had no desire to push himself into a mission without considering it for a while. He was curious, however. Ancients, for all their flaws, did make the world a little more interesting for people like him. His immediate task took priority, though, and he turned his focus to the meeting he'd agreed to attend.

This time, he wouldn't go unarmed. His clothes were better suited to a man who would visit the villa of a noble and certainly far better than what he had worn the last time. He could afford to look a little more respectable.

Still, his new axes wouldn't form part of his arsenal on this excursion. There would be enough time to test their edge on some unwilling victim later but for now, he needed something that was a little less eye-catching.

His dagger and seax were fitted into his belt and hidden from view, although still easy for him to access when needed. In the end, he would be expected to be armed.

The ax hanging from his hip would be enough to draw all attention away from his other weapons. If someone wanted to disarm him, that would be what they took and so would hopefully leave him with the other available for combat.

There was little point in waiting as it would take most of what was left of the day to learn what the lady needed from him, so he navigated the streets again. He strode toward the villas that were still protected by the walls and followed the instructions left for him in the contract.

The way the city seemed to fall away and give space to the luxuriant gardens and tall buildings with marble pillars made him wonder how much coin had gone into it. It seemed certain that those with means wanted the city to remain separated between those who could afford the luxury and those that could not.

These musings kept him occupied while he followed the clear instructions to the entrance of one of the larger villas. The stately home was closer to the count's palace than the others had been.

A larger group of guards waited for him there and immediately reached for their weapons when they saw him.

"My reputation precedes me," Skharr noted and folded his arms in front of his chest.

One of the guards, a woman, fell back and vanished inside the villa as the others stood their ground.

"We know who you are, barbarian," the apparent leader

answered and took a step forward. "And your violent tendencies as well. You'll have one chance to leave before we close the gates and summon the city guard."

The warrior decided it was a little gratifying to know that none of the five assembled in front of him had any intention to fight. It was wise of them, although he did feel the need to exercise his fists against someone at this point.

"I was summoned," he said finally, his posture non-threatening but also unyielding. "I assume this is the home of Lady Tamisen? I was told that she had need of my services."

"Should the Lady Tamisen have need of fighters, she would turn to us for assistance."

"So she does live here, then."

"Keep walking or you will find out why she would turn to us for fighters."

"I thought you intended to call the city guard."

"Well...we will...and—"

Skharr raised an eyebrow. "So which is it? Will you piss yourselves and call for help, or stand your ground? It tends to become rather slippery underfoot if you try both."

The guards exchanged uncertain glances, at a loss now that their leader's authority had been stripped so effectively from him.

Before they could speak, the barbarian fixed them with a stern look.

"Your lady paid two silvers for me to present myself to her. I have done what was needed to earn those. Whether she has the satisfaction she expects from the meeting is up to you, as I will not return the coins."

Once again, the group exchanged glances, their hands still on their weapons. The uncomfortable silence dragged on until the guard who had left earlier returned. She seemed a little red in the face like she had sprinted in the full weight of her armor.

Ignoring the barbarian, she stepped close to the leader and

whispered something to him. He frowned at her, surprise and displeasure warring in his face.

"She asked to see me, didn't she?" Skharr asked with a smirk.

"Fo...follow me. And don't wander off."

The warrior wondered if he had destroyed the man's authority with his men for the future or if it would all pass once he was gone and there would be nothing to remind them of what had happened. Either way, it would be a lesson learned for all of them, and it had little to do with him. If he hadn't been challenged, there would have been no confrontation.

Then again, these men had the responsibility to challenge any who tried to enter their employer's home. He was unsure as to why the guard had made a scene of it, but he had certainly dealt with it in a more aggressive manner than he needed to.

"I must apologize," the man said as he guided him through the gardens of the villa. "It is our responsibility to ensure the safety of Lady Tamisen, and a man of your reputation... Well, we had to be sure that the lady truly did want to see you."

"I understand," Skharr replied. He wondered if an apology was expected from him in return but before he could decide one way or the other, the guard came to a halt.

"Lady Tamisen insisted that she meet you alone," the man said before he bowed jerkily at the hip and turned away to return to his post at the gate.

Skharr took a moment to look around. He stood on a patio covered by a wooden structure that allowed vines to grow thickly enough to block the sunlight, at least to a point. Delicate garlands of flowers descended from above.

"You came armed?"

He had heard light footsteps approaching and despite what the guard had said, he had expected to find the woman attended by an entourage, however small, but she was alone. Deep purple robes adorned her form, and her pale, milky skin was almost translucent. It contrasted sharply with her vivid red hair that had been swept into curls that hung down her back.

"I assumed some fighting was expected of me," Skharr explained and took a step back. "Wiser to come prepared."

"I can appreciate that, although there would be little reason to arm yourself after we met."

"Perhaps. And perhaps I would have come prepared anyway as I do not know what you will ask of me."

She smiled and he took another step back. Her eyes were interesting—a deep green that likely turned brown when there was less light—and he found it oddly difficult to read her character from her appearance. She was taller than Svana had been, with a leaner aspect to her that was a little more regal and stronger than the delicate flower the other woman had attempted to portray herself as.

"And I thought I had made my intentions rather obvious in my conversation with the guildmaster."

The warrior shrugged. "I am not pleased to be known as a commodity, and if Svana chose to share the nature of my agreement with her, I assume she did not do it lightly. With that in mind, I will not take any work from you lightly either and would like to see what you plan to pay me with."

The woman narrowed her eyes and realized what he was asking for after a moment of thought. "You wish me to bare myself to you? Now?"

"I have little doubt that I will be in more danger this time than the last. And under those clothes, you might hide a figure less worthy of risking my life over."

She scowled and shook her head. "You're rather blunt, aren't you?"

"Barbarians must maintain their reputation."

In truth, he wouldn't have been as direct about it without the simmering need that had built inside him since he started sharing his bed with Ingaret. His choice would have extended to any woman willing and alive, but the lady didn't need to know that.

Finally, she laughed. "I'll be honest, your blunt approach is rather refreshing compared to the unsettling attempts by others to conceal their intentions through what they think is a clever turn of phrase."

Without another word, she drew her robes back, let them sink to the floor, and revealed her marble-like skin completely devoid of any other garments.

Skharr made no attempt to hide his admiration. Her regal form didn't change once it was exposed and she seemed more powerful because of it. The slim build remained curvaceous but showed signs of physical exertion—likely combat training—that took nothing away from the femininity of her body.

She smiled when she saw him staring and recovered her clothes gracefully from where they had fallen. "I trust it will be enough in payment?"

He took a deep breath and drew a rein around his desire for the moment. "Indeed, although if you promised the same payment I demanded of Svana, I will still need a gold coin."

"Why?"

"The guild has a cut of any reward I claim, and I doubt they will partake of what I will. Theros will take what is owed, after all. There will likely also be a need for clothes and perhaps a healing potion or two."

"Clothes?"

"Blood soaks in and stains. If that is the case, what I am wearing will not be acceptable among civilized company. Holes will work toward a similar end."

"You were wounded?" she asked and took a step forward once her clothes were once more in place. "Do you have any scars?"

"Potions tend to not leave those. Although if I have any new wounds, you are welcome to see them."

Rejecting the overtures of a lord appeared to be in popular demand among the noblewomen of the city, especially since it seemed they had a champion to call on now.

Skharr wondered if there would be this kind of work for years to come or if the nobles would be more circumspect and only pursue those women who wanted their affections.

He smirked at the thought of lords curtailing their desires—as unlikely as him giving his allegiance to the hairy-assed Janus, he decided.

As entertaining as that impossibility was, he turned his attention firmly to the guards who surrounded him and escorted him into a small courtyard in front of the lord's mansion.

The men had been far more amenable to his arrival than last time. A few even stared openly at him like they couldn't truly believe that they saw him in the flesh.

Or perhaps they simply couldn't comprehend that a man in his position was stupid enough to involve himself in the business of the gentry a second time.

A chair had been set up beside a small table in the courtyard. Various servants surrounded it, each with their own tasks. A few took turns to fan the man seated in it while others served him food or drink.

The lord had a military look about him, but the robes he wore suggested that he had no intention to fight anyone. He even grinned and stood when he saw Skharr approach.

"Ah, the mighty Barbarian of Theros!" he shouted as his men led his visitor closer. "I am rather impressed that you chose to come yourself. Most others would avoid such entanglements... although I suppose you are not like the others."

The warrior's eyes narrowed as the guards backed away. "You...knew I was coming?"

"Well, word spreads quickly in this city. When a woman I

court met with you personally, I assumed it was only a matter of time before you paid me a visit. Although it could have been one of the three—maybe four—others who are courting her too. Lady Tamisen is extraordinary, is she not?"

He was not too proud to admit that he was thoroughly confused but saw little point in telling the lord. Instead, he simply waited for him to continue.

"Anyway, I hope you understand that I will not risk the lives and health of the men in my employ to test your fighting skills."

By now, he was truly curious about the man's attitude. It simply didn't fit with his expectations and limited experience with the upper echelons.

"As the tale was told—according to the word of Lord Tulius— he traded blows with you and left you in a sorry condition. While he delivered a few significant blows, his magnanimity prompted him to leave you alive and him in a generous mood toward his bride-to-be."

Skharr scowled. It didn't surprise him that the man had lied, however.

"Fortunately for you, Tulius is known to be a lying cheat of a bastard, and the tale quickly fell to pieces once it was discovered that he was looking for more men to protect his villa after a few had died mysteriously or were too injured to continue their service. As such, I did hope to see your skills for myself."

"I am confused." The barbarian looked at the guards, who continued to keep their distance. "Do you intend to fight me on your own?"

"Gods no. I have led a few campaigns in my younger years, but I am not ashamed to admit that I would fall well short were we to exchange blows. However, the captain of my guard has made certain claims when he demanded that I pay him more for his services, and I wish for those claims to be proven first. Should you beat him, your contract will be fulfilled and you will have my solemn oath as Vereen Marhart, Viscount of Yarrow, that I will

discontinue any pursuit of the Lady Tamisen's hand. If you fail...
Well, we shall see."

He shook his head. There was simply no way to anticipate
what these people would be like, and he had a feeling he had been
conscripted into a fight simply for the lord's entertainment.

Still, it felt as though fighting one man would have fewer
consequences than facing all of them.

The guard in question stepped forward. With dark skin and
his curly, black hair cut short, it was immediately apparent that
he was not a local. He wore no armor, but the ivory hilt of the
longsword at his side was certainly familiar.

As was the medallion he wore around his neck.

"A blademaster?" Skharr asked and unhooked his ax from his
belt.

"You've seen my like before?" his opponent asked as the other
guards spread out so they would all have a clear view of the fight.
Even the servants looked as interested as the lord did as they
studied the movements of both fighters.

"Two," the barbarian admitted. "I only ever fought one,
however."

"And you survived. Impressive."

"Gouged the eyes out of the man. Took his sabers and sold
them."

"Interesting. I would expect a Mantis-style fighter to have left
you with at least a dozen weeping wounds before he finally killed
you."

He nodded, his gaze focused as the man drew his blade.
"That...was how the fight went. He talked a great deal while he
waited to kill me. Got too close and I did the killing first. I don't
suppose I can coax you into making the same mistake?"

The blademaster laughed and twirled the blade. The footwork
looked similar to the bandit the warrior had encountered,
although the overall style looked different. The single blade was
perfectly balanced and gave his opponent all the range he would

need to keep him at bay. With both his hands holding it, he would be able to shift it faster than Skharr could move.

Not only that, the speed he evidenced meant he would have to close the distance between them quickly and open himself to the possibility of grievous injury if he wanted to win.

Most fighters avoided injury at all cost. He had made peace with his body being in pain many years before.

His gaze still focused on his adversary, he drew the seax from his belt, grasped it in a backhand grip, and stood his ground while the blademaster studied him closely.

He was careful to offer nothing to indicate the kind of fighter he was. The man would have to start fighting if he wanted to see that.

As if reading the thought, his adversary rested the sword on his shoulder and took a few steps forward before he flicked the blade out toward his neck.

All he needed to do was take a step back and watch the blade whip past him. The other man failed to press his attack and chose instead to rest the blade on his other shoulder and circle again.

Skharr could hear the other guards placing bets, although he couldn't afford to give them the attention necessary to hear what those might be. Coin changed hands as they continued to watch the fight unfold.

It was at times like these that he truly missed his bow.

The blade flicked forward again and this time, arced down to catch him across his left shoulder. It was much closer than the first strike had been, which left him with no other option but to raise the seax to block the attack.

He met it squarely but the weapons clashed hard enough to force his hand down. Immediately, the sword twisted in an attempt to swipe across his neck again. He raised his ax to block it, hooked it with the blade of his weapon, and forced it away before he swung in an assault aimed at the blademaster's head.

It missed, but barely, and the man took a hasty step back. A hint of surprise showed in his features as Skharr moved quickly to close the distance between them and the seax flashed out to catch the man on his hamstring. His opponent took another step back and ducked under a strike to his head from the ax before he spun away and gained some distance.

The barbarian brought his hands up again in a defensive stance but grimaced when a sharp pain jolted down his arm.

He looked down at a thin cut over his shoulder that seeped blood. It surprised him because he hadn't seen or felt the sword strike.

The blademaster had blood on his skin too. He had barely avoided having his head severed, and a shallow cut over his jawline made him wince.

"Rather fast for a big man, aren't you?" The guard flicked his blade to the right and the left before he twisted it over his head in an unfamiliar stance. It didn't alter the length or sharpness of the blade between him and his adversary, however.

"No other way to stay alive," Skharr replied. His wound didn't inhibit his movement, fortunately, and the bleeding had already slowed to a faint trickle. It would increase if the fight lasted much longer, though.

It meant that he had to find a way to end the fight soon or he would have a few more wounds, and the next one could open a vein or cut a tendon.

He knew a trick that hadn't worked with the other blademaster, but perhaps it would work in this instance.

Taking the role of the aggressor this time, he lunged forward and as the distance closed between them, ducked under a swing aimed at his head. He thrust his hand forward and released the seax to spin it toward the man's leg.

A deft defensive motion brought the longsword around quickly enough to intercept the smaller weapon, although an incision bled red on the guard's thigh when the blade came a little too close for comfort.

The sword twisted as the blademaster leaned in and attempted a forward thrust into the barbarian's chest. Skharr countered with his ax and attempted to push it to the side, but the tip of the longsword sliced effortlessly through his clothes and opened a wound over his chest. It wasn't deep but it stung enough that he gritted his teeth.

He lurched forward and attempted to catch the blademaster off balance, but the longsword swiped over his side as it was returned to a defensive position. His adversary shoved his attempted blow with the ax aside and swung toward his arm as he made a second attempt.

This provided an opening—not much of one, but it was there.

Instead of following through with the strike, he released the haft of his weapon and hurled it toward the blademaster. The lack of balance in the weapon turned the blade away from the guard, but the haft struck home and delivered a hard blow to the man's head above his eye.

The sword sliced his arm, but Skharr had already surged into an attack with no other weapons but his bare hands. It would have to be enough.

His right arm wound around the blademaster's like a constrictor and squeezed him with all the power he could muster without allowing the sword to come free again. He was only able to get in close because the man's line of sight had prevented him from seeing the attack, and it was the last desperate opening he would have.

An attempt to draw back by his adversary was quickly thwarted as the warrior dragged him into the path of his fist and pounded it into the man's skull above his other eye. A wound appeared over the bone, bleeding and blinding him as he delivered another crushing blow into the guard's gut before the blademaster finally released his sword and it clattered noisily at his feet.

Skharr used his advantage, pushed into motion, and pounded

his right elbow into his opponent's jawline with the force of a battering ram. The blow lifted him off his feet and he fell heavily and moaned in pain.

"Enough!"

The warrior paused, reluctant to lose the opportunity to press his advantage against the man on the ground. The guard met his gaze with no fear in his eyes. He was ready to fight to his last breath, but it appeared it wouldn't be necessary.

"Both parties have proven themselves." Vereen stood from his chair, his expression pensive. "I dare say that without your desperate measures, you would not have been able to best my man but victory is yours, nonetheless. I will send him to my physicians before I increase his pay. As for you... Well, my word stands. I will abandon all pursuit of Lady Tamisen."

"Glad we could come to an agreement." Skharr picked up the fallen sword and offered his hand to the downed man as well.

The blademaster paused for a second before he took it. "You have absolutely no style to your fighting. Neither does a hammer on the anvil, however. Your speed, aggression, and desperate maneuvers all seemed calculated."

"I always fight for my life," he replied, helped the guard to his feet, and handed him his weapon. "Do the same and you'll find you have an edge over every opponent you face."

"Noted."

A couple of the others moved forward to help their captain, who was still unsteady on his feet.

"You appear in need of some medical attention as well, barbarian," Vereen continued. "Might I suggest the services of my physicians to you before you return to report your success?"

Skharr studied the man carefully, but something in his gut told him there would be no attempt on his life while his wounds were attended to.

"That...would be appreciated," he muttered finally and flexed his arm with a grimace.

CHAPTER SIX

The nobleman's physicians certainly knew their craft. They relied on a combination of medical knowledge and magic and used a handful of potions Skharr did not recognize. Still, the pain ebbed quickly and once the bleeding had stopped, a few dabs of another concoction soothed the wounded areas, and a third healed them completely.

"Viscount Vereen does enjoy watching blood sports," the healer told him and completed her work deftly. "Our services are required to tend those who don't kill each other attempting to impress him. He pays his men well, but I cannot fathom the mind of those who act as his guards willingly."

Skharr had to admit that he couldn't fathom it either. Even among his people, fighting was always a matter of necessity, and while some enjoyed it—himself included—there was no time that combat took place simply for entertainment.

It would have been considered distasteful—even among barbarians, he thought with a smile.

Still, the healers worked quickly and the weapons he had thrown during the fight were handed to him on his way to the gate. None of the guards were willing to hold his gaze, which meant that more than a few had lost coin betting against him.

In all honesty, he didn't care. They had likely seen these little fights before if they were comfortable enough to risk coin on the outcome. He was more curious as to whether the blademaster would see an increase in his wages. Lords like Vereen tended to not take the failure of those in their employ lightly.

When he arrived at Tamisen's villa, he realized that a young woman with black hair and tanned skin was already waiting for him at the gate. Small and delicate and with none of the frills and ornate decoration he had come to expect from the ladies in this city, she was still utterly beautiful to behold.

She was no doubt one of the servants.

Before Skharr could speak, she stepped forward but kept her gaze lowered.

"Lady Tamisen has instructed me to bring you to her upon your return, Lord Skharr."

"I'm no lord," he protested, but the girl had already turned to move toward the gate and expected him to follow her.

He did, although a few curious glances were cast at them by the guards he passed.

His guide was quick on her feet and he had to increase his pace to keep up with her as she led him deeper into the property than he had been earlier and into the mansion, although through one of the side entrances.

Even in the glow of the setting sun, everything about it looked radiant as it caught the light and reflected it in hues of purple, gold, and silver.

Too much coin had gone into building these homes, he mused dispassionately, but he had little time to take in the sights. His guide was already leading him through the passages reserved for servants and from there, into the main chambers of the house.

She finally reached a door and pushed it open.

"She awaits you," the girl whispered.

"Thank you," he answered. He received no answer from her as he stepped through the doorway but honestly hadn't expected one. It closed softly behind him.

Torches were already lit within to illuminate the room alongside a few scented candles. There was no fireplace, however. He assumed that was because the city was never cold enough to require them.

Movement from the side of the room immediately drew his attention as Tamisen stepped away from where she had stood and inspected herself in the mirror.

Aside from a pearl necklace around her neck and a silver bracelet, she wore absolutely nothing. Even her red hair had been styled to ensure that nothing impeded his view of her naked body.

"Welcome back, Lord Skharr," she said and advanced toward him.

"I am no lord," he responded roughly, but the reasoning for his protests vanished immediately when the scent of her perfume enveloped him. He couldn't place the precise fragrance, but it and the sight of her were enough to make his body react to the point of distraction.

There had to be something magical about it, he thought vaguely, but the notion was set aside when she pressed herself against him and stood on her toes to stretch up and kiss his neck.

"You are a lord tonight," she whispered as she took his hand and lifted it to her breast. "You will be fucking a lady."

That seemed reasonable enough, although a part of him realized that his brain seemed to have lost both the will and the ability for logic.

With a smile, she smoothed her hands over his chest and slipped her fingers under his shirt to pull it aside, holes and all.

"I should...probably bathe first," he mumbled hoarsely, but it felt like someone else entirely had spoken from a great distance. "I wouldn't want to..."

His voice trailed off once she finished with his shirt and focused on his trousers.

"Wouldn't want to what?"

A good question, he thought dazedly and tried to recapture his earlier thought. Unfortunately, it took a moment as his mind wandered again when her tongue flicked his nipple lightly.

"I am not clean. I would not want to…dirty anything."

She laughed. The low sound vibrated against his bare skin as she placed her lips on his chest again.

"I want you smelling like a man," she whispered and the soft flutter of her breath teased his skin. "Not of roses and lilies but as a man should."

Skharr ran his hand through her hair, pried it loose from the ties that held it contained, and let it fall like a fiery waterfall over her back.

"As the lady desires."

"I am no lady tonight." She looked into his eyes, her gaze hooded as she drifted her hands between his thighs. "And I expect you to not treat me as one."

He smirked at the request, which seemed like the most reasonable one she had made of him so far. Enthralled, he stood willingly as she dropped slowly to her knees in front of him.

———

"Won't you stay the night?"

Skharr paused while donning the new clothes that had been provided for him. In the rush since his return, there hadn't been time for him to do anything other than discard those he had worn earlier, and there was always the assumption that they hadn't managed to match his size.

These, however, were a perfect fit.

"I thought you were sleeping," he answered simply, pulled the shirt on, and grimaced when it slid a little too smoothly over his skin.

Tamisen smiled and rolled to slip out from under the silken sheets before she stretched with delicate grace, likely meant to entice him back to the bed. "I did need a few moments to rest after our…exertions, but I thought you might stay for the night. I can have my servants bring food for us if you wish it."

He let his gaze linger for a moment on what she displayed so openly and couldn't deny that he was incredibly tempted. A whole night of passion with the woman was certainly something to look forward to. As was the food that would be provided in a villa like this, but he couldn't shake an uncomfortable feeling.

It had crept in and driven him to move away from the comfortable bed once they had finished.

The healing potions had done their work and the injuries that had been inflicted were no more, but as with all the other times, he could still feel the wounds like ghosts that lingered to remind him of them. He traced his fingers over his shoulder and recalled the slash he had taken there.

"Well?" she asked, shook her hair enticingly, and walked to where he stood to press herself against his side. "You are more than welcome to stay for the evening if you wish it—although with the condition you left me in, I might require a few of my attendants to step in and finish if our lovemaking this afternoon was any indication."

That was certainly tempting, but Skharr disengaged from her and collected his weapons from where they had been hung over a nearby chair.

"Believe me when I tell you that I wish with every ounce of my being that it wasn't true, but I have business to attend to before the morning." He strapped the seax and dagger to his belt. "Besides, I fear you might not want word to be spread that you entertained me for the evening. From what I've seen, word travels quickly in this city, wherever it might originate."

"I suppose you are right," she whispered as she retrieved a silken robe and drew it over her body. "Even so, a woman has needs, no matter what her station, and I rather enjoy your particular method of sating them."

Skharr looked around and finally found the single gold coin that had been paid to him for his services. "I am pleased that they met with your approval, Lady Tamisen. And do consider me if you need more help to deal with unwanted suitors, although I would appreciate it if you kept my name from any others who might want similar services. It would only be a matter of time before I find myself facing someone who kills me for my efforts."

"Of course," she murmured and traced her fingers over his chest as he finished his preparations. "I might even need your services without needing your services next time."

He smiled and bowed stiffly at the hips before he exited the room. While he could accept that the compliment suggested by the statement was sincere, it was doubtful that he would see the woman under the same conditions again. A brief night of passion was one thing, but his presence there more than once would mean an affair and that carried certain implications that would bode ill for her in the future.

One of the guards escorted him to the gates, and the barbarian knew any one of a handful of taverns nearby would suit his need for a meal, despite the time.

The sun had only set about an hour earlier so most of them would still be serving their patrons and would have food of decent quality to offer.

Once again, the prickly sensation on the back of his neck told him he was being watched but in the darkness, it was even more difficult to pinpoint the origin of it.

Still, his tensions had been effectively relieved by the Lady Tamisen and he now cared a great deal less about who was following him and why. They would slip up eventually, and all he had to do was remain on his guard.

MICHAEL ANDERLE

The food at the tavern he selected proved to be of good quality, although the wine had been watered down to reduce the drunkenness of the patrons. It was the first time he'd ever seen an establishment that wished to restrict how much their patrons drank, but he chose not to question it. There was no point in drinking himself into a stupor at this point in the evening. Besides, perhaps he had it wrong and they did so to encourage their customers to drink more.

He relaxed over his meal and considered his situation. If someone were following him, it might be a good idea to let them think he was drunk. It seemed logical that if they meant him harm, they would likely take their chances when they thought his wits were gone.

The barbarian leaned back, having enjoyed the side of pork that had been roasted over an open flame, and ordered another drink. Shortly thereafter, he requested another.

Skharr made a show of walking unsteadily toward the door when he was finished. He was careful to not appear overly drunk to the point of suspicion but enough to make anyone watching think he intended to return to his home to sleep it off.

His gaze scanned his surroundings and he hummed a tune softly as though unaware of potential danger.

Oddly enough, the drunken feeling he'd pretended seemed to become a reality. The warrior halted, leaned against one of the buildings, and drew deep breaths.

Something was wrong. It would take more than three goblets of watered wine to diminish his senses to this extent and an unsettled feeling settled in his stomach.

The world began to blur around him and his hands trembled.

"Fucking...goblin-sucking...she-bitches from the hells," he whispered and shook his head as he forced himself away from the building. All he needed to do was put one foot in front of the other until he reached the Mermaid. Once there, he would be able to recover and perhaps take a potion to soothe the effects of whatever had caused this.

It took a moment for him to realize that his feet wouldn't respond. He scowled at them and tried to will them into movement, but they remained heavy and sluggish. The one that did finally move caught on one of the cobblestones.

"Fuck and—"

The fall seemed to take forever, but once he landed, he wasn't sure why he'd wanted it to end. His cheek had struck painfully against a stone and he could taste blood in his mouth.

A shadow flitted out from the darkened side streets and advanced rapidly on him.

"Knew you...were there...bastard," Skharr slurred and struggled to keep his eyes focused.

They showed no inclination to cooperate either and all he could hear was someone calling his name.

CHAPTER SEVEN

"Skharr!"

The voice seemed to come from a mile away. What certainly didn't feel like it came from a great distance was the blow that caught him across the jaw. It was open-handed but hard enough to force a reaction from him.

His heart pounded and blood rushed in his ears as he looked around and tried to determine the source so he could retaliate as his instincts pushed him to do.

Unfortunately, his body didn't seem to be able to respond. He managed to move slightly but with no coordination, and what he had intended as a roar emerged as a low moan and he simply flopped onto the cobbles again.

"You've been poisoned, you big idiot." This time, someone caught him by the shirt and turned him.

It was dark and he couldn't see well enough to determine who was standing there, but from the voice, it was probably a woman.

Another hand struck him on the side of the head. It landed a little higher than before and closer to his temple.

"Ow! You…godsbefucked goblin-turd. S-stop doing…that!"

"Stop flopping about like a damn grounded fish and I'll stop

68

treating you like one." The voice grew more familiar with every passing second. "Can you stand? Because I doubt I can carry you to my horse so you'll have to help me to help you."

Skharr shook his head in an effort to clear it but with little result. Still, some power remained in his body—enough that he would be able to stand, at least, with a little help.

"There we go, you big bastard." The woman groaned. She had more power in her frame than he would have thought. Too many cobbles distracted him, however, and he swayed and staggered as he struggled to maintain his balance on the uneven surface.

"Who...who poisoned me?" he asked and grimaced as he slurred the words again.

"Enough time for that. Keep those legs moving, you big lug."

The barbarian nodded. It wasn't like she needed to tell him but the reminder certainly helped him focus.

"And up on the horse."

She helped him lift his foot into the stirrup. He would not have been able to mount and ride properly, but it seemed as though the woman had no intention to let him ride.

With a quick shove from her, he sprawled across the horse like a corpse. Footsteps traced her path around the beast until she stood over him and studied him to make sure he was secure in his ignominious position over the saddle.

"Sera?" he asked when he finally realized where he'd seen her face before.

"At last. I thought you would have a better memory of my face after our adventures together."

"Ad...adventures..."

Something was wrong as it grew dark again. He could no longer see where she was, although it was easy to feel the horse moving.

Troll-sucking godsbedammed poison, he thought belligerently and winced at the effort it took. He needed to think about what it meant that someone had used that against him. It was the weapon of the nobility, not a simple street assassin.

Caro wouldn't struggle under the burden despite the barbarian's weight. He was a warhorse and a little older in years, which was why she had been able to acquire him at such a reasonable price. Warhorses—fully trained, young, and ready for a fight—were bred for combat and to be ridden by knights into actual battles.

Sera patted the old beast on the side of the neck as they continued to move through the streets to where she had established her quarters.

They weren't large. Her sister had chosen to live her life in luxury. She, on the other hand, needed to be on the move. While she loved Verenvan, she hated nothing more than to remain inside the walls for too long. It was why she had chosen the regular work of escorting folk to the mountains and back. It paid less than other work she could have taken, but it was also somewhat safer as long as none of her clients had become a particular target.

The horse snorted and shook his head and she looked at another man who rode down the street toward them. The initial instinct to reach for her weapon was put aside when she recognized the horse before she did the man.

He failed to see her as he dismounted, tied his mount to a nearby fence post, and moved to the door to bang his fist on it.

"None of the lights are on, Regor," she called, still leading Caro toward him. "That should tell you there is no one ready to let you in."

"I assumed you would be sleeping," he responded. "And I needed to wake you."

"Why would I need to speak to you if I was asleep?"

"Perhaps you should tell me. When your crow arrived at my

house, I assumed you were in the mood for company in the middle of the night."

"I am." Sera patted the man slung over her saddle.

"A drunk?"

"Likely, but not this time. You remember Skharr, do you not?"

Regor's eyes widened. "Well, that explains the size of him. What happened?"

"He's been poisoned."

"Shit. How?"

"I'm not sure. Did you bring your medicines?"

The young man nodded. "Yes. Yes, I did."

"Then help me. I don't think I'll be able to carry him into the house on my own."

He strode toward her and helped to drag the unconscious Skharr off the saddle. Even with two of them, it was a struggle to move the massive man from the horse and into her home. Sera was breathing hard and had sweated through her shirt by the time they laid him on the bed.

It at least looked like Regor was in a similar condition, which showed that they had both put similar effort into moving the barbarian.

"You'll want to strip the bedsheets," he commented once they had caught their breath. "If I don't specifically know what poison it is, there will be only one cure for it."

"Mustard root?"

He nodded. "Honestly, he might have preferred to die."

"You remember how he helped us. We owe him our lives. Once that debt is paid, he'll be more than welcome to take his life however he pleases. Slitting one's wrist is rather popular, although a few men prefer to be dropped from a great height and others prefer to merely charge into battle. Skharr would most likely prefer the latter if I know him at all."

"How did you know that he was in danger?"

"A…someone alerted me to his danger and I've trailed him to

make sure nothing happened to him. I didn't follow him everywhere, which would of course be when he was struck. I'll need to go to his room in the Mermaid and collect his things."

"I'll help him in the meantime. But see to the sheets before you go. As I said, once he ingests the root, the ensuing mess will not be pretty."

"Yes." Sera scowled. "I was afraid of that but keep him alive. I'll be back. You have your weapons on you, yes, if anyone tries to break in?"

He patted the sword on his hip. "Will you tell me what kind of danger I should expect?"

"Nothing, I hope. I'll explain everything when I return."

She could tell that he wanted to ask more questions, but like Skharr, the man owed her his life. The unspoken agreement was that he would help her, not as a way to pay it back but because they both kept each other alive.

Once she'd roused the staff and instructed them regarding the bedding, Sera stepped away from the building and glanced casually around her for anyone who could be watching her house. Someone wanted Skharr dead, and they would not expect him simply to keel over. If she knew anything about him and his people, they were far hardier than most.

The guild captain remained alert and watchful as she started through the streets. She found nothing to concern her, however, only the common groups of urchins who waited for drunks they could steal from. A handful of more professional robbers drew away the moment they laid eyes on her.

She could understand that. They wanted soft targets, and a woman with a sword at her hip was to be avoided at all costs.

Most of the city guard patrolled closer to the walls and the wealthy areas of the city, as well as the port. The remainder of the city relied on those who could be bought with coin, and she had taken some work of that kind herself when she'd first started. It wasn't particularly easy and the pay was shit, but they always needed hands somewhere so the work was plentiful.

Sera had survived her time there and made a name for herself before she moved on to greener pastures. The city had destroyed so many and few had walked away from that life. She and her sister had been among those who managed to succeed, but she was under no illusions that this was a common occurrence. Both she and Micah had the help of their blood kin, those very interested in seeing them both succeed.

The Swilling Mermaid and the famous sign of the woman with her breasts exposed was a familiar sight, and one she'd seen too many times. She knew it better than most. When she slipped through the door, the sound of revelry issued from inside despite the later hour.

The owner was usually a little more vigilant, but he was distracted by a group of drunks who tried to start a fight. He had been in the market for a couple of the guilds to defend his business, but he discovered that too many people were too afraid of being banned from the Mermaid so they mostly behaved while inside the walls.

Skharr had carried a key to his room. She would use it to collect his things, although Horse would probably be better off where he was.

She slipped up the steps when the owner looked away and remained in the shadows, her hand on her sword as she advanced. His room was supposed to be empty, but candlelight seeped through the cracks in the wood.

With her hand resting lightly on her weapon, she placed the key in the keyhole and twisted it slowly.

"Stay away!" a woman said from within.

With a frown, she slid the blade out in a single smooth motion and stepped inside. The familiar thrill that came before combat rippled over her as she looked around the room for any potential attackers.

The single occupant didn't look particularly dangerous. The barbarian certainly knew how to choose his women, she thought with a smirk. She looked a little thin, although she filled her dress out in all the right places, and her thick, dark curls were in something of a mess. Sera assumed the woman had been preparing for sleep before she heard the latch of the door lift.

As a reaction, she held a stool up, ready to defend herself with it although it wasn't clear how.

"No need to attack me," the guild captain said. She lowered her blade and slid it slowly into its sheath before she raised her hands. "I mean you no harm."

The woman maintained her tight hold on the stool and shook it a little as if to remind the intruder of its existence. "Then don't break in."

"I wasn't...breaking in. That was not—never mind. Who are you and what are you doing here?"

"Asks the woman who broke in?"

"No. It's what the woman with a sword wants to know."

"Oh... Right." The stranger lowered her stool. "My name is Ingaret. I... Skharr allowed me to stay here most nights while I regained my feet in the city."

Sera nodded and looked around. "I suppose such arrangements aren't unheard of in this city."

"What arrangements?"

"Are..." She paused and looked around the room. "Are the two of you not...uh, close?"

"Close?"

"Sexually."

"Oh. No! Nothing like that. He...well, I did offer, but Skharr refused. I think he might have thought I would have been unwilling had I not been desperate and in need of help. He chose not to."

"I...huh."

"You appear surprised. Have you and he been...close?"

The captain narrowed her eyes. "What? Of course not."

"Then why are you here? I assume you used his key to enter. Why else would he trust you with it?"

"Because...no, that doesn't matter." She studied the woman closely and noticed the brand on the inside of her arm when she placed the stool down. It was a mark she knew although most in the city didn't, of course. All things considered, it was difficult to be a part of the city's rancid underbelly without running into people of that ilk.

Ingaret had no doubt worked for them, and Skharr had stepped in to make sure she didn't have to go back. He was a little brutish, but Sera had already seen a hint of heroism in the man.

"So, he's not fucking you, then?" the woman asked.

"No, I'm not fucking him. I worked with him and owe him my life. When..." She paused, grasped her sword again, and turned quickly to the door as it started to open.

Thankfully, a familiar face peered through after a timid knock. The innkeeper looked confused by the sight of two women in a room that was supposed to be occupied by a man, but he made it a point to not ask any questions.

Instead, he nodded to her. "Evening, Miss Ferat. Expecting trouble?"

She realized that her hand was still on her sword and released it quickly. "Always. Is there trouble, Felix?"

"Of a sort. A message has come in for Master Skharr from the Theros guild. I don't suppose you would know of his whereabouts?"

Sera nodded. "He's been poisoned. I have a physician attending to his welfare and I thought he might need his possessions, which explains my presence in his room."

"Will he be all right?" Ingaret asked.

"Aye, eventually. Although I suppose he'll feel the worse for wear over the next few days."

Felix looked at the two women and shrugged. "I don't want to be involved in the business of nobility. Tell me no truths and I'll have to think of no lies."

"I have missed you, Felix."

"And I you, Miss Ferat. Would you need an escort to your house?"

"It's unlikely, but I appreciate your concern. What message came for him? I think I can deliver it."

"A boy came in—he's familiar. I've seen him trying to sneak some coin from my patrons in the past, but it seems Skharr chose him for some personal work. He said he'd seen the two swill-sucking bottom-feeders who had given Miss Ingaret trouble moving about the street, so he took notes and wanted them delivered."

He handed her a few strips of leather that had been scribbled on with coal. The handful of addresses were easily recognizable as headquarters for the criminals of the city.

Whoever the barbarian had come up against were not men to be taken lightly.

"I'll make sure he sees this." Sera tucked the strips into her pocket. "Will there be any other business? What about the costs for his horse to remain here and the room to be held in his name? I could cover them or, if it would be better for you, I could move everything into my stables."

"Your stables, miss?"

She smiled thinly. "Will there be any further costs?"

"If you need them, I have hoarded as many anti-poison potions as I could get my hands on. They're not cheap but they should be effective. I tend to use them on those patrons who indulge too heavily in my brews. Those who can pay, that is."

With another smile, she shook her head. "While I'm sure your prices are more than fair, my man already has that in hand. All Skharr needs to do is be careful of where he eats and what he eats."

"There should be no costs aside from holding the room from next week. He has paid for another week already."

Sera nodded, took three silver coins from her pouch, and handed them to the innkeeper.

"I said—"

"For your silence and for you to deliver a message to the guild. Tell them I will see them tomorrow on Skharr's behalf before the full-day requirement to pay is over."

"Of course, miss."

She moved through the room and collected everything that appeared to belong to the barbarian.

"I'm going with you," Ingaret declared once she had finished and moved toward the door.

The captain opened her mouth to tell her she couldn't but paused to consider it. Skharr had protected her from dangerous people. Leaving her alone there would likely also leave her in harm's way.

"Fine. But you help me carry his things."

She handed one of the bags to the woman, who initially struggled under the weight of it as Sera led her down the stairs and toward the stables.

There was still no sign that anyone had followed her, and she didn't like it. If someone had no interest in her, they were very likely already aware of Skharr's location.

Hopefully, the men guarding her house would keep him safe for the moment.

They entered the stables and she knew the gazes of the stable hands were all focused on her as she strode through to the stall where Horse was located.

"I still don't know why he didn't give you a decent name," she muttered under her breath as she pulled the door open.

The animal didn't so much as spare her a glance and continued to chew placidly on a mouthful of hay while she saddled him and slid on the strange bridle which seemed to have no recognizable purpose at all.

"Can I have some help here?" she asked and stared at the stable hands.

"You won't get him to budge if he don't want to," one of the boys shouted. "If he wants to follow you, he will. If he don't, you wouldn't be able to drag him out."

"Don't be ridiculous." Sera shook her head, took the bridle, and tried to pull the stallion toward the door.

Horse planted his feet firmly and stared at her while he chewed. Another tug brought a snort from the beast but not a single step.

"The big'un who comes here always talks to the horse like it can understand him," another boy added. "If you wants him to follow, you's has to talk to him. Ask him to follow."

Another tug showed that she certainly wouldn't persuade him to move in the conventional way.

"Come on," she muttered. "I...need you to move so I can return to my house. Think you can do that?"

The only reaction from the stallion was a snort.

"If I may?" Ingaret stepped inside, slipped around Sera to move beside the beast, and patted him on the neck. "We need to go, Horse. Skharr is hurt and sick, and he needs you to come to him. We don't have much time."

Horse stopped eating and nudged the woman's arm gently before he turned and followed the reins that Sera held without resistance. She shook her head in exasperation as they moved out of the stables.

Once outside, she laid the bags over the horse's back and they continued their walk.

It seemed as though Horse was more eager to leave than they were. He leaned his head forward and tugged at the reins.

"All right, all right, we're coming," Sera remonstrated and patted him on the neck.

CHAPTER EIGHT

The bed was little more than a cot that had been brought in for Skharr. The fact that it was still standing under the weight of the huge man was a demonstration of its strength and the skill of whoever had put the godsbedammed thing together.

Regor felt the temperature of the wet cloth he had put on his patient's forehead with one hand, sighed, and removed it. The man was a raging fire. He still didn't know what kind of poison had been used but it had acted far too quickly for it to be cheap, especially given the barbarian's extraordinary size.

He placed another cool cloth on his forehead before he dipped the first one in cool water again and washed it. Mustard Root had been added to absorb the venom, and while it was effective and would rapidly deal with whatever poison had been ingested—especially since he'd spooned a little of the tea he'd made from it into him—he knew for a fact that things would get messy very quickly.

"I don't like seeing you like this, big man," he muttered as he prepared another vial of the paste. "A part of me had come to see you almost as an Immortal—or at least someone undefeatable. An unstoppable force, that's how I see you. I know you're human, but it was like you didn't see it. A pity you had to find it out like this."

Skharr twitched, shook his head, and mumbled something in a language the young man couldn't understand.

"No," the warrior whispered finally and his head whipped from side to side. "No…not…not Therena. Not…not Therena."

"Is he awake?"

Regor bolted from his seat, his hand on his weapon, and frowned at a young woman who wore clothes he had come to recognize as belonging to servants of the household.

He felt a little embarrassment at his reaction, but after the warning from Sera, he did not intend to take the matter of Skharr's safety lightly. His hand relaxed on the dagger at his side.

"No," he answered after a moment. "He's dreaming. Feverish, too. He's fighting the toxins, however, and with help, he should be…"

His patient began to shake on the cot and he let his sentence trail into nothing.

Both he and the woman stepped closer and rolled the barbarian onto his side seconds before a vile liquid spewed from his lips. Regor shoved a bucket beneath the cot as Skharr heaved and began to vomit the contents of his stomach. It wasn't a pretty sight, and most of it splashed into the bucket, but not all. The foul smell filled the room quickly and even the young mercenary couldn't help but cringe and cover his nose.

They finally relaxed when he lowered his head onto the bed and muttered unintelligibly again. He left him on his side. It had been unwise to position him on his back, but once they had manhandled him into the bedroom, it was all he could do to get the man onto the bed.

This night had certainly not unfolded in the way he had thought it would. The whole peloton was taking time off between their trips to the mountains but Sera's crow had flown in with a message for him to hurry to the woman's house.

It wasn't quite a villa but it was certainly larger and more spacious and luxurious than any other house he had seen in the city.

"Lady Ferat has returned," the servant said and scowled at a few splatters of vomit on her dress. "She and another lady brought a horse into the stables."

"If she has returned, why has she not come to see him?" Regor poured water into a cup and drank it quickly. He drew a deep breath and immediately regretted it when the smell assailed him again.

"Lady Ferat said she had business to attend to on the warrior's behalf," she continued. "The woman who came with her has been provided with quarters, and she asked that he be moved to a proper room."

"I hope you are all ready for those proper rooms to be soiled something fierce," he replied and pushed from his seat when a couple of other servants entered to help carry Skharr to new quarters.

"I've seen the effects of Mustard Root before, sir." She smiled as they lifted the cot. There were three of them, and even then, they had difficulty with the tremendous weight.

"Did Lady Ferat tell you what kind of business she would be dealing with?" Regor asked as he stepped forward to help the servants.

"No, but she did say she might be in need of your services herself before the night ended."

He nodded. "I was afraid you'd say that."

———

She had seen places like this before.

Thankfully, she had never worked in one of them, but she had unfortunately worked for those who would spend their time in such places—men who wanted to take their pleasure away from wives and commitments. There was always the potential for consequences, of course, although those possibilities decreased in proportion to a rise in the price.

Sera settled into a crouch beside one of the windows. Men stood guard outside, but they always watched the streets and never looked at the rooftops.

Micah had taught her many things about how to avoid being seen. The masters who had instructed her with the blade had taught her the rest. She was certain that she wouldn't be seen and especially not this late at night. Those guards who were in place appeared to struggle to stay awake. Of course, they were addicted to various roots as well and had no doubt partaken of their particular favorite, which meant they would be violent if they encountered anyone.

But it also meant they would be jittery and distracted by their imaginings and so would pay little attention to anything that happened around them.

It gave her the opportunity she needed. She stood directly above the group, verified that none of them were looking toward her, and inched around the building.

There were a few other locations in the area that the boy had mentioned, but he wouldn't have come close to this building and with good reason.

The guild captain grasped the side, adjusted her balance, and circled the building to listen and peek through the windows. All of them were open since no one could bear to keep them closed in this heat.

Sera moved away from those from which sounds of sex issued —loud, enthusiastic moans from the women and rough grunts from the men.

There were a few with only men or only women inside. These were the kinds of establishments that catered to any needs and desires. Those who availed themselves of what was on offer tried to tell themselves that no victims were involved and these weren't crimes, but she knew better.

Still, as distasteful as they were, they weren't the criminals she was looking for.

Despite the sounds she would far rather not hear, she was grateful that the windows were all open and she tried to choose those behind which the rooms seemed a little quieter. While she didn't know exactly what she was looking for, she was reasonably sure she would know it when she saw it.

Of course, the answer was fairly obvious when she thought about it. There was nothing in the building quite as easy to identify as a large brawler of a man who looked like he had been trampled by about fifteen bulls with their balls tied and being whipped with fresh reeds.

Or, she thought with a broad grin, Skharr's loving touch.

"I can't say I don't miss the bitch," the other man said, "but I did manage to keep her from finding any other kind of work in the city. It won't be long before she crawls back to us."

"How…how long?" The larger man looked like he had trouble speaking and held a wet cloth to his jaw. His eyes were glassy and pupils dilated, a sure sign that he ingested the same roots and herbs the men on the street did.

"Not sure."

"But I…I want her. I want her now."

"I know you do, Yurunn, but we can't force her. Not yet. You remember what happened when we tried that. You got your jaw broke by that big fucker."

"It hurts."

"I know it does. But I went to the bakery where she was working and spoke to the baker. It was easy to convince him that she was free with her favors for any man who would look at her twice and drop a couple of coins, including barbarian trash. Once I made sure he knew she wasn't good for their business, he sent her packing. The slut went crying back to the Mermaid."

"Did you follow her?"

"Of course not. I like living, thank you very much. I'm not stupid enough to be seen around that fucking filthy barbarian-loving place. When she reached the doors, I left. That was all I needed to see. She simply has to realize that she won't find any sanctuary in the world unless it's in our arms."

"Good." The injured man nodded, leaned back, and picked a leaf up from a plate on the table next to him. He chewed on it slowly. "But she needs to come back to us soon. I miss her."

"I know you do. And that means we need to find another way to rid ourselves of that godsbedammed protector. Get some rest, Yurunn. You won't heal unless you rest. Those leaves the doctor gave you should be enough to help you to sleep."

Sera eased away from the window and let the men continue their conversation about whatever leaves the "doctor" had seen fit to give his patient.

She'd heard enough. With the mark Ingaret bore, she knew the woman had worked there before, or at least an establishment like it. It explained why Skharr hadn't taken advantage of her as most men would have.

Some might have even considered that they were doing her a favor. The barbarian had the same needs as most men did but appeared to be a little particular about where he had them sated.

With slow, cautious movements, she shifted her grasp and inched to one of the lower rooftops that would be a little easier to perch on.

Skharr had picked a fight with these two. Or, rather, it appeared they had picked a fight with him and it hadn't ended well for at least one of them.

But she needed it to end. Calling her people in to deal with them would bring no real resolution. The criminals responsible would vanish like rats and emerge somewhere else to simply continue their filthy work and peddle the same flesh.

Someone else needed to get in there and beat some sense into them. She recalled the kind of conversation she'd had with her sister about such matters. Some lessons needed to be taught very physically and very personally.

Sera had learned that if she intended to teach those lessons, she had to do so herself.

She took a deep breath, considered the options, and shook her head and mumbled as each particular option was considered and discarded.

The sun would rise in a few hours and she wanted to return to the safety of her home before dawn to check the progress Skharr had made in his recovery.

It needed to be a quick lesson, then.

As always, circumstances would decide how she went about it. She would not be able to approach the entrance of the building without being challenged, for one thing. And the initial challenge would be followed by many others if she dawdled. There would be no point in that.

Thankfully, she'd dressed for the occasion—a mask pulled over the bottom half of her face and a hood that covered her hair and partially obscured her upper face in shadow. It had been a while since she had used the garb Micah had acquired for her. A gift, the woman had said, although she never thought she would need to use it.

The captain dropped onto the street away from anyone who might notice her and kept her hood down low so that, in the darkness, they would not be able to see her mask until it was far too late.

It took a couple of attempts but she managed to stumble and lurch fairly convincingly like she was drunk. Her efforts finally caught the attention of the two men who guarded the entrance to the building.

"Oi!" one of them shouted as she approached and tripped clumsily over the cobbles.

Sera ignored them and tottered toward the door, mumbling

gibberish that would make them think she was drunk or drugged like they were.

"You needs a password to get in there," the other man grumbled and caught her by the shoulder. "And from the smells of youse, I'd say you cain't afford it."

Her sword was hidden in her robe but very easy to access, especially since they anticipated little to no trouble from a woman and a drunk one at that.

She drew her weapon and it slid clear of its scabbard with a soft hiss. The blade continued into a deft sideways slice that inflicted a diagonal wound across the first man's throat.

Before the second could react, she reversed her strike and the guard's head tumbled away. His body sank slowly to its knees and sagged on the cobbles.

It always brought satisfaction to engage henchmen like these. No matter what she did to them, she never had a reason to feel bad given that they were responsible for doing much worse to others.

A quick search in the pockets of the first man—who still clung to life with his hands clutched over his throat to contain the blood and air that bubbled between his fingers—produced an ugly, rusted key. She had no interest in the rest of their possessions, and they would be picked clean of everything they owned, including their clothes, before the sun came up.

All she needed was the key.

The guild captain paused a moment to wipe the blood off her blade on the first man's sleeve before she sheathed the weapon. She didn't anticipate a need to kill anyone else this night— although if that changed, she would have little compunction about drawing her weapon again.

For now, though, she could move faster and attract less notice with it sheathed.

The key fitted smoothly into the lock and with a quick jerk, the door opened into a narrow, contained room where two more guards were stationed.

Neither looked up from the bones they were playing. Perhaps they assumed the only people who would be allowed in were those who had the password.

A woman who wore almost nothing at all was the first to notice the new arrival and took a step forward.

"Good evening, how may we—"

Sera held a hand up to stop her greeting. The two men noticed her mask, and after a few moments for their addled minds to process it, began to reach for their weapons.

Both carried studded clubs, although neither would have time to raise them in their defense.

She circled the woman, moved in low, and swept the legs out from under the man closest to her. He landed heavily and the floor shook with the impact as she drew her sword.

The other already had his club in hand, but he had no time to raise it before she swung the pommel of her weapon across his cheek and followed it with her elbow in his gut. She drove every ounce of power she had a little lower and to the right than most would have.

The man's body stopped working the way it was meant to, although it took a moment for him to realize it. After years of abusing various roots and spirits, his liver was enlarged and vulnerable and he fell and groaned in pain at her feet.

"This is no commentary on your skills," Sera told the shocked bystander as she drove her boot into the face of the fallen man to ensure that he was unconscious. "I am sure you would have provided a lovely evening, but I am afraid that I would not be your type or you mine."

The woman nodded and the guild captain moved on. She wasn't sure if the whore thought she was a man or not, but in the end, it didn't matter much. Those who spoke of what happened would describe her as massive—perhaps even much like Skharr, a thought that brought no small amusement. There would be no shame in their defeat with tales of that ilk.

Well, less shame, even if they knew better.

No other guards patrolled the building and once she'd gained her bearings, Sera was able to navigate through the halls without getting lost until she reached the third level. None of the patrons in the rooms had heard anything, and the woman below hadn't alerted anyone to her presence yet.

She still had time, but there was no way to tell how much. If she could find the two scum-swillers and deal with them without delay, she could easily make her escape.

The room she had been looking for was at the top of the building and larger than any of the others. It was likely one of the few benefits allowed to men who worked for the crime families of the city, although she had to press her ear to the door to make sure they were still in there.

The big one continued to complain, although his voice slurred far more than before. He had no doubt ingested more of the leaves that would dull the pain of what Skharr had done to him.

It seemed she was left with the smaller and craftier of the two. She didn't believe he was one to be taken lightly, however. Any man working for the families would have blood on his hands, but she doubted that he was the more skilled fighter of the two.

If he was, Skharr would have left him in a much worse condition.

Sera pushed the door open slowly and peered around it to make sure there were no others in the room with them before she stepped inside. There was no point in making assumptions at this point, especially when someone could have been out of sight, waiting to thrust a blade in her back.

All the training in the world could only help her avoid that, not survive it if it ever happened.

As expected, she found no others in the room. The two men

appeared to have a genuine friendship despite the despicable work they had taken on. She could respect that, but they still needed to learn how to treat people beyond their friendship with respect.

They only noticed her when she was already inside the room. The larger one—Yurunn, she'd heard him called—gaped at her, unsure whether what he saw was a result of the roots he had taken, and pointed a finger at her.

His companion turned and his eyes widened as he immediately reached for a dagger he carried on his belt.

The guild captain moved in a blur and the pommel of her blade struck him hard in the stomach to force the breath from his lungs. She held the sheathed blade in both hands, hooked the man firmly behind the knee, and lifted it to almost flip him completely.

He failed to land on his feet and fell on his stomach instead. His head followed a second later with a loud thud.

The larger man struggled to stand, but it was no easy task. Thus far, he'd managed to accomplish little more than a series of groans while he pushed on the chair where he was seated.

She tilted her head and simply watched him until he had almost succeeded before she lashed out with her foot.

Her target had not been the man, but the chair. It skidded across the room and left Yurunn with nothing to support his weight. He remained upright for a second longer until all the strength seeped from his legs and he fell to join his comrade.

"Now then, are you both listening?"

The larger man was still conscious but the other was not. She nudged him in the ribs and when he failed to respond, the nudge turned into a kick that dragged a groan from him as he rolled over.

"I hope the two of you realize how lucky you are." She deliberately masked her voice as a rough growl. "I am more of a precision instrument when it comes to this type of business, while the man who would have come in my stead would have been more like a maul that would crush you and everyone else in this building. I am willing to let you live, of course, but if you so much as whisper a word about Ingaret or so much as cast a shadow on any part of her life, I will find out. More importantly, I'll tell Skharr and let him finish the beating he dealt your friend. Do you understand?"

Neither man appeared to be in any condition for a response and she didn't intend to wait for one either. The barbarian had probably left them with a similar warning when they tried to attack him, but she hoped this warning would have more impact.

As long as the warrior didn't have to start a war with the criminal families of the city, it would be worth it.

She stepped to the open window, climbed lightly onto the ledge, and jumped onto one of the nearby roofs. Her business there had been accomplished.

CHAPTER NINE

The house was still being cleaned when she arrived. People scrubbed vigorously and a few of them complained about the smell.

Sera scowled and decided she could understand their whining. The mustard root Skharr had been given was meant to purge the poison forcefully from his body. It was effective but a thoroughly unpleasant experience and perhaps worse than the toxin itself—without the death part, of course.

Regor was right. The barbarian might not thank them for saving his life in this particular case. The only reason why she hadn't taken the potion from Felix was because the poison had already taken hold. For the potions to have an effect, they needed to be administered early before the worst of the signs appeared. Not only that, this was the only treatment they knew of that could work on everything, while other potions required them to at least know what they were dealing with.

In this case, it was a mess, but she had done what was necessary to save his life and it would be worth it.

For the moment, however, she needed distance from the stench that had begun to permeate the rest of the house. Her servants would clean to be rid of it, but mustard root was pungent when mixed with poison.

She slipped into the kitchens instead, where the smell of baking bread, cooking sauces, and rich spices were enough to cover the worst of it.

It was early enough in the morning that a handful of the workers were already in the kitchens preparing meals for the rest of the staff, as well as starting preparations for her breakfast.

Two young women laughed together as they kneaded bread. They didn't hear her come in, although that was her fault. She still wore the light boots she'd used to sneak into the brothel. With the sound of work surrounding her, Sera discovered that the conversation between them was as necessary as the aromas to distract her from what had engulfed the rest of the house.

"Did you see the size of him?" one asked. "That can't be human —maybe a troll or one of the desert orcs. You know, the ones they bring out as their champions to intimidate people when they come to visit humans?"

"Orcs can't be poisoned," the other responded and shook her head. "They are immune to almost anything that would kill them that isn't made of steel and swung hard. They had to develop that since they needed to eat anything and everything that they came across in the fucking deserts."

"That is a myth," Sera commented as she stepped beside the two women. "A myth based on the fact that poisons that kill humans do not kill orcs. As you said, they have adapted to their environment to be able to consume almost anything but some things can poison them."

She suspected that other households would have discouraged servants from interacting with their employers, but she had never been like that, not with the people she trusted to care for her home while she was away. Which, she reminded herself, was most of the time these days.

"Truly?" the first woman asked and continued to knead the

bread on the counter in front of her. "How do you know?"

"I traveled with a couple of orcs and I learned that vanilla gives them all a bad case of the shits." She sat on one of the nearby stools. "Apple skins are more deadly, however, although they seemed to enjoy them. Peeling the apple still presented the danger of the possibility of death, and they reveled in that. Merely because something doesn't kill humans doesn't mean it's safe for all creatures, Eska."

"Well then, what do you suppose would kill an elf?" the other woman asked.

"I've cooked for elves and they aren't too different from humans that way," Eska told her. "Stick with me, Ren, and you'll learn a thing or two."

Sera chuckled. "You should know that the man who is being cared for is, in fact, human. Not troll or orcish in any way."

"He's big enough to be non-human," Eska replied. "Big enough to be an ox."

"Stronger than the oxen I've seen," Ren added, her hands working rhythmically and without conscious thought. "When I went to take food to the physician you brought, he reached out and pulled one of the doors from its moorings. With one hand."

"I think the ox might have been comelier as well."

That brought a laugh from Sera. "Not every man is graced with the looks of a young god. You should know that."

Eska shrugged. "It would be one of my wishes if I ever found a djinn temple. Imagine if there were men handsome enough to increase the humidity in Verenvan. Now there is a dream."

The guild captain could only smirk in response. "It is curious how your desires are both hilarious and base at the same time."

"We are simply taught to admit that which you folk in high places have been taught to ignore and avoid," Ren said.

"Please." She snorted. "Your father practically begged me to take you on after he discovered you with...what was his name?"

"Roberto, I believe," Eska interjected.

The other woman shook her head. "No, Roberto came later. Thomas was the one my father found me with. He was a dreamy bastard and with a cock to match."

"Fiorn was rather dreamy as well if I recall." Eska paused in her kneading to reminisce. "All the muscles in all the right places."

Sera nodded. "But it was Roberto who finally drove your father to let you go."

"He was a little young," Eska remembered, "but rather poised. I thought of taking him for a ride myself, even though I knew his mother."

"I knew her too, although I was a child then," Ren replied. "They were all comely, however. Still, I believe Sera can do better than either of us."

"I have no intention of bringing a stud home to put in my pasture."

Eska nodded and resumed her work. "The man does have enough muscles. I imagine he would leave you sore in all the right ways if he put his mind to it. If that were what you had in mind, of course. You might have to leave the candles unlit for the duration."

She narrowed her eyes at the woman. "That isn't why I helped him. I owe him my life and that of my men as well."

"Be that as it may, there is no reason why you might not consider other possibilities." She brushed her thick brown hair from her eyes and walked to one of the nearby cupboards. "A few of the ladies in this house have made use of my herbs in the past and you might consider the same path." She took a small wooden box from the back of the cupboard and tossed it to her employer, who caught it deftly without missing a step.

"What is this?"

"Protection in case of emergency. I imagine if you see him in a moment of weakness, you might feel the need to put a bag over his head. This would allow you to use your body, not your eyes. You will thank me."

Sera laughed and threw the box at the woman, who ducked under the perfectly aimed projectile and let it sail into the wall behind her. The container remained intact, however, and Eska retrieved it quickly.

"Suit yourself." She laughed as she returned it to its place. "But trust me when I say that you'll want…"

Her voice trailed off and the gazes of all three women drifted toward the door as the sound of what was happening above them made Sera immediately think of the dragons that were still rumored to wander the Yakul mountains while she had been training there.

Some had told her that the roars that echoed off the mountainside were merely the wind cutting through the caverns in the high peaks. Even then, the thought of one of the winged monsters that had driven so many other civilizations from the mountains was enough to send chills up any spine.

The sound of Skharr being sick had a similar reaction. The only time that she had needed to take the root had been one of the worst experiences of her life, and not only because of the snake that had bitten her.

"We've already lost three sheets that will need to be burned," Eska muttered and tried to focus on her work. "And I have my doubts about the bed as well. The chances are it will need to be burned as well."

"The ox of a man has had fits as well that might break the bed a good deal sooner," Ren added.

The guild captain could appreciate their concern, not only for the man but also for the condition of the house even when he had recovered. They had been with her almost since she had taken possession of it, which had been years earlier. She made a point of giving them working conditions that most other workers in the city would kill for. It was the very least she could do.

Sleep would not last for her, not today, but a few hours were necessary.

Sera knew how dangerous it was to go without it, even if her mind was occupied with other issues.

It was still morning by the time she dragged herself from the cot she had chosen for a brief rest.

She would sleep fully when Skharr was no longer dying and she didn't need to worry about an assassin trying to get into her house to kill him again.

A few platters with food had been set out for her, but she wasn't particularly hungry—although it wasn't because of the stench. It was interesting that there was nothing foul-smelling in the house.

Tremendous work had gone into making her home livable again, mostly in the room to which Skharr had been moved.

The guild captain collected the food and made her way upstairs, listening for any sign that the patient was still in a fight for his life. When she heard none, she pushed the door to the room open.

The foul smell still lingered there, stronger than anywhere else in the house, although it was now manageable and tolerable enough. She looked in at Regor who was seated close to the bed and watched the barbarian like a hawk. The young man looked exhausted but then again, so did his patient, who lay peacefully on the bed.

A new bed, she realized, dragged in from another room. The original had likely been taken out to burn with the sheets that had been ruined.

"Good morning," she whispered as she approached Regor. "I'd ask how you are feeling but the answer is rather clearly painted all over your face. Did you get any sleep last night?"

"Did you?" He paused and looked at Skharr. "I...apologize."

"No need. You have been awake all night dealing with the big fucker. For myself, I managed a few hours after I returned home last night, but I wish I could say it was enough."

He smirked and narrowed his eyes as she placed the platter of food on the table for him.

"Get some food in you," she said quietly. "And then some sleep. I had the servants prepare a room up for you in case you needed it."

"I appreciate that. It has been a long night, to say the least, and I did not look forward to a ride to my home."

"Then worry no longer. I'll make sure the big bastard doesn't pass away in his sleep. He is sleeping, is he not?"

"The worst of it does appear to be over." The young man approached the sleeping giant and placed his hand on his forehead. "The fever has passed, which generally means his body has won the fight and merely needs rest to recover fully. I had no idea if he would survive the night. I remember when you—"

"There...there is no need to bring those memories up."

Regor laughed. "Well, then. Once the fever passed, someone sat with him to spoon water and other liquids into his body while he recovered. I already showed Ingaret how to do it and she should take over from me in a few minutes. I will eat now and find some rest in a short while."

Sera nodded. She had almost forgotten about the woman, even though her little trip into the swamps of the city had been to make sure her life would be a safe one from this point forward.

Ingaret. It was an interesting name, reminiscent of the mountains.

"Well then, since I am not needed, I must attend to some business for Skharr at the guild," she stated and patted his back in passing. "Thank you for all your help, my friend. I don't know if I could have done this without you."

"You most certainly could not have done it without my help. But I owe the man my life as well."

She grinned and shook her head. "I'll see you later. Get some rest."

It was as likely as not that the man would do no such thing, but she wasn't his mother and the only time she could order him to rest was when he was under her command. For the moment, there was nothing to compel him to obey her word.

Her clothes were simple, and she wore only her sword to indicate that she was no common merchant or housewife as she took one of the horses from her stables. The rush of the morning was past, which left her a clear path to the hall where Pennar most likely waited for her.

Or for Skharr, depending on whether he'd received her message or not.

Sure enough, the old man called her name and gestured for her to approach the moment he saw her.

"I've been looking for you," he all but snarled and gestured impatiently for her to dismount. "A group is preparing to run a dungeon, and I thought you might be interested. In fact, I thought Skharr might be interested, so if you happen on the man, tell him to reply to the messages I've left for him."

"He is...currently unavailable," Sera replied. There was no telling if the assassin had worked for one of the guilds or not, which meant it was best to not share any information on his location. She trusted Pennar, but many ears were listening that she did not.

"Unavailable, huh? Well, there should be time for him to join, but he'll owe the guild for the contract he is currently working before he can take any new ones on."

Sera tilted her head and looked around the hall. "How much would he owe for his current contract?"

"After the last one like it, he paid a gold coin, although I wonder if that might not have been an accurate representation of how much he made on the damn job."

"How do you mean?"

"The giant fucker might have implied that he'd taken a night of passion over actual pay, and the implication was that this would be a similar job. Although if he is indisposed, it might not have gone well for him."

The guild captain scowled and shook her head. Many in the guilds didn't mind taking flesh as pay for their work, although it always made her feel sick to be associated with them.

"I'll cover his pay. When he recovers, he'll have to repay me." She took a gold coin from her pouch and handed it to the man. "Do you know of anything...any contracts that came in that might have Skharr's name on them?"

Pennar shook his head. "Even if there were, I would not be at liberty to discuss them, but I make a point to not take any contracts on guild members."

"Would the other guildmasters be of a similar mind?"

"No. What happened to Skharr?"

"I should not discuss it. Just in case."

The guildmaster nodded. "I understand. I'll make inquiries, but there is no promise of answers. If someone is looking to kill him, they might be smart enough to do so away from the guilds in the underworld of our city."

That made sense and was where her instincts leaned as well.

"Do you have a copy of the contract for the dungeon? If I see Skharr, I'll be sure to pass it along."

He took the scroll from his desk and put it into her hands. "Send the man my best. There are many in this city whom I would see dead, but he is not one of them."

She smirked and pocketed the scroll. "If it makes you feel better, I feel the same way about you, old man."

"And yet you never fail to take the opportunity to bring my age up."

"I wouldn't want you to die. That does not mean I won't mock you from time to time."

He laughed. "Get out before I use the names I have for you."

"Save them for when we're drinking together. You're more

creative when you drink."

———————

Breakfast waited for her outside. Denir was like a mother and tried to make sure she ate and slept regularly. He had no power over her when she was out in the world, but when she was within the walls of her home, the man did everything he could to make sure she lived a healthy lifestyle.

While he never said anything outright, she could feel the silent judgment in his eyes after she'd had two goblets of wine and looked for a third. He would have poured it if she'd asked, but there was always a hint of annoyance from him that made it uncomfortable for her.

Which was why she tended to drink excessively when she was beyond the walls and his influence.

A knock on her door drew a raised eyebrow and Micah looked up, breathed deeply, and shook her head.

"Denir? Come."

The door opened and the distinguished-looking man stepped inside.

"If you intend to pester me about eating my breakfast, you should know that it can wait until after I've finished with these reports."

"Of course, Dame Ferat." It was said in the familiar tone of someone who pretended to not be as involved in her life as he was. "I was here to announce that you have a guest. One of your men from the wharf."

"Oh. Well. Send him in."

Denir bowed and stepped out of the way as a young man entered. He smelled of fish and enough hard work to make him sweat profusely in the heat of the city.

"You can shut the door, Denir."

"Yes, miss."

The door closed and she was alone with the man. She continued to look at the papers on her desk. "Did you have something you wanted to share, or will you simply stand there like a pissant all day?"

"Sorry, miss. I have news for you."

"Well, as much as I enjoy the suspense, why don't you share what you know and allow me to reward you for your work?"

"Yes. Yes! I...well, the news might not be what you hoped for, miss. The man you wanted dead—the giant—was...well, he is not dead."

Micah froze with a sheet of paper in her hand and put it slowly on her desk.

"Is that so?"

"Aye. He took the poison but before it killed him, someone came along. A woman with a horse was there, helped him up, and took him to a large house on the edge of the Palatine."

She didn't want to show that she knew exactly who the man was talking about. There was no need to let the people in her employ know anything she didn't want them to.

"And you know he survived?"

"Some contacts inside her house say it was a close call, but he survived and is resting peacefully this morning. I can continue to watch him if you like."

A few moments of thought were followed by her slow nod.

"Yes. You do that." She searched inside her drawer for a small purse full of silver coins. As much as the youths she employed liked having coin, she knew they were likely to be killed if it became known that they carried gold on them. They were greedy but in spending their coin, it was better if they had silver and copper.

It was a policy among her people, and they knew it well. She tossed the pouch to the young man, who caught it and made it disappear in his clothes before she could blink.

"Thank you for the good work, Triam."

"Thank you, miss." He bowed his head in deference to her before he backed out of the door again when Denir opened it for him to leave.

The old man had listened to the conversation, she had no doubt. Of course he had.

She stood from her seat and followed her retainer as he escorted Triam out of her house and held the door open for him to leave. The chances were that he would go off to spend his coin on any one of the many vices there were to be found in the city.

"Should I handle him like the rest, miss?" Denir asked once the boy was out of earshot.

"No. Leave him in the swamp. I don't want the body found. He'll merely be another urchin who disappears from this city every day."

"Of course, miss." The old man closed the door again. "It would appear that your sister is intruding on your business. How will you deal with that?"

Micah shook her head and stared down the hallway but didn't focus on anything in particular. "She must have realized that the man has a price on his life, but I didn't expect her to interfere. And I cannot kill him while he is under her protection. I would not treat my sister that way—not to mention that I am unsure if I would survive her wrath, even if she does not survive mine."

"She does have an odd morality to her that I find curious."

She smirked as they wandered to her office. "She is a lunatic with aspirations of being a good person, no matter how deadly. I will have to find a way around that." She reflexively clutched the ribs Sera had broken the last time she'd seen that kind of rage in her sister's eyes.

"As you say, miss. For the moment, however, might I suggest that you indulge in some breakfast?"

"You're like my mother, Denir."

"I am worse than a mother, Dame Ferat. I would have thought you would have learned that by now."

CHAPTER TEN

H is head hurt with a low, throbbing pain, the kind he was only too familiar with, usually on the mornings after a night of revelry and excessive drinking. Skharr had never allowed himself to drink too much on a regular basis, but a few occasions demanded it.

It had been a while since such an occasion had arisen, and all he could do for the moment was groan as he held his head and waited for the pain to pass.

After a few long minutes, he realized he would be waiting for a while. He shook his head very gently and kept his hands pressed to his temples as he inspected his surroundings.

The room was not his at the inn. He decided it would have been too much to ask that he make it to the Mermaid. It was not small, however, and reminded him of one of the rooms he had been in at the various villas around the city.

Although, he thought around the pain, it was a little smaller and lacked the pretentious nature of the owners. The structure was solid and small details indicated that the home was lived in, but it wasn't as luxurious as he had somehow expected.

With a low groan, the barbarian pushed up from the bed he was on. The sheets were fresh and clean and everything felt the same, even him. He looked at his bare chest and realized he had been washed.

Memories of the night before had begun to return. Fighting. Healing. Fucking. Eating and drinking.

From there, the rest was something of a blur. Sera had been there. Somehow, he'd hurt himself when he landed on his face. The bruising remained tender beneath his probing fingers.

"Fucking cobbles," he muttered under his breath and examined the rest of his body. There were no other signs of injury aside from the myriad of scars painted across his torso.

His brown hair was a mess of tangles that would need to be brushed thoroughly before he tied it back, and his beard was a little longer than he would have liked.

"Been here more than a night," Skharr noted aloud and tugged what was growing on his chin.

"A little longer," someone said from the door of his room.

Skharr turned to a young man who stood at the door. He remembered him wearing armor and weapons while they escorted a small convoy out of the city. Although he now only wore a shirt, trousers, and light shoes, his face was unmistakable.

"Regor? Is that you?"

"In the flesh." Regor stepped into the room and nudged the door shut with his foot as he carried a tray in both hands. "You were very nearly not with us in the flesh if you take my meaning. That poison was strong. It would have to be to kill a man your size, and it came close. It took some very expensive herbs to purge it from your body and it was…messy. I needed to wash you a few times while you were recovering."

"How long have I been here?"

"A few days. It seemed like you were conscious here and there, but you were feverish and hallucinating. I didn't know how much was spent on that poison that was put into you, but I would say it was worth it."

"Feels worth it," Skharr replied.

"Who is Therena?"

The barbarian froze and fixed his gaze on the floor as he stretched his arms. They felt stiff like he hadn't used them in a while, which was more or less correct, he acknowledged.

"You repeated the name constantly in your sleep. I assumed it was someone or something important to you at some point in your life."

He sighed and shrugged off-handedly. There was no good time to talk about what happened and he had no desire to start in this strange place.

"Where am I?"

Regor looked around the room. "This is Captain Ferat's accommodations. She moved Ingaret into quarters of her own and Horse into the stables."

"Stables? Her...accommodations?"

"Aye. You know. Living quarters. Home, if you feel emotional about that kind of thing."

"I know what accommodations mean. I am...they are more luxurious than I would have thought a mercenary captain would be able to afford."

"Believe me, we all had the same thought when we discovered where our captain lives when she isn't traveling with us. Her father would not allow her to live in any kind of squalor, although he never did care much about putting his name to hers."

"Her father?"

"That is her news to tell," Regor replied, poured water from a pitcher into a clay cup, and handed it to him along with a few seeds. "Your stomach will feel a little unsettled and those entrox seeds should settle it enough for you to eat. And believe me, you'll need to eat."

When the man mentioned it, Skharr noticed that his stomach was rumbling to remind him that he needed food in him before too long.

"It is a good thing I still have a few secrets to share," Sera said from where she stood at the door.

The barbarian scrutinized the woman carefully, and not because of the unexpectedly civilian garb she wore. Despite the unusual attire, her blademaster medallion still hung around her neck and her sword was sheathed on her belt.

A mysterious father and benefactor did make him curious, although he was never one to intrude on the lives of others unless it pertained to his own.

Regor looked quizzically at the two of them and immediately came to a decision to leave. "I'll check…something in the kitchen, I suppose. Perhaps see if they have enough to feed the giant barbarian. Swallow the seeds, Skharr."

He did as he was told and washed them down with the water the man had given him before he beat a hasty retreat—with the tray, unfortunately. It seemed Sera wanted a word with him in private.

Common sense told him, though, that it was unlikely that she would use the opportunity to share something of her origins with a man she barely knew. He could understand that, having the same reticence when it came to revealing too many details about his life. While they had been involved in an adventure or two in the time they had known each other, the fact remained that they were still mostly strangers drawn together by circumstances.

"I suppose I have you to thank for saving my life," Skharr muttered and rolled his shoulders. "Poison is not a weapon used often, at least not by the people I tend to make enemies of."

"That should change the longer you stay here. People in civilized places seem to become more civilized in their manner of killing people. Not that I approve, of course, but I don't have to. Fortunately, Regor had mustard root in his possession. It purges the poison forcibly from the body very effectively."

He nodded. "I've seen its effect."

"You haven't seen its effect on a barbarian before, I can tell you that."

"No, I suppose I have not."

She chuckled and gestured with her head. "Let's get you something to eat. I can talk while you chew."

"Will you talk about how a mercenary captain is able to afford such a large house while she travels around the world, escorting not so wealthy merchants through the wilderness?" The question surprised him as much as it did her, as he hadn't intended to pry. He stood and grimaced at the weakness in his knees when he started to walk again. His whole body was sore, which made it difficult to take the first few steps and drew a groan of pain.

He gritted his teeth and forced himself to move a little more until his body became more cooperative. As he pulled a shirt on, his stomach rumbled to indicate how hungry he was and he joined her when she left the room.

Food provided sufficient incentive to continue his efforts, and Sera fell in beside him with a hand on his arm like she expected him to fall.

Skharr's first reflex was to wave her away, but he felt like he had the strength to only rival a three-day-old foal with the way his knees quivered at every step.

"It's not a story I share willingly," she explained as they moved down the steps. "My mother was a concubine to the Emperor—one of the few he truly loved, or so she told me and my sister. However, it became clear that he needed an alliance to maintain his power, one that would give him sons to solidify his dynasty, and all his concubines were sent away to different cities. Those who had children were cared for like my mother was."

"Your mother is no longer of this world?"

"No. And when she died, the creditors took everything she owned, including me and my sister. They had little use for children our age and left us to scratch our living from the swamps. It took our father five years to find us. We were sent to different schools to enhance our training and given coin to support ourselves when the studies were finished. My sister made good use of that coin and established herself in the swamps. I was a little more modest. I have a home and investments to support the house and the people who work in it, but I never felt at home here like my sister does."

"You prefer to travel?"

"And the guild provides me the opportunity to do so while earning money in the process. Meeting wondrous folk, hearing their stories—"

"And carving into them with that sword of yours." Skharr patted the weapon on the pommel. "You know, I did run into another of you blademasters. He was protecting one of the lords of the town—a lord who wanted me to fight him to prove my mettle and his."

"I assume by the fact that you're standing that he is not?"

The barbarian shrugged. "He inflicted a few significant wounds, but I managed to sneak in a couple of tactical strokes that hurled him on his ass. When I moved in for the kill, the lord intervened and said we had both proven our points and that I would not have won if I hadn't been willing to risk my life."

"He sounds like a terrible person." Sera opened the door to what looked like a small dining room, where chairs stood around a table laid with a modest yet robust meal for two.

"Nobles in general are terrible people," he noted. "From what you tell me of your family history, I imagine you feel the same way."

She nodded. "Agreed. Although I suppose if we looked for technicalities, that would mean I am a noble as well."

"Your attitude is decidedly...not." The warrior took his seat, helped himself to a few slices of bread, and slathered them with butter and the selection of jams and preserves before he attacked them hungrily. "The attitude is what makes them terrible people. From what I heard, the man enjoyed making his guards fight for sport—to the point of drawing blood and even killing a few of them."

The guild captain shook her head, selected a few pieces of cheese, and fitted them between pieces of bread before she took a bite. "Do you barbarians have any semblance of nobility?"

"Some, I suppose. Leaders of the tribe are elected at every full moon, but those chosen have proven themselves in some way or another. They wouldn't have the kind of absolute power over the Clan your nobles might, but it is as close to the concept of nobility as you might understand."

"Were you ever that kind of nobility?"

"I can be if I ever return with enough coin to justify my return."

"Justify your return?"

"The Clan is pragmatic above all else. Youths are sent away to fight in foreign wars and bring home the coin and food that will support those who remain in the mountains. You'll find, once you tear away all the different blankets of morality and flowery poetry, that your society lives by the same rules. At least my people don't bother to conceal it."

Sera opened her mouth as he wolfed down the bread and followed it with cheese, dried meat, and fruits.

"How do you plan to survive your time away from your tribe, then?"

"I've made a few fortunes in my life. Fighting wars for the most part, although I have avoided them in my last few endeavors."

"I assume that has something to do with not wanting to return home to scratch a living out of rock, snow, and whatever caravan happens across your path?"

Skharr shrugged. "Home is home and will always hold some degree of appeal, but no, I never wanted to return. I suppose that might be selfish of me, but many others never returned either."

"By choice?"

"Unless they chose to die, no."

"Are you willing to stay away long enough to die so you can stay away?"

"I have many reasons to not return. Disliking how my people live their lives is the least of my concerns."

Sera narrowed her eyes. "Will you ever tell me what the real reason is?"

"One day, perhaps." He did not want to discuss it further. There was no point in doing so. "Why did you do this for me? I'm not wealthy—at least not as rich as you are—and it would take years to repay you."

"Wealth does not impress me, DeathEater," she replied as she stood. She likely wasn't as hungry as he was. "I admire courage, skill, and those who help others who need it rather than take advantage of them. You protected the people in the convoy. I would have lost them all had you not acted, so I owe you their lives and my own. The way I see it, I might be master inside these walls, but your experience makes you master outside them. We might be able to help each other in that respect."

He smirked and took another mouthful from the plate he had served himself. "Do you expect me to join you beyond the walls again, then?"

"That was the idea, but you still need to regain your strength. Regor said it would take you a few days to be ready to travel once more, and we are leaving two days hence. You'll not be ready for it, I don't believe. But you could leave the city—and those who want to kill you—behind. And you might even make some coin from it as well."

She placed a scroll on the table in front of him.

"Ivehnshaw Tower," Skharr muttered. He knew what it was almost before she showed him the scroll. "I heard they were trying to arrange a group to venture there as happens every year. What is it about this dungeon that attracts so many adventurers when so few others would go to the other ones?"

"The fact that there are known survivors who walked away with more coin than they could ever spend in a thousand lifetimes, with the promise of more waiting for any who would return. The appeal of a known reward contrary to the hope of one is enough to drive those desperate for coin and recognition in the world."

"It almost sounds as though you are saying I am one of those desperate for coin and recognition in the world."

"You are desperate for something, but it is not coin or recognition. I will make my peace with your reason being that you do not want to remain in a city where all wish you dead."

"What about Ingaret? What will happen to her?"

"Oh. Ingaret. Well...I had a word with the men who were tormenting her. As it turns out, they tried to ruin her life, lied about her to those who employed her, and threatened any who would not accept the lies."

Skharr looked down and his scowl deepened as he put the last of his food back on the plate. "I told them. I said—"

"I know. Well, I assumed as much. And I invaded their little establishment and beat the same warning into them again. As much as it needed to be done, you don't want to be involved in a war with those who run the underbelly of this city. Hopefully, I avoided exactly that. If it happens that the war begins, you may count me on your side, but until then... Well, leaving them alive appeared to be the most peaceful solution."

"How will she be able to live if I'm gone?"

Sera smiled and patted him on the shoulder. "Your loyalty to her is admirable. I decided she would be better stationed here.

We have work available and I pay my people well, along with providing them with places to live and protection from the dregs of our society."

That was something, at least. He nodded slowly and finished his last mouthful. "I suppose I knew I wouldn't be able to watch over her forever. I appreciate you helping her."

She smirked. "Well then, you can repay me by making a full recovery and finding yourself a place where half the city is not trying to kill you."

"I can make no promises."

That drew a laugh from her. "You should know that I also brought your horse to my stables, as well as all your possessions. He refused to move until Ingaret told him you were poisoned."

"Of course not. He would never trust anyone to simply walk him out of a stable without any knowledge of where I am. He has more loyalty than that."

"You'll have to tell me how you taught a horse to understand your words."

"He is my brother and my equal and always has been. Why would I not treat him as an equal?"

The woman made no response to that. "Well then. I have business to attend to regarding the convoy I will be escorting. I'll leave you to...assemble yourself, I suppose."

"I'd like to see Horse."

"I thought you would. You'll find him in the stables. I made sure that he has been treated well during his time with us."

He made a mental note to check that they weren't pampering the stallion too much, but he hadn't finished his meal yet. The guild captain left to see to whatever business was required of a woman in her position, but he felt as though he hadn't eaten anything for the past few days. Of course, he hadn't, and the table was a great deal emptier by the time he stood.

Interestingly, his body felt weaker and more tired by the time he had finished eating. The need to lay his head down to rest was difficult to resist, but Skharr pushed it aside and forced himself to wander the house in an effort to find the stables. This proved to be something of a frustrating challenge as it was larger than he had anticipated, and with his unsteady legs, he had no desire to explore.

"Are you looking for something, sir?"

He turned to a woman who stood a few feet away from him. It annoyed him that he hadn't heard her approach. Perhaps the poison had affected him more than he was willing to admit.

"I...I was looking for the stables. Need to make sure Horse is all right."

"Of course, sir. Follow me."

She looked like a servant and dressed like one as well, although he felt justified in his paranoia and made sure she remained in front of him at all times.

"It's good to see you on your feet again," she said as they walked at a pace that wouldn't strain him. "There were moments when we feared you would not rise from your bed ever again."

Skharr nodded. "Appreciated. Although I fear the process of healing might take a little longer than I'd like."

"There's no need to rush into any battles yet, good sir. You've been through quite an ordeal and you'll need time to recover fully—although, from the looks of you, I would say it won't take very long."

He realized that she was watching his movements closely from the corner of her eye as she opened a door that led them out of the house and into a small courtyard.

"How do you mean?"

"Well...you are rather more imposing and impressive on your feet than you were in bed, although I assume you can be rather imposing in that realm as well."

"Oh."

There was no need to answer that.

"The stables are right over there." She pointed to a smaller building connected to the house. "You'll find your horse inside waiting for you."

"Thank you."

"Of course. Let me know if you need any more help."

The barbarian nodded and continued slowly toward his destination. A few hands worked in the morning sun, although they paused to watch him approach the doors. Skharr waited for them to shout some kind of challenge to stop him from entering but none came and he pushed inside.

The stables were rather larger than he had thought they would be. Ten stalls provided ample room for the horses they housed and there was additional space to walk them indoors. This was something he had only seen in stables located in cities that were more likely to see snow and low temperatures in the winter months, which allowed the animals to be exercised without the uncomfortable necessity to do so in freezing weather.

He wasn't sure why it was needed in Verenvan, but there was no point in questioning it and he shrugged and stepped into the stall where Horse waited.

The beast had lived in comfort over the past three days, that much was clear. A thick layer of clean wood chips covered the ground, and a fresh bale of hay and a bucket filled with clean water was available for him. Along the side, an empty bucket stood with bits and pieces of apples still inside.

"They have been spoiling you here, eh, Horse?"

The beast snorted in response and turned to nudge him in the shoulder as he found a stool to sit on. Standing had begun to feel like a chore in his condition.

"I'll be fine and only need a few days to recover. Besides, it's not like you'll complain about remaining here. You're being spoiled and there are even a few mares to keep an old horse company. You could not ask for more if you wanted to retire somewhere. I doubt you would find a better haven, to be honest."

Horse shook his mane, nudged him in the shoulder again, and nibbled gently at his shirt.

"I might need your help for one more mission, however." Skharr patted the beast on the neck. "Another dungeon, and considerably more dangerous than the last one we went to. Although I did take the lion's share of the danger in that one."

This time, the nudge almost knocked him off of the stool and he laughed and pushed him away.

"What do you say? We'll need to leave in a few days, so you'll have more time to enjoy being pampered like a rich horse. But once we leave, things will be back to our usual fare."

He pulled the scroll out, broke the seal, and looked through the details that had been provided for the tower. It appeared to be similar to the last one, although there were a few terms he wasn't sure he understood. Unlike the first dungeon, it looked as though the fact that others would be involved meant there were certain terms all participants needed to agree to before joining.

Horse snorted and leaned into his hand.

Skharr laughed. "Yes, we'll return here more than likely— should I survive. If I do not, you could probably find your way on your own, yes?"

The stallion stepped away from him and shook his mane again.

"It's not pessimistic. Realism is a sound tactic to prepare oneself for all eventualities."

He pushed from his stool, still feeling a little weak on his feet, and scratched the animal's forehead in farewell before he left the stall. Three or four steps later, however, he needed to lean on the walls as he walked slowly out of the stables. He could feel the gazes of the stable hands on his back as he returned to the house.

And not only the stable hands, he realized. The same woman waited for him as he approached the house.

"Is everything to your satisfaction, sir?" she asked and hurried forward as if to assist him to remain on his feet.

It was annoying and all the more so because he wasn't sure if he needed help or not.

"Horse is certainly happy. What was your name again?"

"Oh, my name is Eska," she replied with a small smile. "What is his name, by the way? I've only ever heard folk call him 'horse.'"

"Horse is his name."

"Oh. Truly?"

"Why not?"

She shrugged and pulled the door open for him. "Most folk would give their horse a noble name of some kind."

"Horse is a noble name."

"Well, yes…I suppose."

He needed to move the conversation along, he realized. "Could you help me? I am not sure what is meant here…"

Eska moved closer as he traced his finger over a particular line in the contract.

"Do you need me to read you the whole thing?" she asked.

"No, only this one. Equal liquidation of all assets acquired between all surviving contracted parties."

"Huh."

"What?"

"Nothing. I…uh, merely assumed you couldn't read at all."

"Why?"

She flushed a little sheepishly "I…well… Barbarians usually— Never mind."

Skharr nodded. It was good that the perception of him being a stupid barbarian remained despite what might be called familiarity.

"Do you know what that means?" he asked and pointed again at the line he had difficulty understanding.

"Ah, yes…it means that any treasure you find will be divided equally among all members of the group."

Eska slid her hand under his shoulder as he began to ascend the steps. He experienced a mixture of annoyance and shame when he relied on her a little more than he would have liked to reach the top. As if sensing his discomfort, she remained silent as she guided him along the hallways.

"Do you think you'll be in any condition to join a party leaving the city?" she asked as he reached his room.

Skharr shrugged and breathed a little deeper than he would have liked. "I suppose I'll find out."

CHAPTER ELEVEN

"Hah! The barbarian himself! Welcome back!"

Skharr grinned as Throk hurried toward him. Dwarves tended to be very physical in their greetings, which meant that he wrapped his powerful arms around his midsection and squeezed as tightly as he could before he released him and stepped back.

"It is a pleasure to be back, Master AnvilForge," the barbarian replied and drew a deep breath.

"All is well with you? Not to be impolite, but you've lost much of your color. And you appear a little less powerful in the shoulders. Still strong enough to rip a human in half but like you'd struggle with an orc."

"I made some enemies who thought to poison me. If not for the help of friends, I likely would not be here today."

"And I would have lost the one customer who inspired me and my kin to the finest work we've had in decades. Decades, I tell ye! Who's the godsbedamned assfucker who tried to kill you in such cowardly fashion? Poison—pah!"

"If the truth be told, I do not know." He laughed as he was guided into the back of the shop. "Although I will leave the city for a while, so I hopefully will not have to deal with the offenders in the foreseeable future. And speaking of leaving the city, I am in need of a few weapons of decent quality if I wish to survive the trip and I hoped you might have something for me."

"It will be months still for us to have your ax ready for combat," the dwarf replied when they reached his office. "We have started the work but most of the materials have yet to arrive."

"I am aware of that, but I require more practical choices that you might have. I need a proper shield, for one thing, and perhaps a spear. I have been involved in a few fights where range would have suited me well. As I recall, there is no matching the dwarves when they mount their shield and spear walls."

"A man after my own heart." Throk laughed. "You would not happen to be among those who would venture into the Ivehn-shaw Tower, would you?"

"It would appear that most know more about that business than I do."

"It has become something of a famed expedition over the years, and most of the adventurers looking to arm themselves come to me. They spend a great deal of coin on greatswords and armor, but none of them request the weapons that will keep them alive."

"Does that mean you can help me?"

"Aye, and I can do you one better. Of all those inbred fuckers who are risking their pit-swilling lives, I would say you are the most likely to survive, so I think you are in a position to help me. I could lend you the weapons and armor you need free of charge. I'll give you my best and should you survive the tower, I will be able to sell everything that was used by the mighty Skharr Death-Eater in his quest into the Ivehnshaw Tower for a profit to those who have a mind for such things. I might even be able to knock some of the price off your ax if you bring them all back."

Skharr nodded. "That is a surprisingly reasonable offer from you. I suppose you have more on your mind than simply a desire to sell famed weapons and armor."

"I am endeared to you, DeathEater, and I would hope that you remain with us for many years to come. Besides that, you'll have the best chance to survive carrying my weapons and bearing my armor. Now, let us find something that will suit your particular fighting style."

He narrowed his eyes as the dwarf began to rummage through those weapons and armor that were on display in the office. "You haven't seen me fight."

"I don't need to see you fight. I see your balance, the way you walk, and the power you have, and I can deduce that you rely on power and speed over actual technique. Would that be correct?"

His scowl deepened but he eventually nodded. "I thought you might have a saber or a sword that might suit." While he did still have the longsword he'd taken from the Dark Knight, he was loathe to take it into another dungeon. Aside from the fact that he wasn't sure how effective it would be in confined spaces due to its impressive length and size, it was also the kind of weapon that might tempt others to simply stab him in the back in order to acquire it for themselves.

"Swords are useful but limited. In a full combat situation, you'll want weapons that match your abilities completely without needing to compromise. You enjoy the use of axes and bows, yes? But I would like to introduce to you something new. The maul."

Throk lifted a heavy-looking hammer from a nearby table. It had been carefully crafted with markings made to imitate the head of a bull. The front added little to that and was simply comprised of four small spikes meant to crush anything they came into contact with, but the back extended the carvings into the bull's horns and formed a long, thin spike that protruded from the weapon.

The haft was carefully carved with a variety of dwarven runes while steel reinforcing rods added weight to it.

"It would take any dwarf two hands to carry this one," the blacksmith stated as he handed it to him. "It might be a little too heavy for most humans, but a man like you would have no difficulty carrying it with one hand and using it as one might a war hammer to crush skulls, bones, and even doors if you have a mind to do so. It would also allow you to carry one of these."

The dwarf pulled out one of the heavy shields Skharr remembered them favoring. Its edge was rimmed with steel that had been sharpened and curved slightly outward to make it almost as much a weapon as a defensive tool. The center was framed with the embossed likeness of the same bull as the hammer.

It was large enough to cover most of a dwarf's body and was therefore large enough to cover the barbarian from neck to groin, which was all he needed. It too was heavier than most shields he had used, but he was large enough to carry it using the center grip without difficulty.

"Do you like what you see?"

Skharr smirked. "It has been many years since I have carried weapons of this quality. I am usually forced to take those I find among the fallen on the battlefield, or weapons and armor made for those light in coin."

"Those days are in your past, I am happy to say, at least for the moment. Now, for the spear…"

He selected a longer weapon from the table, hefted it, and replaced it before he chose another. It looked heavier and sturdier and was a little shorter, and only the spearhead rose above the barbarian's head. The blade was longer and thinner than most he had seen in the past, although what appeared to be steel reinforcement ran the length of the haft to the base, which ended in a spike.

"It's long enough that you can bury the base in the ground and use it like a pike," Throk explained and demonstrated the movement with more than practiced efficiency. "But it's also light enough for you to use with one hand if you care to keep your shield in hand, and the balance allows you to use it with far more movement if you carry it with both hands. It's longer than a longsword, lighter, deadlier, and more versatile, I think."

"Do dwarves have an aversion to swords?" he asked and weighed the weapon, which seemed well-balanced.

"No, but you have to admit that we find them less effective. I can craft the finest sword you'll ever find, of course, but swords were always meant as secondary weapons—civilized weapons— and we both know you are something beyond civilized, yes?"

Skharr nodded. The spear was certainly a fine weapon and exactly what he had in mind if he were to come up against another blademaster.

"I'll take them all and some armor if you have it to spare—and if you have any that will fit me."

"I'll make it fit and will have the weapons and armor delivered to you. Where are you staying?"

He frowned when he realized he had no idea of the address. "Do you know the Ferat house?"

"Dame Ferat?"

"I...do not think so. Captain Ferat, yes?" Sera had mentioned a sister and he assumed she was the Dame Ferat mentioned.

"Ah, yes, that does make more sense."

"How?"

"Far be it from me to spread gossip about the various mercenaries who make their living in this city."

"But there is gossip to spread."

"Indeed."

"Say no more. But the house does belong to Captain Ferat."

Throk laughed. "Noted! Gods, it has been years since I've felt this way! Feeling excited to work for a human has been a foreign sensation of late!"

"I hope your enthusiasm continues."

"You plan to raid another dungeon, then?"

Skharr smirked. "Is that disapproval I hear?"

The mage responded with the faintest shrug. "I would merely have thought that you would have learned your lesson by now. You must have earned enough coin to retire and live a life of some comfort, but you choose to continue to risk your life on ventures that many would consider foolish."

"I have found that the City of Verenvan is as dangerous as any dungeon I have escaped from."

"I doubt any man who tried to kill you would have been as effective as a dungeon could have been."

"No, but a poisoner was almost successful. They would have succeeded had someone not intervened at the perfect time."

"Yes, I suppose that is the logical way to go about it. If they can't find anyone brave or stupid enough to try to slip a dagger in your back, of course." The mage shook his head like the concept rather disgusted him as well. "How did you survive?"

"I was fed a mustard root concoction."

"A brutal but effective method. I suppose you are still recovering from that?"

The barbarian nodded.

"I would suggest, should there be a next time, that you use one of my anti-venom potions, although those must be applied as quickly as possible once you realize you have been poisoned, as they might not avoid damage to certain parts of your body. There are, of course, other methods that are a great deal more effective."

He looked at the table the man had set up for himself in the Guild Hall. "Are any of them among these?" He gestured vaguely at the potions on display.

"Well yes. I would hardly have use of them myself. This one, in particular, is one of the most effective."

Skharr leaned closer to the item the mage had placed on the table for him to see. "What is it?"

"I don't think you want to know."

"Try me."

"Mule testicles, spelled and infused with the nycrophilic venom of the Krondor spiders."

He could only imagine that his reflexive expression depicted pure disgust. "And how would it work if I needed it to?"

"You simply take a bite from it."

"I think I'd prefer the mustard root," he muttered. "Or failing that, death. The taste alone…"

"From what I hear, it tastes like an over-spiced pork sausage," the mage explained. "A little dry, of course, but not quite as horrid as you might think."

"And I'm sure I've needed to taste worse for survival in the past, but I would still pass on it nonetheless."

The man finally grinned and tugged his graying beard gently. "Yes, I believe that to be the wisest course."

"So…"

"No, it's simply some food I had reserved for a midday meal."

"What would you have done if I had accepted it?"

"I would have continued to conjure oddities about it until you changed your mind, and if you failed to do so, I would have eventually told you the truth."

"Out of sheer curiosity—"

"It would have involved the spelling. Likely something along the lines of the monthly flow of a virgin, preserved fish guts, and the urine of some mystical creature or another."

Skharr gagged and shook his head. "I am glad I didn't push the issue, then."

"I am grateful for that as well. My imagination regarding what folk think constitutes magical is unfortunately a fertile field that would have allowed me to continue for days."

"Well then, now that we have moved past the realm of fictional cures, what would you have to offer that could help?"

The mage held up two vials with a purple liquid inside. "These anti-venom potions should work against most poisons. There might be a few magically infused toxins that would be a little more difficult to heal, although these will still slow the effects."

The warrior nodded. "I'll take those."

"And there was something else I wanted to speak to you about. That trinket you sold to me before...well, I was able to study it and found that it had more than a few magical properties to it."

"I assume you do not mean to pay me more for it now that you know what it is worth."

"Of course not, but after I was able to use the spells I learned from studying it, I thought it would be only fair if I offered you the first opportunity to hear the results. It was almost miraculous, I have to say, given the way the spell is formed. I almost didn't believe it."

Skharr folded his arms and scrutinized him cautiously. "Will you continue to expound on the quality of the spellwork or will you tell me what it does?"

"I forget, folk like you tend to be all about the effects and less about how they come to pass." The mage looked annoyed and shook his head. "I still have not studied all the effects, but those that were the easiest to replicate involved healing of a human body. In fact, if you were to wear it long enough without sustaining injuries, I speculate that it would even rejuvenate your body and restore it to a more youthful condition."

It was an incredible claim, and he now understood why the man had tried to lay the groundwork for him to believe him.

But there was still one problem. "Honestly, I don't see how likely it would be for me to go that long without injury."

"A fair point, but at the worst, it would still slow the effects of aging, leaving your muscles stronger and more vital for longer, keep your bones from going brittle...that kind of thing."

Skharr nodded. "I'll take one if you have it to sell. Provided it is not out of my purse range."

"I'll make it fifteen gold coins for you," the mage replied.

"I've learned that I get what I pay for in terms of these magical charms."

"In my case, I would gain other benefits. One would be that I will be able to see the effects of these spells on a human body, which would allow me to alter it according to what I might need. There would also be the fame of arming and preparing Skharr DeathEater, Scourge of Dungeons, in two of his successful runs."

"It is odd how you are the second person to think you will profit should I be successful in this venture."

"And two of us cannot be wrong." The man managed a smile as he pushed one of the charms toward him. "Altogether, I'll need you to pay me twenty-five gold coins."

"Worthwhile, but still expensive," Skharr grumbled under his breath as he retrieved his pouch from under his shirt and counted out the coins required. His supply was a good deal lighter by the end of it, and he pushed the payment toward the mage as he collected the items he had bought.

"Always a pleasure, DeathEater."

"Likewise."

The Guild Hall still bristled with action, but a trace of fatigue seeped into his body as he moved away from the stalls. Sera had been right. He would need a few days to recover his strength, which had been thoroughly sapped by the results of the assassination attempt.

"Pardon me, sir!" said a small, shrill voice behind him. "I have a message for you from the Theros Guild."

CHAPTER TWELVE

S kharr turned to a young girl who stood in front of him, her eyes wide as she looked into his eyes like she was uncertain as to precisely what he was.

It was a common reaction, especially with children, and he waited for her to come to terms with what she saw before he said anything.

"A message?" he asked finally when she simply continued to stare at him in bemusement.

She shook her head as if to clear it. "Yes. Yes! A message from the Theros Guild. The word from Guildmaster Pennar is that you are to meet the group heading out beyond the walls, and you can be escorted by a caravan to where they are gathering."

He looked around the Guild Hall, unsure of what he had heard. Pennar wasn't one to alter arrangements without warning, not unless he had good reason to do so.

"Did he happen to mention why there was a change of plans? The contract clearly states that the group will assemble here in the Guild Hall three days from now."

"He did mention that it had to do with the safety of the members. It seems a few of them had threats made against their lives, so the meeting will take place three days west of the city at a location that will be disclosed inside your scroll. He also told me to mention that the caravan already had possession of your weapons, armor, and your horse, and said the beast would be saddled to avoid suspicion. Does that mean you are one of those with a threat against his life?"

Pennar had certainly made it obvious enough, so he merely nodded.

"He said they would meet you at the Eastern gate before the sun reaches its peak."

Skharr looked out of the massive windows of the Guild Hall and noted that midday was less than two hours away. He could be reasonably assured that Sera would wait for him before the caravan left, but they couldn't linger for too long before those they were escorting grew impatient. Not only that, others would no doubt notice that Captain Ferat's group made no effort to leave and find that suspicious.

Besides, he could only assume she had been behind the decision and had instructed Pennar to send him the message before she collected his things and secured them in the caravan.

He wasn't sure if he was ready to travel again, but he knew for a fact that he was not ready to face another attempt on his life, not if they decided to put effort into it this time.

"Thank you for your trouble," the barbarian muttered. He reminded himself that the squires at the Guild Hall were not allowed to collect coin from those who received their messages. It was an odd tradition and one meant to instill honor in those who worked for the guilds, but he could make no sense of it.

Still, traditions were not to be spat upon, and he turned his attention to the fairly long walk through the city.

Skharr hated that he could feel weakness in his body and forced himself to ignore it and focus instead on the situation he was in. Sera would not push him to move unless she felt his life would be in danger at her home, which meant she had changed her opinion since they had spoken. He had every reason to trust her.

Once again, he felt as though eyes were watching him as he moved into the open, but he couldn't shrug the feeling that he had been made paranoid by the guild captain's warning.

There was no point in holding himself hostage to his fears and he forced himself to not peer over his shoulder at every opportunity.

Too many people were on the streets—not as many as there were in the morning but enough of them to obscure anyone who could have been following him. There were also too many buildings, which meant he had to watch the rooftops as well.

If nothing else, it was a good distraction from how tired he felt.

Before long, however, he finally located those who were following him. The two men were most certainly not skillful. They acted too shifty and darted away a little too quickly when they thought he might be looking at them. Not only that, but their hands strayed under their cloaks a little too often.

They were waiting for something—simply following, keeping their distance, and not approaching him, which meant they were very likely waiting for something to happen. No doubt a few of their friends were moving into position to close their trap. If he had to guess, it would be a cluster of folk closer to the gate, and at least two others with daggers would wait for him to turn his back and slide their blades into it.

He wouldn't give them the opportunity, of course. Weakened or not, he would not wait for killers to come to him when he knew they intended to make an attempt on his life.

It was simple enough to make himself appear a little more wary and he stared openly at the two who followed him when he had the opportunity to do so. The contrived reaction made them nervous as though the tables were turning. His mouth was dry and breathing had become more difficult—like he had spent days running—but there was no reason to play coy with them now.

As he started to approach a small alley, Skharr very pointedly made himself as easy to watch as possible. There was no way to disguise himself even if he wanted to, and he slipped into the sidestreet and scanned the area to make sure no one was waiting for him in there. Satisfied, he pressed himself hard against the nearest wall. He would be difficult to miss, of course, but all he needed was a moment of confusion from his pursuers.

Both rushed into the narrow street behind him and their footsteps scuffed the cobbles as they tried to close the distance again. Perhaps they felt a little greedy and were anxious to take whatever coin was owed for his death and divide it between only two of them.

The barbarian stepped behind the second man to enter the alley with him and resisted the urge to charge after the first. He wrapped his hands around the man's neck and twisted savagely.

At any other time in his life, he would have made the kill only too easily, but he encountered some resistance before he felt and heard the man's neck snap and the body went limp. It crumpled on the cobbles when he released it.

The man's comrade reacted with surprising speed, however, and he spun and lurched closer as he brandished the small dagger in his hands.

"You's a big fucker, ain't ya?" The ruffian smirked and flicked the knife from one hand to the other.

"Not too late for you to walk away."

"S'too late for all of us now. Why don't you fall over and die, eh, barbarian?"

"Stubborn, I guess."

The blade slashed, aimed at his stomach, then swung at his arms instead. The large warrior backed away. The man lacked all subtlety but he was skilled with the knife and had managed to open a small gash in his forearm.

"First blood, eh?" The assassin cackled. "You should give up no—"

The warrior didn't allow him to finish his gloating. Instead, he snapped his fist forward and it pounded into the man's nose. His assailant flailed wildly with the knife in his effort to slice his throat, but he missed and Skharr caught him around the wrist and tried to squeeze it.

His physical weakness was enough that he couldn't bring his usual power to bear and when his would-be assassin realized this, he tried to twist free and regain control of his hand. The barbarian growled in frustration and annoyance and gritted his teeth as he summoned all the strength he could. He dragged ragged breaths in and forced his whole body onto the man.

The weight was enough to force the ruffian back a step or two and as he retreated, his foot caught on the uneven surface and both men landed hard on the cobbles.

Skharr grimaced at a sharp pain in his arm and for a moment, he feared the knife had stabbed into the flesh. He looked at it quickly and realized that he had merely twisted his arm when he fell.

Instead, the blade had found purchase in his attacker's torso. It was buried to the hilt in the center of the chest and a little to the left, which explained why he had ceased his struggle almost immediately and gaped almost in shock.

The warrior had seen the look too many times from men who genuinely and without a shadow of a doubt knew they were dying.

He grunted and pushed off the man but needed a few seconds to recover his strength. The assassin's eyes fluttered shut when he died, although his fingers still twitched where they held the knife handle.

"I…need…to stop this…"

Each word emerged as a struggle. His lungs were burning and the fatigue in his body continued to build. Finally, once he no longer heard the blood rushing in his ears, he dragged himself slowly to his feet.

"Need a drink."

There was no time for it, unfortunately. Despite the spots in front of his eyes, he could see that the sun was rapidly climbing to its peak for the day. Every inch of him wanted to stay and rest, but he reminded himself that he would have time for that once they were on the move.

The gate, at least, was not too far away and he managed to not stumble along the route. He had to keep telling himself to watch for other potential assassins as it was unlikely that he had killed them all.

Thankfully, before anyone else could think to waylay him, his gaze settled on the familiar faces of Sera's peloton. They stood ready and seemed to be watching for him, although he couldn't see the woman herself.

Regor was there, already mounted, and held Horse's reins.

"It took you long enough," the man noted with a chuckle, although his mirth faded quickly the moment that he saw the wound in Skharr's arm. "What happened to you?"

"Ran into some godsbedammed troll-fucker's knife," the barbarian told him and scowled at the injury. The bleeding had already stopped so he didn't think it was too serious. "Thankfully, he had the good manners to run into it as well."

"I imagine it took a little convincing."

"Not as much as you would think."

He wanted to make light about it but wasn't able to resist leaning on Horse with a sigh of relief when the beast moved close enough.

The mercenary handed him the reins as the group began to move toward the gate. "Are you sure you would not prefer to ride? I am sure the beast would not mind carrying you a short distance."

Horse seemed to agree, nudged him, and nibbled the hem of his shirt.

Skharr shook his head. "Won't ride a brother. Let him continue to carry his fair share of the burden without adding me to it."

"If you say so," Regor replied and urged his mount forward as the convoy continued out of the city.

If any others were waiting for him, they failed to make an appearance, and once they were beyond the shadows of the walls, he leaned a little more heavily on his four-legged companion.

"See?" he asked and patted Horse's neck. "No need to worry. We shall get through this without too much difficulty."

The stallion snorted as if to voice his doubts.

CHAPTER THIRTEEN

S kharr knew the hammer had been designed with a dwarf's hands in mind. So was the shield he carried, as well as the spear.

But that did not alter the fact that these weapons were some of the best he had ever laid his hands on—which he was willing to admit was a rather low measure, of course.

With that said, the assumption that he would return from the tower made him realize that he would have the money to invest in better weapons from this point forward in his life. He wouldn't sell the longsword, of course, but it would be wise to have quality alternatives for certain circumstances.

He would have to, he decided. Nothing else than the best would meet his current expectations.

Regor was already on his feet again, his sword and shield in hand as he adjusted his hold on both and clanged them together loudly.

"Come on, then!" he shouted. "That was a lucky blow."

The barbarian tilted his head and hefted the hammer with a smile. "If you say so."

"What else would you call a strike that makes me stumble into a rock that tripped me?"

"Those who complain about luck are those who are left covered in dust. You should have kept a better eye on your footing and your surroundings. Your feet should move constantly so I—or any other—would not have been able to deliver a firm blow to your shield."

"Were you this good a fighter at my age?"

"No. I was probably as good as you are when I had seen twelve winters, but I had been trained to kill from the day I could walk so there were different expectations. For instance, I expect that you can probably fish better than I can. I know for a fact that you are a better healer than I."

Regor paused, wondering if he had been insulted or not, and decided to simply move past it. He shrugged and grasped his weapon a little tighter.

The sword slashed forward in a flat swipe across the barbarian's stomach but hammered hard into the shield and bounced away. As had happened already a few times, the young man was now closer to his opponent than he would have liked and pressed his shield forward to regain some distance.

Skharr returned the favor, shoved his shoulder forward, and thrust him back a step. He immediately followed with his body low, used the spike on the opposite side of the hammer's head to hook the back of his opponent's leg, and lifted it until he was on his back again.

"You should also avoid entangling yourself with those stronger and larger than you," he pointed out, tucked the hammer under his arm, and proffered his hand to help the other man up.

Regor hissed and pushed some of his curly brown hair from his face as he accepted the help gratefully. "And so you were fighting for your life from the moment you could walk, yes?"

The warrior shrugged. "There is little else to do in the mountains. What little farming can be done is possible only in the summer months, and most of those with able bodies are out raiding in the winter. Those who must remain must learn to do one or the other."

His companion chuckled and shook his head. "It is odd. Folk see that part of you and only that. You are more than merely a barbarian."

"And yet less of anything else. Besides, folk tend to underestimate a simple barbarian, which allows me an edge."

"Yes," the young man agreed. "A simple barbarian whose recovery is bordering on miraculous. When we left the house a week ago, you were barely able to walk and had to lean on Horse for every step you took beyond the walls of Verenvan. And yet here you are, as healthy as you've ever been like you hadn't been poisoned at all."

Skharr looked at his hands. He did not miss the feeling of weakness that had hung over him during the first few days after the convoy left, but Regor was right. His recovery had been a little too rapid. He knew his body well and it should have taken at least a month to feel as strong as he did now.

"A mage might be to thank for that," he admitted and drew the charm from under his shirt where it had hung around his neck. "One I've encountered before. He said the charm would help heal my body of wounds, and were no wounds to occur, it might perhaps even restore my body to some semblance of youth."

Regor nodded slowly. "So…only healing wounds, then?"

He laughed. "Aye, most likely. Although I have to say that the cold nights and the hard ground aren't as easy as they would have been ten winters ago. I am a few years shy of old, but a little youth in these bones would not go awry."

"Or maybe you growing older would make things a little more even between us. You know, I spoke to the mage you mentioned. He was in the Guild Hall, yes?"

Skharr nodded.

"He tried to peddle something like donkey balls to me. Said

that they would cure all ailments and disease. I was tempted but once he started describing how the spelling went, I couldn't go through with it."

The barbarian shook his head and was unable to suppress a laugh. "He tried to peddle the same goblin crap to me as well. When I challenged him, he finally admitted that it was his lunch and that he used it to entertain himself with the unsuspecting travelers he encountered."

The young man froze for a few seconds before he laughed as well. "That misbegotten prick. I'll tear his arms off when we meet again."

"You can't deny the man his amusements. Or maybe you can and I'll be amused watching you try to attack a mage. That should provide good entertainment."

"You're an ass as well, I should add. I need something for the bruises. How do you feel?"

Skharr shook his head. "You never managed to bruise me."

"Ass."

"Well, it is true. You'll need to improve your form somewhat if you think to give me pause. Blademasters like Sera are generally the kind who would inflict damage, and it would make things a little more interesting. Speaking of which, you never did tell me why she did not join us on this convoy."

"She mentioned having business to attend to in the city—the kind that would be easier if she didn't have to worry about your safety all the time."

"I thought I would be safe at her house."

"It seems she changed her mind."

The warrior was curious about what would make the guild captain question the safety of her home. More importantly, what would change her mind and yet still compel her to remain in the city—and in that same danger. Still, there was little point in pushing the matter any further.

"What will you do now?" Regor asked and traced his fingers

lightly over the bruise on his shoulder. "We won't move for another few hours. Do you think you can find anyone else to train with?"

"I don't think any of the others would risk it. I think I'll go for a run."

Regor raised his hands in a gesture of acquiescence and returned to the camp as Skharr collected his weapons and strapped them to the saddlebags on Horse.

"What do you think, brother?" he asked. "Do you feel up to a run, or are your old bones too tired for that?"

The stallion nudged him almost a full step back and snorted.

"You're right." He chuckled and patted the beast on the head. "You could trot faster than I could run, I suppose."

Once the weapons were secured in the saddlebags, he settled himself into a brisk pace with Horse behind him.

He hadn't been entirely honest with Regor. The warrior had never heard of any spells or charms that could make people feel younger and he certainly hadn't believed it when the mage had suggested it. Still, the idea had begun to grow on him and the possibility seemed far more realistic when he started to run.

It wasn't until the poisoning that he realized how much he took his strength for granted, but it felt strangely different now—not quite new strength but a return to that closer to his youth. He hadn't felt this much energy in his body in years.

The wind rushed through his hair and energy coursed through his veins and he laughed with pleasure. It occurred to him that his run was taking him farther from the camp than he would have liked to go, but it wasn't like he couldn't track them if he needed to. He could easily move faster than the convoy too.

Skarr ran farther from the path and Horse followed at a light trot. He looked calm and almost uncaring about the route that they had taken.

For years, the barbarian had given little thought to the reality that he would probably outlive the beast. It was calming to have a brother like him at his side and so made it difficult for him to consider that he would have to find a replacement soon.

But this wasn't the time for that, he reminded himself. For now, all he could think about was how far he could run before his body began to tell him to stop. He wasn't sure how long it took before the burning in his muscles and his lungs finally drove him to a halt next to a small stand of trees.

His breathing began to slow and he stared across the open fields that spread to the west. It was mostly lowlands there, webbed with hundreds of rivers that enriched the soil and had made it the target of dozens of wars in the past until one group finally managed to break through. Emperor Rivar was credited with ending the last war over the lands with a marriage that had solidified his claim over the region, although many more marriages and alliances had been forged to keep it.

Over the course of the last three hundred years, a tenuous peace had held.

The mountains towered above the lowlands in the west. About fifty or so clans vied for survival in the region and received support from a handful of lowland nobles when they needed the clansmen to join them in some fight or another.

And beyond those was his home.

He didn't feel particularly homesick but seeing the mountains in the distance did wonders to remind him that it was there.

Horse nudged him in the back and stamped the ground nervously to bring his mind back to the present.

"I know. We'll return shortly," Skharr muttered and patted the beast's neck. "I merely need a moment to catch my breath and, of course, bask in the fact that we are on our own for a little while—oi!"

His exclamation came when the stallion nipped at his fingers and pawed the ground again. He shook his mane and looked nervously around. The warrior had learned to trust the beast's instincts and immediately began to search for any sign of what had unnerved him.

Finally, he saw something that flew high above them. Its great height made it seem smaller at first, but as it began to swoop toward the earth again, he realized it was almost Horse's size, although lean and more gangly and with long wings that allowed it to glide in an easy descent.

The closer to the ground it got, the more of it he could see, although it looked like it had no interest in the barbarian or his horse.

It uttered a screech that made his skin crawl and plummeted faster toward a small wagon that moved slowly along the road—the same road his caravan would travel on soon.

"I suppose they might need our help." Skharr growled at the pervasive sense of menace and opened the saddlebags to retrieve the throwing axes as well as the war hammer and hang them on his person. Defense wouldn't be much of an option against something that could simply fly away.

The shrieks continued to issue from the creature as he pushed toward the road and moved as quickly as he was able to. He relished the rush of the burn in his muscles and the way his whole body seemed to somehow unite in the effort.

As he approached, he narrowed his eyes to study the scene. Two men on horseback attempted to drive the beast away. All they carried were swords, however, and the predator remained well out of their range, flapped its enormous wings, and opened its mouth to reveal rows and rows of teeth the size of knives, ready to carve into them.

Suddenly, as the creature moved upward again, it spewed a stream of something from its mouth, but it wasn't fire as he'd expected. A glowing quality to it was odd enough, but it was green and it sank quickly into the ground around the horses.

As they walked over it, they reacted in terror and pain and

immediately began to neigh and kick and bucked their riders off as they attempted to escape the substance.

Smoke rose from the hooves and the men's armor as they struggled to move clear of it and told him it was some kind of acid. Which, he reasoned, meant the beast was some type of draconid. The presence of only two limbs suggested it was a wyvern, perhaps, although he had never seen any that could spit acid before.

"By all the fucking goblin-infested seven hells." He snarled, yanked one of the throwing axes from its sheath, and hefted it carefully as he approached the road. The beast hadn't seen him yet, but that would change the moment he joined the fight.

Horse had already made the wise decision to stay clear of the combat and stopped well short of the road. He pranced and stamped nervously as Skharr approached in a full sprint and threw the ax as hard as he could.

There had been a few instances and opportunities to practice, but the flight of the weapon was still a pleasure to watch and it whistled cleanly as it cut a smooth path toward its target.

His aim was still a little off, unfortunately, and the weapon sliced into the beast's wing instead of its head, which was what he had aimed for.

It screeched again, this time in agony as the weapon gashed the membrane of the appendage to leave a hole in it. The beast tumbled and landed hard, rolled away from the road, and tried to protect itself from the second ax that whipped above its head.

"I surely miss my bow," the barbarian muttered as he yanked his hammer from his belt. The other two guards turned to look at him, unsure of what had happened but unwilling to look this particular gift horse in the mouth.

Their armor was severely damaged and showed signs that the acid continued to melt through it. He shook his head and surged toward the creature. There was nothing quite like living through all the dangers in his life only to die from an attack by a hungry wyvern.

He didn't want to kill it. The creature looked hungry and had likely only attacked the wagon because it had a nest full of eggs that had to be sustained. Wyverns preferred to hunt in mountain rivers where they could dive into the water and snatch salmon from the depths.

Or maybe this was a different kind. He had never seen one that spat acid before.

"Stay back!" Skharr roared and retreated a step as the beast rushed from the tall grass and launched another stream of the foul substance at the defenders.

The barbarian grimaced. He should have chosen his spear instead of the hammer if he had to kill it.

Reluctant to try for a fatal strike, he held his ground as the wyvern stood as tall as it could. It was a few feet larger than he was and when it flapped its wings, the wind rushed around them.

"I won't run," he told it and remained motionless with the hammer poised as he waited for it to act. Any sign of movement, even the slightest twitch in the jaw, and he would move away to avoid the acid that would certainly come next.

The wyvern stared at him with large beady eyes fixed in an unblinking stare, one predator watching another and waiting to see who would back down first.

He knew what it would do before it did. It was wounded and outnumbered, and while the wing was injured, it could still fly. With a few flaps, it became airborne again, circled away, and flew toward a thicket over a hill, likely where its nest was situated. It would hopefully find some kind of creature there to feed on.

Or perhaps it wouldn't. It was a beast that would have to find its way, but it would not eat the horses and men he was protecting.

He grasped his weapon a little tighter and looked around for his axes. One had landed farther up the road, and the second was somewhere in the grass. He would find it but would have to wait for a moment.

"We appreciate your help, sir," one of the guards told him and still tried to brush away the acid eating into his armor. "Haven't... needed to deal with anything like that. Not ever."

"Wyverns not this low," Skharr noted. "Like mountains."

"Not anymore," someone said from inside the carriage. "There are too many humans in the mountains. They are being driven away from their perches and they have to fight for what land they have now. It is a sad situation, but every sight of a changing world can be sad to see, I suppose."

Skharr recognized the voice and the familiar figure who stepped out. The elf was hard to forget, and she looked almost the same as she had before. Her clothes were in a similar flowing style and almost identical in color to what he remembered from their first meeting.

She was smaller than a human would have been, and the familiar and yet unfamiliar features and bone structure made her oddly and impossibly beautiful.

"You," she said as she descended from the carriage and approached him. "I know you. I remember you."

"I am difficult to forget," the barbarian admitted ruefully and glanced at the guards, who were immediately uncomfortable with their charge so close to an armed man.

"Yes, you are the barbarian. I remember when my family first came to Verenvan, you were there to greet us."

"I had just arrived in the city myself at the time."

"Yes, but you were there to greet us. And here you are again to save me and my men from the attack of a monster. Bearing... some magic of your own, it would appear."

He narrowed his eyes, unsure of what she was talking about until she pointed at his neck. His charm had fallen out from under his shirt and now hung free over his chest.

"Aye," he admitted and tucked it away. "Much needed."

"You will join the others in their search for Ivehnshaw Tower, will you not?"

Startled, he nodded slowly. "How—"

"Others have passed us, telling us of their destination and carrying weapons and trinkets like yours. I made the assumption. Correct, yes?"

"Yes."

"I have a gift for you." She returned to the carriage before he could stop her, although she was not inside long. When she emerged, she held a dagger in her hand.

"What is that?" Skharr asked.

"A dagger of health."

She put it in his hand and he was not able to resist when she wrapped his fingers around it.

"Why would one need a dagger that heals?" he asked and studied the weapon.

It was small and delicate like she was. The blade was about as long as his middle finger, with silver filigree running down the blade and into the oaken handle to finally appear as a silver snake with emerald eyes on the pommel.

"A cursed blade is not something to take lightly," she explained and slid a sheath over the blade, a small leather piece engraved with the same silver that traced through the rest of the dagger. "This must be stabbed into your heart to keep you from death."

"So...it heals? By stabbing myself with it?" It sounded somewhat backward, but he was loathe to offend her in his confusion.

"It might," she admitted. "There is no limit to what it can do. Similar to a wish, it will bring whatever you want most in the world into the world. For most who are dying, their wish is to not die. However, it must be activated by pushing the blade into one's flesh."

"So I couldn't simply push it into the flesh of some other bastard?"

She smiled and shook her head. "A cursed blade demands its

price but in some cases, you might find yourself willing to pay it. Unfortunately, I must continue on my journey, although I know we will see one another again before too long."

Skharr nodded, still unsure of what she was talking about. It was odd to encounter an elf again, but he had no aspirations to see her in the future.

Which made him wonder how she knew she would see him again.

The carriage began to move and as he retrieved his weapons, the convoy trundled up the road toward them.

"I guess we'll see our people after all," he muttered to Horse as he slid the weapons into the saddlebags.

CHAPTER FOURTEEN

The odd dagger the elf had given him nagged at his thoughts. He knew he had no fear of magic but he was afraid of unsheathing it for some reason.

In the end, he could probably sell it if he didn't intend to use it —hopefully to someone who wouldn't stab themselves for a wish of some kind.

The mage would probably take it, and as Skharr knew what the blade did, he certainly wouldn't sell it for anything less than its full value.

But that would be a matter for later. He hid the blade deep inside his saddlebags, away from where he was tempted to use it himself.

Even knowing it was there felt like a temptation, although he was certain that his wish would never be to avoid dying. He wasn't sure the blade would help him in any way and decided it would be best to simply put it out of his mind.

"I'm afraid that here is where we will have to part ways," Regor commented as he moved forward to ride next to him. "Unless, of course, you are willing to finish the escort with us.

You'll miss the dungeon, most likely, but you will find yourself in safer hands. Trust me."

The barbarian smiled, pushed a few errant strands of hair away from his face, and tucked them behind his ear. "I fear we will have to part ways here, and I'll hope we see each other again. Hopefully after taking everything that I can carry from that fucking curse-spawned tower."

"I'll drink to that," the young man commented, took a skin from his hip, and tipped a few mouthfuls down his throat. "It's only water but the sentiment remains."

Skharr patted the man's horse gently and stood aside as the convoy started to veer away from him. They moved in a northerly direction while he remained precisely where he was at the crossroads.

The fact that there were crossroads—and heavily trafficked ones at that—already told him there was enough space for a small settlement to be established nearby.

There were no walls and it looked like the town—or possibly village would be a better word—had simply sprung up from the roads and the rivers that meandered through the area and from one day to the next had simply started to grow.

The barbarian assumed some lord or another had claimed the lands and sent soldiers to patrol it, but this was as large a settlement as he had ever seen that didn't have any walls—or at least some kind of fortress.

That would change come the first large-scale onslaught from the outside. It would be bandits or perhaps a lord's army that was looking for food and revelry, but it wouldn't take long.

No walls meant it would be easy pickings for any force large enough to attack.

Although that would not happen in the foreseeable future. At present, the influx of visitors ensured that any group would think twice before they launched an assault.

He and Horse approached slowly and he scowled when he realized how many outsiders swarmed the settlement. Hundreds had assembled and some even chose to make camp outside the town, although he hoped it was only because they didn't want to pay what he was sure would be exorbitant prices at the local inns and taverns.

Skharr decided that he wasn't in the mood to make camp outside with most of the others, although he could guess why so many folk had gathered there. It was where the scrolls had told most of the adventurers to meet to prepare. He had expected a smaller group—twenty at the most—but it would seem he was one of hundreds.

If they organized, they could probably launch an assault on the tower. No matter how much magic it held, he doubted that anyone would have the power necessary to resist an attack by hundreds, especially centuries after they had died themselves.

But there was always greed to be considered. The promise of reward beyond each adventurer's wildest dreams would be considerably diluted by the numbers that had gathered, and those who had come were looking for treasure that would allow them to never have to work again.

More than one overtly hostile gaze followed him as he led Horse into the town. The fact that they were all armed and carried charms and magical items of all types and qualities confirmed that they would join him on the raid on the tower, but it appeared that they wouldn't be willing to share their treasure once it was found.

Perhaps that was why so few people made it out of the gods-forsaken hellhole. The moment they saw how much coin there was to share, they all turned on one another until eventually, there wasn't anyone left for the magic inside the tower to kill.

As he approached one of the inns, he realized that most of the folk who would join the quest had made camp outside, which left rooms available at least. Skharr found the inn that looked the most respectable and he and Horse entered the courtyard.

"You joining the rest of them fools, then?" the innkeeper asked. "Well, my name is Horus, and if you have the coin, I have the best food and shelter for you and your companion before you throw your lives away on this pointless quest."

"Pointless?" he asked.

"Aye, well, there have already been those who escaped with more coin than they could spend, which generally means there ain't no more to claim for those who come after. Not that I don't appreciate the business, of course. Winter months are coming and I would see fewer folk coming through here otherwise."

"Magic remains," the barbarian noted. "The tower still appears and disappears. Survivors lost their memory."

"That's what all the others say." Horus shook his head, poured ale from a jug into a couple of mugs, and pushed them to a young woman who waited to serve another group. "And I suppose the fact that they all end up dead themselves—or at least that is the most prevalent assumption—could indicate that there might still be something to kill in there. Of course, it doesn't mean there is coin in it for any others who might survive."

"You think they might meet another end?"

The innkeeper shrugged. "You see the types this kind of quest attracts. The most likely end they meet is at the hands of the other adventurers. There might be something in the tower as well, of course, but another thought might be that the others simply never found a way out. The doors closed and they starved within. Those who did come out claim to have no memory of how they accomplished it, so it is all rumor and myth at this point, and I don't have sufficient time in my day to consider it. But back to the topic—have you an interest in one of my rooms and a stable for your horse, perhaps?"

"Both would interest me." He showed the man his pouch. "But it would depend on the price of the rooms and the stable."

Horus nodded. "Given the number of people in our town, I think three silver pieces would be enough for a room and another two coppers for your horse to be stabled with us until you choose to leave."

It was expensive, especially in light of the remoteness of the town, but he had come in expecting something like that. With so many people there, folk like him were bound to set their prices high and he doubted that he would find anything cheaper in any of the other reputable establishments in the city.

He took three silver coins from his pouch, placed them on the counter, and instead of the coppers, he added a gold coin.

"Would this be enough to keep my horse stabled and fed?" Skharr asked. "I'll not take him with me and should I not return, I would need him to be stabled for the duration of the winter months. After that, he should be set free and will find his way home from here."

"Well, that is an...odd request," the innkeeper answered, but avarice gleamed in his eyes as he studied the gold coin. "I'll keep him until the weather is warm enough for travel, and then he will be released, you have my word on it. Might I ask, though...why would you bring a horse on an expedition like this if he will not assist you in it?"

"He already has. But he's old and most likely won't survive a trip into the tower. I would see him well fed—and given a good supply of apples if you can spare them. As for myself, the room for a few nights. What options have you for food?"

"We have a few wild boars roasting over the fire and you'll get a fair share of that, as well as potatoes and cabbage soup all for a single silver piece, which will also buy you about as much ale as you can drink. Although you will be charged another copper extra for every mug past the fifth."

Skharr doubted that he would drink all five mugs of ale, but he was willing to put it to the test as he placed another silver coin on the counter.

"Very good, sir. My girl will find you and lead you to your

room once it is ready. For the moment, you should choose a place to sit and enjoy your meal."

The barbarian did as he was told and glanced around the common room. More than a handful of patrons were already present, most enjoying their evening meals. The majority looked armed and armored, which meant they were likely all on the same quest as he was.

"Oi, you—big lad!" a deep, booming voice called from the other side of the common room. "Come and join us if you've a mind to!"

A dwarf seated at one of the longer tables gestured for him to approach, joined by almost a dozen humans who also waved in welcome.

"You're with the Theros guild, aye?" the dwarf asked as he approached. "You've something of a reputation for dealing with dungeons as far as we've heard. Care to share a few stories and maybe some advice for fellow travelers over a mug?"

Skharr took the seat offered to him and studied his new companions quickly. They had the look of characters who had been in a fight before, even the dwarf. If he were to guess, he would have said they looked like they had been soldiers once and had turned to the guilds for work once the fighting ended.

"Not sure if my experiences will help with what we'll face," he replied softly as one of the young women hurried forward and placed a mug in front of him.

"As like as not, but we'll be entertained with a good story nonetheless." The dwarf laughed and took a swig from his mug. "S'true that you from the Western Clans? An actual DeathEater?"

He nodded slowly and sipped his ale. It was rich in taste and more than a little heady with a hint of honey mixed with the flavor, likely to mask some of the bitterness from the hops.

"An actual DeathEater," he admitted.

"Ah, well. A shame we don't have you on our team, then," one of the humans commented. "We could likely use a character like you to tear through whatever magical fucksuckers are lurking in the tower."

"Why are you joining the venture, then?" he asked carefully.

The dwarf shrugged. "We are all in need of coin for one reason or another—a fairly desperate need too. When the work in the city doesn't quite fill that need, we needs to find ourselves other ways to make the coin."

"Desperation, then." Skharr drank from his mug again and enjoyed the taste more this time.

"What brings you here to fight the same fight?" The dwarf extended his hand. "The name is Kondel, by the way. Kondel TowersSon, at your service."

The barbarian took his hand and shook it firmly. "Skharr DeathEater at yours."

"We knows who you are," one of the humans pointed out.

They were interrupted when at least ten men in full plate armor strode into the inn, shouting, singing, and laughing as they advanced on the innkeeper in a group. They carried swords and various banners that indicated their houses of origin, and Skharr immediately caught the glare they cast at the group he was with.

"Godsbedamned fucking knights," Kondel muttered and spat on the floor next to the table. "We passed them on the way in. They tried to pick off the weaker bands. Thin the herd, they said. Back where they come from, they have some kind of vows that are supposed to make them honorable, but all they are is ruffians and mercenaries—and not even the braver kind either."

He nodded. "There's only one kind of knight in shining armor. The kind who never had to use it."

"I'll drink to that."

The rest of the group agreed loudly and each took a long draught from their drinks as a platter of food arrived for him.

"Fuckers like that won't think twice about riding over you twice with the carriage carrying all their clothes." The dwarf snorted, picked up a double-headed ax that leaned against the table next to him, and shook it at them. "Come try that shite with me and I'll introduce you to the salty taste of your insides, ya fucking cowards!"

The knights ignored them and left the inn and it appeared that Horus told them he was full and could not accept all members of their team.

Skharr noted that the dwarf's ax had the same bull sigil that had been etched onto his weapons and armor.

"You were supplied by AnvilForge as well?" he asked.

"Aye, the best smiths in Verenvan, although expensive. I managed to purchase the ax a few years ago—some of their finest work—and it's still as sharp as the day I bought it. You using their equipment too?"

He nodded. "They agreed to supply me, although I fear it might cost me more than I can afford."

"If they outfitted you, there must be a team they agreed to do the same for," one of the humans noted and frowned as he picked something from his teeth. "I've not seen any group in dwarf gear, so is the Theros team simply taking their time in arriving?"

The barbarian smirked. "A DeathEater is his own team and does not need anyone to surround him."

The group laughed but stopped when they realized he was not laughing with them. He merely enjoyed the rich food that had been provided with a calm expression.

"Well, if you've a mind to join a team, we're more than happy to accept someone of your experience," Kondel said and sipped his drink again. "Traveling alone in these parts is a dangerous prospect for all, no matter what their origins."

He pretended to focus on the food in front of him, but he couldn't deny that he was tempted. It was always easier to work the dungeons as part of a team, especially after his experience the last time.

"I might take that offer," he said and bit into a thick slice of boar meat.

"Well, if you do, we'll leave sometime tomorrow in the morning," Kondel muttered around his mug. "Always glad to have someone with real dwarf armor in the fight with us."

Sera truly disliked having to wear this skin.

It was a metaphorical skin, of course, but it felt as alien as if it had been a literal one. There was nothing about being a noble that she enjoyed aside from the fact that she likely never had to worry about going hungry or being cold or exposed to the elements, at least not while she was in the city.

But sometimes, it was necessary. A few words with Pennar had told her who Skharr had worked for on the night of his attempted assassination, and she would narrow down the list of who the assassin might be before she made any serious accusations.

Which meant she would pay Lady Tamisen a visit, and that required more than her usual light armor and sword.

Of course, there was no rule against ladies carrying weapons, especially if they had been trained in a particular form or discipline, and a lady with the skills of a blademaster was not to be ignored.

But all the rest had needed to be replaced. Instead of light and comfortable clothes, she had been provided with silks dyed purple and red to match her complexion. The servants appeared to enjoy dressing her like a prim and proper lady, but Sera had never felt so uncomfortable.

The carriage finally came to a halt and she could hear guards speak to those who waited outside the villa. It was, of course, their responsibility to ask who sought to gain entry and why.

She smirked when her man replied in no uncertain terms that Lady Sera Ferat was there to speak to Lady Tamisen and that her business was her own.

The guards stepped back and she was allowed to disembark from her carriage. She swept toward the gate without so much as a glance at the guards, although she could tell that they studied her carefully—and inspected the sword she carried at her hip.

"Lady Tamisen will meet you momentarily," one of the servants called and she did her best to not acknowledge the woman who had spoken. Nobles behaved in a certain way and she did not intend to break with tradition yet.

The guild captain was guided into a small meeting area out in the open where servants were already setting out refreshments for the unannounced guest.

Tamisen herself appeared in a few moments. The woman looked a little ruffled but tried to hide it as she attempted to be the best hostess she could be.

"Lady Ferat!" the woman called with a small wave while she pushed her long, curly red hair away from her face. One of her ladies hurried behind her and tried to draw her hair up in a more functional style that was more befitting of her status.

"Lady Tamisen." Sera smiled as they greeted each other politely with an exchange of kisses on each others' cheeks. "I was hoping you would be home. More importantly, I hoped that my people inquiring as to your whereabouts would be enough warning of my arrival."

"That is my fault, unfortunately." Her hostess gestured for them to sit as the servants finished setting out the refreshments. "I'm afraid you have not been seen in proper company for so long that I assumed you would not be coming. It is refreshing to see you among your peers once more instead of the—forgive my bluntness, but the dregs who fill the guilds."

She forced a smile. "Your bluntness is forgiven. Although I would think you would have more appreciation for the dregs of the guilds, given the company you have kept of late."

The woman flicked her hand quickly to send the servants

away and out of hearing distance, although the impish grin that touched her face was far from bashful.

"You heard of it, then? I did try to keep it a secret, although I suppose word would inevitably come from somewhere. I would hardly consider the barbarian to be the dregs of the guilds, however. Head and shoulders above, I would say."

Sera didn't want to admit that she was right about that, at least. "Did you hear that he was poisoned soon after he left your house?"

Her hostess leaned forward and narrowed her eyes. "What? No! Of course not! Is he well? Alive?"

"I barely managed to save his life. Are you saying you had nothing to do with his attempted assassination?"

Tamisen shook her head vehemently. "I would not even know where to begin. Besides, I was far more interested in the man for his many…assets. He removed an unwanted offer of marriage and provided a delightful evening besides. After Lady Svana recommended his services to me, I wasn't sure I could have resisted. I don't suppose you've ever entreated him for his…assets?"

She shook her head. "I owe him a life debt. He saved mine and that of my people."

"That is a pity," her companion muttered, picked up a piece of fruit from the table, and studied it intently. "You can only marry once, and a ride like that is better enjoyed before than after."

The captain forced a laugh, shook her head, and tried not to show how annoyed she was at the woman in front of her.

Nobles. She would never understand them despite technically belonging to their ranks.

CHAPTER FIFTEEN

"Are you sure this is the place?" Skharr gazed somewhat dubiously around the location where they had recently stopped. Aside from the cool winds that swept from the mountains, he wasn't sure what exactly he should look for.

"Aye," the dwarf grumbled and peered at his scroll. "This does appear to be the place if this map is any good."

"The map would have been followed by hundreds of adventurers over the years." He shook his head. "There might have been something here, but how do we know it will lead us to this... Tower of Ivershaw?"

"Ivehnshaw," Kondel corrected as the others in their party began to circle the area as if that would bring something to reassure them. "And it is where all the others came. I saw them a long time ago when I was only forging weapons for the group that left. I saw them enter when the portal came, and then they vanished with it."

"Did they ever come out?" he asked and studied the dwarf carefully.

"Not one of them did. But I have heard that some have in the past, which is why so many come every year."

The barbarian nodded. All the legends and rumors that surrounded the tower were exactly that—legends and rumors. There was nothing of substance to confirm its existence, even though they searched for something that could indicate where it would appear.

He had not been in full armor for a long time, and the dwarves had put considerable effort into what he had been loaned. The gambeson was light and fitted easily to the pauldrons. The helm was a work of art, of course. Designed with the sigil of the bull in the front, it made it seem as if he were the bull, complete with horns that curled behind his head.

Which, he thought after a moment, made it look a little more like a ram, but it was certainly better if he found himself in a fight. Horns protruding from his helm like that would be too easy for a foe to grasp and yank in any direction.

Horse wasn't with him to assist with his burdens and he did not want to have to carry everything on his own. He wasn't even sure how long they would have to wait out in the open, much less inside the tower. How much food they would need for the duration was something to worry about as well. While he knew he could hunt in the wilds and kill his food even without the bow, he doubted there would be deer, boar, and rabbit in the tower.

"When is it supposed to appear again?" one of the mercenaries asked with a frown.

"Soon," Kondel answered and hefted his weapon. "And if you need any kind of proof, there it is."

Skharr looked toward the path they had approached on where the others who wanted to join them on the quest advanced slowly. He studied them briefly and it appeared as though not all intended to go inside. Some among the groups had already begun to erect tents and stalls to hawk their wares and others seemed only curious and wanted to watch the adventurers enter.

"So when you say you were a blacksmith when you watched it, you mean you were among that crowd?" he asked the dwarf.

"Aye."

"What is the appeal?"

"You want to see them on their way, wish them well—it is something of an event. The fact that you can make coin at the same time is simply an added advantage."

The barbarian nodded, but his attention had already moved elsewhere. Something was wrong, although he couldn't be sure what he was looking for. He moved his hand instinctively toward his weapons. The shield hung from his back, along with both of the throwing axes, while the hammer was attached to his belt.

He already had hold of his spear so he tightened his grasp on that instead. It had doubled effectively as a walking stick and he had used it to carry a few of the food bags, but he quickly loosed them and readied the weapon. Something moved in the tall grass on all sides, and he didn't like the fact that he couldn't see more than ten feet around them.

It took the dwarf a few seconds to realize that he was no longer listening to him. Kondel had continued to expound on how much coin he had made the last time he was there, but when his large companion hefted his weapon and looked warily around him, he fell silent and took his double-winged ax from his belt.

Skharr was surprised to see that he carried it with one hand and a small shield with the other. It was an effective size but it was crafted in a way that would allow him to take hold of it with both hands if he needed to.

Eventually, the warrior was able to identify what had caught his attention. Something rattled in the grass over the sound of the wind. He knew the noise, which was no doubt why it had immediately triggered an alarm in his mind. A few flatlands existed in the mountains where he had grown up and it was always a warning. The snakes there liked to leave their rattlers up while they remained buried in the sand, away from the sun but still on the hunt for their next meal.

But whatever stalked them now was not underground and instead, used the grass to remain hidden.

He spun when a couple of the members of his team fell. They simply dropped where they stood without something dragging them down, and he shifted his spear in that direction in search of the familiar target.

Finally, it appeared. It had advanced when it saw Kondel turn his back to look toward his fallen comrades.

The beast was much larger than he expected it to be and it slithered closer through the grass and raised its head. The bright, venomous-yellow eyes with dark slits for pupils flicked from side to side as it searched for an opening in the dwarf's armor. It opened its mouth and bared its fangs, which dripped with a milky liquid.

The warrior roared and drew his spear back as the serpent advanced on the dwarf, in part as a warning but also to distract the beast before it could strike.

Sure enough, the massive head swiveled to try to find the source of the sound as he advanced on it. The fangs extended and some of the fluid was ejected from its mouth.

Skharr knew he would be grateful for the range his weapon would give him. He darted to the side, thrust the spear from the angle he had chosen, and drove the blade through the creature's throat and out the other side.

He could feel the sinuous power in it and even with the wound, it would not be enough. "Ha! You're as fucking ugly as Janus' hairy one-eyed serpent," he yelled as he drove forward and thrust his adversary to the ground. He yanked the spear out and stabbed again to deliver the killing blow between the beast's eyes.

Once he was assured that it was dead—although its long body continued to squirm and writhe in its death throes—Skharr drew his spear out and looked at the others in their group.

Those who had been knocked off their feet had already regained them and had their weapons out while they tried to identify a target. Kondel, however, seemed to be rooted where he stood with his shield up but his ax down as if he hadn't expected to have to use it.

"Are you well, dwarf?" he asked and used the tall grass to wipe the head of his spear clean.

His companion did not respond immediately and stared numbly at the massive snake that now twitched frighteningly close to him.

"Nah," he responded at last, cleared his throat, and shook his head. "I'm as godsbedammed far from well as an orc-fucked goblin."

He followed the dwarf's gaze to the fallen creature. "Afraid of snakes, are you?"

"You would be too if you saw the creatures that made their homes in our caverns."

"I have been in the dwarven caverns before. I don't remember any snakes."

"Well, I do. Some of them are large enough to fill a tunnel on their own. They rush down and eat everything in their path, although their nests are considerably worse as they hatch hundreds of younglings and simply wait for something to fall inside."

"Wouldn't have thought a dwarf would be afraid of the dangers lurking under the mountains."

"Fuck you. How's about that?"

Skharr grinned and patted his shoulder. "I suppose it is an acceptable response."

The dwarf cackled in response. "Nice work on your part, though. Fought many snakes in your past?"

"Run from them for the most part."

"So, are you afraid of the monsters that lurk under the ground too?"

"Yes, but I'm no fucking short-assed dwarf."

That earned him a punch in the thigh over his armor. It was hard enough to sting but not enough to bruise, which he assumed was the intention.

The groups began to gather and move closer to where Skharr and his team stood, although a few of the men and women paused to poke and nudge the dead snake.

The knights they had seen at the inn were the last ones to arrive, but they pushed those in front of them out of their way with the kind of rough arrogance that suggested a sense of entitlement.

"We'll be the first ones through the gates," the apparent leader shouted, loudly enough for the others to hear. "None will step in front of us and we shall be the ones to step out, for the honor and glory of Emperor Rivar!"

They were the emperor's knights, then. The barbarian planted his spear in the ground and narrowed his eyes. It seemed they counted on none of the teams being willing to engage in a fight prior to a tough dungeon crawl, and if any did, they were the most likely to throw punches and would all converge on those who challenged their enforced authority.

It was an intelligent move, he was willing to admit, but not one that spoke of the kind of honor knights were so well-known for.

He would need to make a statement, he decided. Better now than when the slime-spawned fuckers bullied anyone who crossed their path once they were inside the tower.

"Those who would stand in our way, stand in the way of the emperor!" The leader removed his helm and carried it under his arm. He had the good looks that seemed to be expected in most knights.

His dark, dusky skin went well with the long, silky black hair drifting over his shoulders. The square jaw and brilliant smile would have made the man a good deal more handsome had his look not been so smug and superior.

Skharr had a mind to make him a little less good-looking and much less smug. He rolled his shoulders and drew a deep breath as he advanced along the path that was unwillingly being cleared for the imperial knights. While he knew there was the potential that his decision might have a poor result for him, it was better to have that now than inside the dungeon.

"Out of the way, you big oaf!" the man shouted and gestured belligerently. "You would not want to run afoul of the Emperor's ire!"

The warrior continued to advance.

"I said out of the—"

He did not let him finish his last warning but surged forward and drove his fist across the man's jaw. The hard impact sent waves of pain through his hand, but the effect was all he had hoped for. He smirked when the bully's eyes rolled back and his whole body went limp before he even knew what had happened.

But the job wasn't finished. The man's companions seemed ready to start a fight, which would put him at a severe disadvantage if he did not act quickly. He caught the falling knight by his breastplate, lifted him almost without effort, and hurled him into the ranks of those supporting him.

Their advance was halted when they had to catch their comrade in full plate armor as he pounded into them.

The pause was all the barbarian needed. It wasn't long before the other groups decided they wouldn't be intimidated either. Dealing with the individual groups while showing signs of strength was one thing. It was quite another after a display of weakness, however, and with their leader incapacitated, the whole group was given pause, unable to avenge their fallen man immediately.

Skharr stood his ground with his hand resting on the hammer at his hip as he watched them and waited for them to try to attack. He might have needed to knock a few more down if they advanced, but the fight faded from their eyes when they realized that the other groups had begun to gather against them.

One by one, the knights retreated and slunk to the back of the line.

The attention of the groups turned toward the warrior and he stared boldly at every man who dared to meet his gaze.

"Any others who wish to cut in line?" he roared across the plain and listened for any sign of contention. There was none, and he turned his back on them and strode to where he had planted his spear.

Kondel was waiting for him, pulled the weapon from the ground, and handed it to him.

"I like the way ye negotiate, DeathEater."

"There is no need to negotiate when you have all the leverage," he replied as he watched a woman approach the front.

Nothing about her indicated that she was one of the mercenaries. She wore no armor, and the only weapon she carried was a dagger strapped to her hip. Her robes were silver and purple, and a sigil on her chest suggested that she was perhaps a herald for the local lord.

She held a scroll in her hand and opened it as she reached the front. "You have all been summoned to venture into the Ivehnshaw Tower. Entering will cost each man a silver coin in tax. The honor is great and the possibility of riches and glory immense, only matched by the risk presented to you all. An escort will be provided for any survivors who wish it, and while there will be no taxes on any treasure found, ten gold coins will be expected to pay the guard for the journey to the safety of civilization. Healing vials will also be made available to them, although be warned that prices will be enough to turn your balls blue. Or your tits if you happen to be a lady."

"No ladies here!" a woman shouted from the back and the

statement was met with a chorus of cheers and laughter from the group.

The herald waited for the amusement to subside before she continued. "Those who have not paid their tax yet will need to do so before entering. The tower will open in..." She paused to look at the sun. "Approximately ten minutes."

Skharr shook his head. He didn't want to part with any more coin, but in the end—if he survived—it hopefully meant coin would no longer be a problem in his life ever again.

Of course, he still didn't know if there was any treasure to be found inside the tower, but he would discover it if it was there.

The moment of consideration passed quickly and he accepted the necessity, drew a silver coin from his pouch, and handed it to the woman. She took it quickly and placed a firm stamp on his guild scroll before she waved him forward to rejoin his group.

Nothing had happened as yet, although he could tell that the teams had begun to grow more anxious for the moment when they would begin the fight of their lives. He dragged in a deep breath and quelled the anticipation building in the pit of his stomach.

"How much coin do you think we'll come away with?" Kondel asked as he spun his weapon idly in his hand. The dwarf seemed genuinely excited to be a part of it all.

"You don't think we are more likely to die?" one of the others asked.

"Why think about that when you can think about what you'll spend your coin on?" another replied with a laugh.

The barbarian shook his head, peered into the sky, and rolled his shoulders. His gaze flicked around as an odd crackle drew his attention and the air filled with the smell of ozone.

Something was happening at last.

CHAPTER SIXTEEN

S kharr realized that he had discerned the changes before the others did. It was a subtle difference, but he could sense the smells and the shift in the air around him that those gathered seemed to not have noticed yet.

But the transformation, when it occurred, came quickly. The whole open area around them crackled and flashed brightly and all those present, mercenary or not, turned away and shielded their eyes. When they looked again, the tower had suddenly materialized.

It wasn't a conventional structure, he noticed—at least not at the base. It seemed more like a mountain that rose sharply skyward until the peak became a tower.

None of those present could be sure whether they would make it to the top or not. The only way to go was forward, and that was through a cave that opened at the base. His group was the first to regain their senses and approach.

While it wasn't his group, in fact, given that he'd joined them in a somewhat relaxed way, they allowed him to take the lead position while the others moved in behind him. The cave enveloped them quickly, and the bright daylight vanished the moment they stepped inside. He looked back, a little surprised, and realized that something around the tower prevented the sunlight from filtering in.

Even so, enough light came from above them at the top of the cavern. What looked like massive chandeliers provided some illumination, although it took a few moments for them to adjust to the change.

The cavern was wide, an area much larger than rooms in most houses, and the barbarian continued to move rather than pause like others to inspect his surroundings. Even the fact that the stone floor was littered with skeletons didn't make him hesitate. Hundreds of them sprawled with their armor still on and their weapons cast around them.

"What do you think killed so many?" Kondel asked and nudged one of the closest with his boot. He scowled when the bones fell apart at the touch.

"No matter." Skharr growled and shook his head. "If we linger here, we will find out. Keep moving."

He looked over his shoulder and realized that most of their team had stopped to examine and loot the bodies, so only he and Kondel continued through the cavern toward what looked like a massive stone door ahead of them. It was easy to see the writing on the doors but reading it was a problem.

The barbarian stepped closer and frowned when he realized that more of the skeletons were piled near the door than anywhere else in the room.

The script seemed to be in dozens of different languages, and he needed to study more than a handful of them before he found one he understood.

"Dwarvish, of course," he muttered.

"What do you have against dwarvish?" Kondel asked.

"You love wordplay and putting in as many floral phrases as you can to make any phrase mean anything you want. It's annoyingly effective at confusing anyone who reads it."

"Well, yes, but there is a beauty to it. Besides, it can't be our fault that so many of you have languages so simple that even a child could understand them."

Skharr shook his head and chose not to reply as he ran his fingers over the writing in an effort to decipher it. He couldn't say he had used the dwarvish tongue a great deal.

Suddenly, the meaning was clear and he backed away from the gate, yanked his shield off his back, and grasped it firmly.

"You seriously think it means that?" his companion asked when he finished reading it a few seconds later.

"Sixty can go in," he confirmed and shook his head with a scowl. "No more, no less. The ranks must be thinned. It'll be a massacre." And, of course, it explained why so many had fallen close to the door.

He gestured for the two of them to move. As unobtrusively as possible, they inched along the wall and away from where most of the fighting would take place.

The other groups converged on the gate and a little time passed in noisy discussion while they studied the various languages to find one they understood. Those polyglots in the ranks were the first to realize what it meant and spread the word quickly. Fights began within moments among those closest to the door and a few men fell victim to fatal wounds inflicted without warning before they gathered their wits sufficiently to defend themselves. The others returned to their groups to explain what would allow them to progress through the dungeon.

"What do you think, DeathEater?" Kondel asked and hefted his ax. "Should we fight to return to the rest of our group?"

"They are among those who started the combat," he answered. "If we try to rejoin them, we will be in the thick of the fighting. They can make their way to us but for the moment, with everyone determined to kill the other, we won't need to find fights. They will find us."

Skharr was right, and it wasn't long before one of the groups noticed the two separated from their group and decided they would be easier targets.

"Keep me in your line of sight," he warned the dwarf and planted his spear at his feet as he watched the five men advance. "I'll keep to your back as much as possible but try to not hit me when you swing."

"You try to not hit me," his companion retorted.

"Of course, but I'm a much larger target."

Kondel could not argue with that, and the barbarian retrieved one of his throwing axes, judged the weight, and focused on the only one of the men approaching without a shield. He breathed deeply and stepped forward before he launched the weapon as hard as he could. Although he still needed to practice his throws with it, the ax flew true and he smiled as the blade buried itself in the man's chest deeply enough to make him stumble to his knees and clutch the wound as blood poured freely.

He drew the second ax and hurled it quickly but scowled when it glanced off one of the shields and clattered across the floor.

"Any more tricks up your sleeve?" his companion asked with a snort.

"Only the one."

Skharr left his spear where it was for the moment. It would hopefully give pause to any who might consider an attack from the side, he reasoned as he freed his hammer from where it hung on his belt. The weight of it felt more comfortable in his hands, and he held his shield out in front and watched those who had already pushed forward in the next assault.

"Yaragrim!" Kondel roared suddenly, rushed past him, and swung his ax into the group that attacked.

The barbarian shook his head and followed. He pushed his shield forward to block a sword aimed at the dwarf's head and swung his hammer easily.

It arced in low, and even though the man wore a helm, the

warrior could feel the impact all the way up his arm. The weapon crushed the bone and battered the man's head until there wasn't much other than mush inside.

The powerful strike brought a grin to his face as he circled the dwarf, who continued to roar obscenities interspersed with battle cries as he goaded the three who remained standing.

He could do little other than protect his comrade and deliver what strikes he could while he watched and waited for an opening.

Barely moments later, his opportunity presented itself when their opponents tried to focus their attacks on the dwarf instead of the barbarian in front of them. He did not intend to waste it.

In silence, he moved in from the flank and thrust his shield into the side of the nearest man. There was no satisfying crunch on the impact but his target crumpled and fell into his comrades, which forced them to lower the shields they had raised to stop the rampaging dwarf.

With nothing in his way, Kondel took advantage, and Skharr was surprised when two of them fell heavily, one missing his head and the other without the lower half of his left leg.

His attack left the barbarian with the last remaining man, who tried to fall back and turned quickly. He had barely taken a few steps when a blow from the large man caught him in the knee. It shattered and as he stumbled forward, the warrior swung his hammer to deliver a powerful killing stroke to the back of his head.

Others surged forward, and he lifted his shield to block a spear that was thrust violently to catch him in the chest.

The collision was enough to destabilize his attacker while he moved not an inch despite all the power in the blow. His companion had executed the legless man efficiently and hurried closer to help him.

"How is your non-violent approach working now?" the dwarf asked with a grin and flicked the blood from his ax.

"Not particularly well," he admitted and retreated to a position where no other groups could flank them.

Another team attacked—six of them this time. The fighting had devolved to include smaller and smaller numbers as the adventurers fell in what was, indeed, the massacre he'd predicted.

More than half were already dead, but more than the sixty who were required still remained. He wondered how many had died in this starting trial of the dungeon over the years.

More than a few, he mused when he glanced at the skeletons that had now been joined by the fresh corpses of this year's hopefuls.

Suddenly, a bright flash of lightning streaked across the room. Skharr raised his shield in time but felt the strike that thrust him back a few steps.

"A mage?" He growled belligerently as he straightened. "By Janus' hairy ballsack—they brought a fucking godsbedamned hell-spawned asshole mage?"

Another bolt, this time of fire, careened across the cavern toward him. It moved slowly but he barely managed to dive out of its path and his shield fell from his fingers as he rolled away from the flames.

Defense was no longer an option, he realized quickly. He needed to attack.

Skharr pushed to his feet and scrambled into motion immediately. He grasped his hammer tightly as he rushed toward his attacker, who seemed to have targeted him specifically. It was a short distance between them, but the man had already begun to build something between his hands—something worthy of concern, he realized as it crackled and spat sparks while it expanded.

In the next moment, the mage's intense focus disappeared and his hands fumbled behind him to try to locate an arrow that now protruded from his back.

"You idiot!" the man shouted. "Where in the piss-swilling hells did you learn to shoot?"

The answer was another arrow fired at the barbarian. It was a decent attempt except for the fact that a mage was there to stop it from reaching its target.

"What are you shooting at, you useless goblin-fucking turd?" the magic-user demanded after a bellow of pain.

Never one to miss an opportunity, the barbarian advanced and caught him while he still fumbled to reach the arrow. He had no intention to help him, however. In fact, the mage would help him against a flurry of arrows. The warrior had lost his shield, but the new human one would do as well.

The man shrieked in pain when another two arrows pierced his back. A spear cut followed and brought Skharr to a halt.

He dropped the corpse, circled toward the spear-bearer, and swung his hammer. The man's helm did nothing to save him and the weapon crushed his skull with ease. He fell to his knees in a rapidly expanding pool of blood.

Life lingered in his opponent's eyes and he considered leaving him alive, but this was no time for mercy. Besides, they needed folk to be dead to be able to push beyond the door.

A powerful strike to the neck broke it with a loud crack and finished him almost without effort. He shrugged and turned away to look for his next assailant.

The archer scowled at him but stood his ground as he reached into his quiver for more arrows. His face paled when he realized there were none left.

"Your luck is as bad as your shooting," the barbarian told him and glanced over his shoulder to check that his friend was not in any trouble.

Kondel had engaged one of the men and was toying with him. He certainly had skill and Skharr couldn't recall if he'd ever seen someone handle an ax with such dexterity and strength.

"Fight me, you goblin-spawned goatfuckers!" the dwarf

shouted before he clipped the man's hamstrings cleanly with a deft reverse cut and buried his ax into his back before he yanked it out without a pause for breath. "Stop sending your misbegotten brats to fight a dwarven elite!"

Satisfied that his short comrade had matters well in hand, he grinned and turned his attention to the archer, who had drawn a sword and now screamed something to stir what courage he had to attack. He waited for the man to swing his blade wildly before he stepped to the side and used the hook on the back of his weapon to pull his adversary's leg up sharply. As he fell, the warrior delivered a single blow to his head with his hammer that ensured his demise.

"Having fun, dwarf?" he asked and studied the groups still engaged in pitched fighting. They seemed suitably focused elsewhere and not on him so he took his time to retrieve his shield from where it had fallen.

"My mood has soured, unfortunately." Kondel growled in what might have been anger and fell to his knees beside one of the older bodies that was little more than a skeleton still wearing weapons and armor. "I'd say this is one of my kin from the armor, although I wouldn't know their name. But my family sigil is here..."

He pulled a dagger from the remains, and Skharr narrowed his eyes as his anti-magic charm shuddered against his chest.

"A magical weapon," he told his friend.

"Aye, my kin are known for it. I'm not sure what it'll do but it should prove useful." The dwarf drew his dagger from his sheath and placed it in the skeletal hand. "Thank ye for the help, brother. Or sister, I suppose. Hard to tell when it's only the bones."

"There's a beard," the warrior pointed out and grunted as he blocked an attempted sword thrust aimed at his chest. He swung his hammer to catch his attacker in his ribs, reversed the weapon, and used the spike on the other side to kill him.

"All dwarves have beards," Kondel replied with a slightly

disbelieving look while he sheathed the new dagger and picked his weapons up. "I thought you said you spent time with my kin in the mountains."

"I have heard so and aye, I did." Skharr lifted his shield and pounded it into the face of the closest mercenary, then crushed his ribs with a strike from his hammer. "But I never saw any women while I was there. I assumed you kept them all hidden—unless…"

"Yes, you walked among men and women and thought they were all men. Well, dwarves, anyway."

He shook his head. It was an interesting snippet to add to the memory of his time with them, but this was certainly not the time to dwell on it or ask further questions.

"Stop!" someone shouted. "Stop the fighting!"

When the two companions looked toward the speaker, they realized it was one of their party who, although covered in blood, stood immobile and pointed at the door.

A gong resonated in the cavern and combat ceased almost immediately as everyone turned to focus on the barrier. It had already begun to pull open and many of those present shifted their feet warily and muttered to one another.

Skharr drew a deep breath, looked around the large space, and noted that it was considerably emptier than when they had first entered, at least of the living. The majority of the teams were dead, although most of the knights were still alive and so were most of the group he had entered with.

"I think this calls for a celebratory drink." Kondel unhooked a skin from his pouch and handed it to the barbarian. "Western Spirit, brewed in the mountains. The kind of shite that will kill lesser folk but immediately raise a true warrior's dick in a salute."

He scowled, worked the cork out, and took a swig. Sure enough, the burn did feel like it would kill some folk, although his nethers seemed unaffected. He handed it to the dwarf and wiped the back of his hand across his mouth.

"As described," he noted, shook his head, and cleared his throat to ease the burning sensation. "Although it seems I might not be a true warrior."

Klondel smirked. "Well, it will put a beard on your face, no mistake," he replied. "But you ain't dead so there's hope for you. Here's to the next round going as well, yes?"

"I wasn't surprised that you called on me."

Sera looked up from the goblet in her hand. The woman in front of her was something of a vision with curly blonde hair and angelic features, and the guild captain happened to know that she had made the marriage market work to her advantage over the past half a year or so.

But that kind of game was only worthwhile if it came to an end, and Svana had found herself a rich and powerful husband willing to turn most of the running of their collective families over to her.

And it all had something to do with the big barbarian bastard, by the sounds of things. Skharr had become involved with people who were as likely to murder him as help him.

"Lady Tamisen informed you of my interest, then?" she responded with barely a flicker of emotion on her face.

"Naturally. Of course, had I been any other person and did not know what I do, I might have been concerned about your questions regarding a man who is not part of the local gentry. But knowing Skharr as I do, I can only question why it took you so long for your interest to pique."

"My interest?"

"I assume you are looking to engage his services. I wouldn't think the daughter of the emperor—even if disowned—would lack marriage proposals. You'll find that a man like Skharr is

MICHAEL ANDERLE

quite capable if you need to sift out the unworthy contenders, and..." The woman shrugged.

"Good for an evening of passion." She sipped her drink. "Or so I've heard. But that is not why I am interested in his well-being."

Svana narrowed her eyes and Sera, for a moment, saw past the façade the woman wanted the world to see of her. Delicate princesses rarely achieved what she did, and the fact that all who saw her could only see the mask was likely the reason why she was so successful.

But it vanished quickly and the woman inspected the polish on her nails. "But what does interest you about the man?"

"The fact that he beat your husband-to-be to a pulp—rather publicly, I might add—with no further repercussions."

"Now, that is interesting." Her hostess leaned forward and tilted her head as she studied her. "Of course, Lord Tulius did get what he wanted in the end. Perhaps not in the manner in which he wanted it, but he still has my promised hand. Even so, if the birds who speak in my ear are correct, your man barely survived an attempt on his life, did he not?"

The captain nodded. Svana was certainly much cannier than she wanted people to realize.

More importantly, it seemed like she was trying indirectly to implicate her husband-to-be in the attempted murder. It was an interesting thought, although she wasn't sure how much of that could be chalked down to simple politicking and rumor-mongering and how much of it was genuine.

"Do you think Lord Tulius was involved?"

The woman shrugged. "I would make no such implications about the man I am engaged to. Of course, Skharr would not be the first person he would have poisoned. He is not quite the man to engage his foes directly if you take my meaning. I think that is why the count favors him."

Sera nodded. "I see."

"You should reconsider using Skharr," Svana continued and

moved expertly past the conversation about Lord Tulius. "The man is undoubtedly worth the interaction. You know, it is a shame that—"

"A shame that you can only be married once, yes," Sera finished for her and nodded. "Tamisen felt similarly about him."

CHAPTER SEVENTEEN

Once he'd collected his weapons and the rest of his belongings, Skharr remained at the back of the group. Although it appeared some animosity still lingered amongst them all, he felt as though an unspoken—if shaky—alliance now existed between those who had survived.

They had possibly realized that they were far from the end of the dungeon and if they were going to kill each other, it would be when it mattered.

Many of them were already exhausted from the battles in the cavern, but none wanted to be left behind so they all pushed forward together.

"How soon before we all start stabbing each other in the back again?" Kondel asked and took another swig from his skin before he hid it again.

"Likely when the next closed door tells them to kill each other," he muttered. "Even so, I wouldn't put it past anyone to try to stick a knife in someone's back."

The dwarf nodded in agreement. "This tunnel is nice work. They inlaid the light-giving stones perfectly to keep it illuminated but not brightly enough to give your head the splits."

"The splits?"

"A pain in the head that makes it feel like an ax is splitting it in half."

"Ah."

"Honestly, how did you survive among my kin without learning any of this?"

"I was needed for my skills that did not involve talking," he admitted. "Goblins were raiding mining expeditions, and I was tasked to clear their parties while your kin worked. In truth, I fear I learned more about goblins than dwarves."

"I suppose that does make sense, although you might have paid more attention and learned a thing or two."

The barbarian could not disagree. "How far do you think this tunnel will go?"

"The writing at the entrance said it would close again in an hour, which means we should reach the end of it soon. With that said, I doubt that whoever built it would have made it easy for any of those who traveled through it."

He suspected that the dwarf was right, which was why they pushed forward at a brisk pace. The absence of vocal complaints seemed to suggest that the other fifty-eight mercenaries who remained felt the same and the whole group continued to half-run, half-jog through the subterranean passage. It wouldn't bode well for their stamina, of course, and he knew the humans would experience difficulties later, depending on how long the dungeon continued and how long they survived.

After what felt like forever, he could finally see the end. The others began to race toward it, although he felt that being the first out of the door might be a costly mistake. Rushing into anything, especially in a dungeon like this, could prove deadly if they weren't careful.

Once they emerged from the rocky corridor, he couldn't help feeling that something was familiar about the area where he stood. The room widened in front of them and something cast a faint light across the whole of it, although many deep, dark shadows might be cause for concern.

It reminded him of the pyramid room from the other dungeon, although this space was considerably larger and the path leading toward the source of the light, whatever it was, was a great deal wider. A dozen carriages could run side by side across the whole of it without being in danger of reaching the rim, but he couldn't see anything beyond the edge except blackness—the kind that dug into the instincts of all living things that relied on light to see and told them to stay away.

Skharr did not intend to test the limit of that. Not unless he had to.

"What do you think is waiting over the edge of that?" Kondel asked.

He closed his eyes and rubbed his temples. "If you're an intelligent dwarf, you don't want to know."

"Sure, but curiosity never killed anyone," his companion muttered and nudged a skeleton near the exit of the tunnel.

"I'm sure that if anyone was curious enough to find out what was there, it killed them," the barbarian muttered. The light made him nervous, exactly as it had in the other dungeon. There was something magical about it and the charm around his neck told him it was something he didn't want to ignore.

"Have you no more curiosity about the world around you, DeathEater?"

"The same rules apply to most of the world, TowersSon." His mood seemed to drop as they continued across the causeway and waited for something to happen. "It's all about benefit, greed, and wanting to have more of anything than everyone else. Not too many who could break that pattern do. All these dungeons spread across the world are from the Ancients who had a mind to gather everything they had and keep it there. In the end, hundreds of years after they died, they are still killing to protect their treasures. With that in mind, I am not entirely curious to find out what kind of greed drove which person to do whatever the fuck they did this time."

Kondel glanced at him with raised eyebrows as strode he onward in silence.

"I think that was the longest I've heard you speak," the dwarf said finally. "And you were drunk last night."

"Was not. Merely…steeped. Slightly."

"And you call dwarvish lettering full of flowers."

Skharr chuckled and shook his head. "Aye, I stand by that."

"But you must feel all you said. Been on your mind long?"

"Ever since I stopped fighting in wars and decided to be a guild mercenary instead. Too many claims about honor and homeland turned into simple petty disputes of the rich and powerful who played with the lives of those who believed their words."

The dwarf nodded slowly. "Well, in the end, as long as you get to be as greedy as the rest, I say look at the world with a little more faith in your fellow beings and you'll see it rewarded."

"I prefer to keep my expectations low and find myself pleasantly surprised."

Conversation from the rest of the group turned their attention to the business at hand and the barbarian stopped when they did. If they were confronted by further culling attempts by their fellow adventurers, he didn't want to be the last one to know about it.

He moved to the front when none of them made any effort to move. Their immobility was odd enough on its own as they had too many among them who wanted to maintain their brisk pace despite the possible dangers they might face. His hand rested on his spear and he held his other ready to take hold of the shield hanging from his back. He frowned when they all shuffled aside to allow him to push through.

"How did we not see this from miles away?" Kondel asked and stepped a little closer to the edge of a vacuum that yawned in front of them.

"Might be something magical to it," Skharr mumbled and leaned forward carefully. His curiosity was getting the best of him despite everything he had said about it, and he peered into the murky darkness and tried to discern something or at least any movement.

Something, he told himself, was always better than nothing. The fact that they couldn't see more than ten feet down was more distressing, he felt, than seeing hundreds of crazed monsters waiting for them.

The monsters could be down there, of course, and they simply couldn't see them.

"Only one way forward," he said pointedly and stared ahead at the columns that rose from the darkness below to create another path for the group, this one considerably narrower than what they had followed thus far.

A glow emanated from each of the pillars, an unsettling light that refused to displace the darkness that surrounded it.

Between the path they were on and the columns was a gap of fewer than six feet across. Still, given what most likely waited for them below, he knew none of those present would simply leap forward with confidence.

They all seemed to wait for someone to be the first. Aside from the darkness into which a misstep would plunge them, no one seemed to trust that the pillars would be there to catch them if they did jump.

Still, there was no other way to advance but across it. The barbarian stepped forward and studied the drop between him and the new path. It was a short jump by his standards. He had made longer ones in his younger years, especially when climbing the mountains of his home.

"Don't think I can make that godsbedamned leap," Kondel

muttered unhappily. "It's as wide as a scum-spawned troll's asshole. Well, I could if I had no choice, but it would be a close thing. I don't want to have to be dragged up by my beard if I miss my step."

Skharr tilted his head and studied both his friend and the gap. "I could probably throw you that far if you had a mind for it."

The dwarf had much the same expression on his face as he judged the distance and his comrade's size and strength. "I...do you think so?"

"Size is not everything but in some cases, it can be the difference between life and death. No need to risk it over something like this."

Another judgment of the distance was all the dwarf needed before he nodded. "Aye. I can do that."

They approached the edge together and Skharr took a firm hold of his companion's shoulder pauldrons and made one last measure of the gap as Kondel drew a few deep breaths. The warrior did as well, and as the dwarf took a running jump beyond the edge, he added a powerful thrust and a last-moment lift. Kondel catapulted toward the far edge.

It was more than enough and he landed on his side and rolled a few times before he stopped himself and laughed loudly.

"Godsfucking she-devils!" the dwarf roared and pushed nimbly to his feet. "Your turn, DeathEater!"

He shrugged, took a few steps back, and made sure there were none close by who would try to trip him as he ran forward. His friend had the right idea of it, and instead of jumping, he dove to the other side. The gap ended quickly and the pathway stretched ahead of him. As he landed, he rolled over his shoulder onto his feet and skidded to a halt, anxious to not go any farther.

The fact that the path on top of the columns was so narrow now made his mind focus on the edge much more. It was slicker than the one they had left behind and he shuddered to think of the consequences of slipping over the rim. He doubted that he would be able to catch himself again.

"Never did like heights," Kondel muttered softly and shook his head. "Although I suppose there are a few fears combined in this particular instance."

Skharr nodded. "I agree. You'd rather be under the mountains than on top. Although I think we might have more to fear here than the possibility that we might fall."

"How do you mean?"

"Magic is coming from these pillars. As I would explain it, they are giving power to something."

"You've seen this in the past?"

"Aye. They gave power to a Lich that hoped to summon a demon with my corpse."

"I assume he was unsuccessful."

"No, indeed. I am, in fact, a demon trapped in the body of a barbarian, looking to enslave the human race and wage war on the dwarves with a slave army that will inevitably see the world burn as a result of my greed."

Kondel shook his head. "You jest, barbarian, but the prophecies have stated that to be the fate of the world. Humans and the summoning of demons. You know this is why the Ancients were defeated in the end—because there was a fear that they would bring about the end of the world through their actions."

"Instead, they left us dungeons to plunder at the risk of our lives." He shook his head and watched as the others managed to overcome their fears of what lay below and their possible inadequacy and leap across the gap to join them. "I wonder if they would have done anything differently if they knew this was how things would end."

"Well, I assume they would want to avoid being put down like the rabid dogs they were."

"I mean what kind of difference would there be if they knew

what would happen to them if they continued on their paths, and would they change it for the better if they did know?"

The dwarf shrugged his broad shoulders. "Fuck if I know. Double-fuck if I care. They are dead, we are not. So we keep moving until one of those changes."

"Is that your positive view of the world then?"

"Aye. And realistic."

Finally, everyone had crossed the gap safely and gathered on the narrower path. Most of them looked as terrified as Skharr felt, although it was likely a mixture of the change in the texture of the surface below them as well as thoughts of what might have happened with an inopportune slip.

They continued to move and the nervousness began to spread among them, especially the knights who remained. They had lost a few of their members, which drove them to be even more aggressive than before.

Skharr doubted that it would be long before they tried to attack the other survivors, and he wanted them in front of him when it happened. He saw no point in taking a dagger in his back if he could have a better chance in a decent fight and even take advantage of the present conditions whenever it happened.

He froze suddenly, narrowed his eyes, and looked around.

"Oh, I know that look," Kondel muttered. "You think something's coming to attack us, don't you? Please tell me it's not hell-spawned, pit-swilling fucking snakes."

"I doubt it," the warrior whispered. It was difficult to listen over the clatter the rest of the group made, but he could discern a sound he hadn't heard before.

"Do you know what it is?" his companion asked. "Your hearing is sharper than mine. Hells, most humans, I reckon. What do your ears tell you?"

He shook his head when he realized that it wasn't something he heard but rather something he felt. It was odd how he made that distinction at the same moment when he realized that the vibrations came from the structure beneath their feet.

Suddenly, a scream shattered the uneasy shuffles and murmurs of the group.

It was one of sheer terror and it echoed hideously across the cavern and almost grew louder when they all turned to see the origin.

More than one of the party cursed when all they saw was an empty space where one of their group had stood before.

"Oh, by the stinking fucking spawn of Janus' hairy armpit," Skharr muttered and yanked his shield clear of his back. "Something's climbing the walls! Back to back and stand away from the edge, all of you!"

The barbarian expected his warning to go unheeded, but the fear in all of them appeared to drive them to listen to any form of leadership. They stepped away from the side of the walkway and a few slipped on the slick surface before they regained their balance and positioned themselves in the center, all facing outward.

As a shape crested the path, Skharr lunged and thrust his spear into it. He would waste no time considering whether it was friendly or not, especially given the bone-chilling scream that seemed to haunt everyone's memory.

When he felt a crunch and almost no give, he wondered if his blow had been effective. But whatever it was, the creature was pushed away from the pillars and tumbled into the darkness. The warrior noted that it didn't scream although he did hear a solid impact with the bottom after a few seconds of falling.

Any other time, he would have considered it a comfort to know there was a bottom at all, but his mind was better occupied by what continued to climb up the columns supporting their route.

He was struck almost immediately by the stench of rotting flesh, which made it very clear that they faced something undead. The Ancients had loved their necromancy and it showed in what they left behind in what would become their tombs.

The monsters looked skeletal but strips of flesh still hung from the bones, the most obvious reason for the smell. A few of them wore helms and had old, rusted weapons in hand, but not all. Others simply stretched toward the mercenaries like their fingers would be weapons enough.

"Drive them back!" Skharr roared and his voice echoed through the chamber as more of the undead swarmed from the depths.

It took his words to shock the group from complacency. A few, including Kondel, shouted battle cries and rushed forward, although they tried to not draw too close to the edge.

The barbarian used his spear and forced the closest of the enemy back by driving the blade through its skull. It stuck and he growled, shook it loose, and grinned when the creature knocked a few of its comrades down before it fell. The eerie silence from the attackers—aside from the clacking of their bones—was only made worse by the fact that their jaws moved. They opened like they were screaming to voice the pain that was mirrored behind the glow in their eyes.

These were men who were never allowed to die but were forced to remain in their rotting bodies for eternity.

He used his shield to shove a few more of them away. Kondel displayed similar expertise and wielded his ax to sever the heads easily. The skulls continued to move their mouths but the bodies immediately lost all power behind them.

"Aim for the heads!" the dwarf yelled and nodded when the others began to follow his example. As the skulls were removed or simply crushed, the remaining bones collapsed and provided no further challenge.

The number of monsters seemed endless, however. Skharr thunked his spear into the floor and it drilled into the slick marble and remained there. His expression grim, he drew his hammer.

The spear would give him a reference point, which would keep him from straying too close to the edge, but he was sure he would have more success with the hammer now that he knew what would kill the turd-sucking bastards.

More clawed their way upward and they would keep coming. They had begun to push each other and a few were dragged off the platform by others that climbed behind them, desperate to join the combat.

"We can't remain here!" Skharr roared over the sounds of battle. "We need to continue moving or they will overwhelm us!"

He was not wrong. A few of their number had already fallen and were dragged screaming to the depths, and there was no sign that the creatures would stop.

Skharr retrieved his spear with his shield hand and moved ahead as he swung his hammer in a wide arc around him to crush the skulls of the enemy and clear a path for the others to advance through the undead ranks.

Some followed suit but others did not, and a few fell behind.

There was no possibility that they could return to recover the fallen. All they could hope for was to escape themselves.

The barbarian waited on the side, wielded his hammer to crush skulls of the monsters around him, and fought to keep the path open while more of their people pushed past him.

Once most were through, he took a final swing before he turned and ran with the rest of the group. A sense of terror filled him as fingers snatched at his arms and feet and tried to drag him back. The bones broke and he continued, alert for any of the undead that crawled over the edge on either side of him.

They had only climbed close to where the mercenaries had been but that line was changing and even more seemed to swarm from the depths. He'd long since given up trying to estimate their numbers.

"Another gap!" someone called from the front, and Skharr knew what waited for them as he pushed through behind Kondel. The dwarf had begun to turn, likely thinking he would not make the jump on his own and would prefer to fight his way out or die trying.

"Not on your whore-fucking life!" he shouted, grasped him by the shoulders, and dragged him along.

The gap was certainly wider than the last one had been, and he knew that if he stopped to think about it, he would doubt whether he could make it as well.

But there was no time to think, fortunately, and he pushed himself into a sprint and launched into the jump with his friend still with him.

With the effort he put in, the dwarf traveled farther than he did and landed hard on the other side. The barbarian narrowly avoided a calamitous fall and threw his weapons down, but his lower half and some of the upper fell short. With the slippery surface, he seemed to be losing the battle.

"No, you don't!"

Kondel managed to grasp his arm a split-second before he began to fall.

He resisted the urge to look down, reluctant to see what fate awaited him there, and the dwarf groaned and strained to drag him the few yards to safety.

His breath came in deep, panicked heaves and he remained where he was on the floor for a few moments. He tried not to think about how easily that could have gone poorly for him.

Finally, once he felt sufficiently recovered, he looked up and saw no more of the mercenaries on the other side of the gap.

But when Skharr counted those who were on their side, he realized that not all had survived.

The monsters remained where they were and stared venomously with their glowing eyes toward the mercenaries who

MICHAEL ANDERLE

had escaped them. There was no sign of pursuit, and he groaned and pushed to his feet before he collected his weapons.

"We need to continue," he rasped hoarsely and patted Kondel on the shoulder. "Thank you. I thought I was for the afterlife."

"You tossed me across the gap. Twice. I think you were owed some recompense."

CHAPTER EIGHTEEN

"What do you think they were?"

Skharr looked up from inspecting his armor to ensure there weren't any holes or gaps that would leave him open to attack.

"What?"

Kondel punched his shoulder and pointed at the creatures that still stared at them from across the gap they had vaulted over. "What do you think they were? You know, before they were turned into violent, murderous, godsbedamned monsters?"

The barbarian scratched his beard idly. "Truthfully? I did not want to consider it."

"Why not?"

"Those creatures do not come from nothing. They are created from the dead, and there must be...thousands under there. I would hate to consider how many were dragged into those depths, kicking and screaming, to become one of them, or the fact that they could somehow effect the same transformations on those in their clutches. How many adventurers do you think died here? How many were unable to escape?"

The dwarf looked into the unnerving, glowing eyes of the

aberrations that watched them fixedly and shuddered. "Aye. Best to not think about it too much."

He nodded his agreement and frowned when he noticed a few cuts in his gambeson, but there was nothing he could do about it without needle and thread. The rest of his armor was intact, as well as his weapons. The dwarves did know how to forge quality armor, not that he had ever doubted them.

"How many do we have left?" he asked.

"Do you think we're all in this with you?" One of the knights scoffed.

"Many of you were willing to fight together before. I don't see why we should not continue."

"Because there will be all the treasure we can carry split thirty ways," another commented.

"Thirty, then," he muttered and made a hasty count of the group. "That seems right. We'll continue moving, and if another path leads us to start killing each other again, we'll thin the ranks again, what say you? It would appear that there are too many beasts and creatures and…things looking to kill us here, and there is no need to include each other on the list until necessary."

The man did not look convinced, but it appeared that none of those remaining were interested in fighting each other at this point. As long as the monsters no longer followed them, all they wanted to do was to rest and recover.

The knight backed away and mumbled something about standing in the way of the Emperor, but he chose not to challenge the barbarian. An uneasy peace settled while the others regrouped in their teams and he made a count of how many were left in each.

Skharr paid particular attention to the knights. They had lost most of their party and only five members remained, including the leader who had tasted his fist before the dungeon had opened.

A handful of dirty looks were cast at him, but there was

nothing to them, not yet, and he gestured for everyone to continue.

Kondel stood with the group they had started with, of which only four had survived. They had not suffered the most losses by any means as some of the parties had disappeared entirely, but it was still shocking to see so many dead in so short a time.

The dwarf returned to him with the two mercenaries in tow. "They are in need. I told them to stick close to us and we'd see them through as long as we were here. You don't mind that I spoke for you like that, do you?"

He shrugged by way of an answer and greeted the other two with a pat on the shoulder.

"We'll stick close and fight hard," the woman muttered and nodded firmly. "We know the two of you are good fighters, so we'll see if some of your luck rubs off on us."

"Fortune favors the bold," he answered.

"Aye, it does," the other mercenary replied. "I was a little sad that you talked that fucking knight down from a fight. I would have wanted a piece of that emperor's ass-sucker for myself."

"If this place continues as it started, you'll have to get in line," Kondel answered and pushed the man forward. "For now, stay the fuck alive and I won't have to drag you out of whatever hell humans go to for a proper dwarvish ass-kicking."

Skharr couldn't help a small smile as they continued along the pathway, although it appeared that no more of the monsters lurked in ambush. It wasn't long before they turned a corner on the path, which led them to another doorway.

Unlike the last one, this was already open for them as they approached, and no gaps or guards awaited them as they moved through. The barbarian could feel the gazes of the others on their small group, although he didn't know whether it was because they wanted to imitate them or slit their throats when they weren't looking.

The aperture led them into a chamber that didn't look quite

like a tunnel. In fact, if it weren't for the lack of windows, he might have called it a hall in some castle or another from the look of the decorations.

"I would say this is where the Ancient who built this tower spent his or her days," Kondel muttered and stretched his hand to the side to pat the stonework. "I would like to meet those who carved it. Truly, its beauty has stood the test of time."

"Aye, put a little magic in them and they'll stand forever," the other man in their group pointed out.

"Dwarves use runes to keep their halls from falling," the barbarian stated. "Keeping something this large this far under the earth from caving in requires considerable magic—and a little luck."

"I've always heard that luck is magic," another mercenary said. "You know, the kind that applies to common folk."

"Could be. I'm not one to comment on that kind of thing."

He knew very little about magic, although that was more intentional than not. The Western Clans hated it and mages as a whole and actively uprooted them from anywhere they happened to appear. It usually did not turn violent. Those who were encountered were very politely but forcibly escorted from the region by any warriors who found them.

There was no point in angering them. They merely weren't welcome among the clans. He had heard dozens of stories regarding why but only once he had left and learned the history involving the Ancients did he understand where the almost religious fear had come from.

"I don't think you'll be able to speak to those who built this," Skharr commented and shook his head. "And I'll wager that you wouldn't want to speak to them either."

"Aye, you're probably right."

They moved deeper into the hall, where the lighting in the walls dimmed to the point where he could see a few members of the group retrieve their torches and light them to illuminate the room that they were in.

It didn't look much different than anywhere else they'd seen thus far, and he could only imagine that the lights had gone out for a reason.

"You expecting something here?" Kondel asked.

"What? Why would I be?"

"You have your weapons in your hands."

He realized that the dwarf was right. His spear was already in his right hand and he'd taken the shield off the hook on his back and now carried it by the rim, ready for a fight. It had been a purely reflexive action but he had learned to listen to the inner promptings.

"Any change in this place makes me nervous," he explained and tried to make sense of it himself. "If the lights are going out, I can only assume it is some kind of warning that we are about to be attacked."

"Either that or it will tell us to start killing each other again," one of the mercenaries said as he lifted one of the torches higher in an attempt to see more of the room they were in.

In that moment, something swooped from the ceiling with an ear-splitting shriek. It looked like it tried to extinguish the flames, and when he looked up, Skharr realized that dozens of eyes stared down at them, all beady and reflecting the light.

"I think we might have intruded," Kondel whispered and grasped his ax a little tighter as all the eyes remained fixed on them. Skharr placed his spear down immediately and drew one of his throwing axes from the sheath on his back.

"How well can you throw those?" the dwarf asked.

"You saw me kill a man with one of them."

"Aye, and a man is very different than something that flies around and maybe tries to haul us into a nest, wouldn't you say?"

While he hated to admit it, his friend had a point. Flying creatures were far more elusive than a stationary, man-shaped target.

"I did hit a wyvern in the wing with one of them. Once."

Kondel sighed. "I suppose it'll have to fucking do."

"I am better with a bow, however."

"Why did you not bring one?"

"Mine was broken and I had to settle for something readily available or join the parties leaving for this particular dungeon next year."

"That…would have been a shame."

The creatures above them had begun to grow more restless and chittered and shrieked as if to scare the lights away. None swooped on the intruders, however, and Skharr found that a cause for concern. He couldn't imagine that any of the monsters in the tower wouldn't attack them outright, which meant these were waiting for something.

Suddenly, they dropped from their perches in the ceiling. He narrowed his eyes as the creatures—about the size of a large dog but with long wingspans—began to fly away instead. They moved deeper into the hallways with no apparent intention to attack the intruders in their domain.

"That is odd, yes?" one of the mercenaries asked and looked around as if to make sure that none of those who were still among them had been attacked.

"Very odd," the barbarian agreed and examined the room. He studied the space for some sign that the creatures might circle and return from another direction but there was nothing to indicate that they would be attacked again.

"Should we…keep moving?"

The question was voiced in a hopeful tone, but Skharr knew the answer was no immediately. Something still moved above the light cast by the torches.

"I don't think we scared the flying creatures," he muttered, lifted the shield, and held it by the handle as whatever now descended brought stones and rubble with it.

A massive beast approached but before it reached the floor,

enormous wings opened and generated a blast of air powerful enough to hurl a few of those closest to it off of their feet.

Most of the torches were blown out but those few that remained quickly returned to normal. Their holders used them to relight the others to reveal the creature that now confronted them.

It looked like a wolf with a long snout and ears, but it was at least the size of a large bear. Black fur bristled over every inch of it except its forelimbs, which appeared to be completely bare and stretched and relaxed like it was breathing in and out.

No, not a wolf. A bat—a gigantic, bear-sized bat.

"I think we know what scared the others," Skharr said with a curse and hefted the ax in his hand. Many things were wrong with the beast in front of them, but the one advantage was that it was not easy to miss.

The first ax flew and it sank into the creature's right arm. The second was launched quickly as well, but the monster elevated swiftly. He couldn't see if the blade struck its target or not, but as it bared its fangs, the front arm extended and reached toward the mercenaries in front of it.

The men flung themselves out of the way but a few were caught before they could escape and the winged arm launched them into the nearby pillars. The crunch of bones breaking was followed by their cries of pain. One of them was caught in the beast's front paw and dragged to its mouth.

"Help me!" the man screamed, fighting desperately. "Help m—"

His voice was cut off when the top half of his body vanished between its jaws, which snapped shut and pulled to rip him in half.

"By all the fucking hells—enough of that, you steaming pile of slime-coated goblin turd." Skharr snarled, snatched his spear up, and moved forward.

As he did so, he noticed that not all the mercenaries were fighting the monster. Those it was not focused on hurried forward through the chamber and left the others to fend for themselves.

"You godsbedamned spawn of Janus' poxy whore!" Kondel shouted after them, but he received no response and they had larger concerns for the moment.

The beast's paw swung again and a couple of their party fell under the blow. None were caught and eaten but they were no less dead and they sprawled lifelessly on the floor.

"You're mine, you ugly cock-sucking dung heap!" Skharr called and drew the creature's attention away from his comrades. He waved his shield to make sure it wasn't distracted by anything else.

He had its attention almost immediately and dove to the left to avoid being caught by the jaws. Still in motion, he rolled over his shield, landed on his feet, and stepped under the monster's sweeping arm as he drove his spear upward into its exposed chest.

While it wasn't necessarily his finest thrust, it pierced between the ribs with a grating sound. A roar from the creature made his ears ring, but he continued to push and used every inch of his body to shove the spear forward and drive the beast back a step.

It flailed and reached for him, but the spear had already emerged from its back.

The barbarian waited, his feet planted firmly in place, until the monster stopped moving. He could almost feel every tick as its heart slowed until it finally went still while he pinned it securely.

When he was sure it was dead, he dragged the spear from the massive body and tried to clean the blood from it. As he turned to see how many mercenaries remained, he realized that they were attending to the bodies.

Even Kondel had dropped to one knee and mumbled a few

words in his native tongue as he closed the eyes of one of the fallen.

"When we get out of here, we will repay you," one of the mercenaries said softly. "Find your family and....and make compensation for your sacrifice."

Skharr looked around, unsure of what his place was in all this. He knew none of them. Even the one he knew best—the dwarf—seemed intent on giving the fallen their last rites.

"What kind of rites does your clan have for their fallen?" Kondel asked as they arranged the bodies and wrapped them in their cloaks.

"Not many," he admitted. "Many die and energy that could be spent on the dead is better spent on the living. But...I am sorry that all these died. I assume that still leaves only four of us."

His friend nodded and looked at the others. "Well, the first thing we'll do is chew the heads off those goblin-fucking, toad-licking bastards who left us here."

As the other groups or what was left of them started to move away, Skharr decided he couldn't disagree with that logic. They had been left to fend for themselves. It didn't matter that they were in different groups as far as he was concerned, but it seemed that each man was there for himself, at least in their eyes.

They continued through the halls and Skharr was surprised to see torches ahead.

"You think they're waiting for us?" one of the mercenaries asked. "Hoping to pick us off?"

The answer was quickly revealed as the group came to a halt in front of a massive door that was slammed shut. Those who had gone off ahead inspected the barrier in the hope that they would find writing on it.

"You self-sucking troll whores should be rotting with the undead for leaving us behind," Kondel told them belligerently.

Skharr moved past the dwarf and approached the door. "What are you all waiting for? Why have you not moved forward?"

"There is nowhere to go," one of the men admitted. "No writing on the door and nothing to tell us how to move forward."

He looked at the group, narrowed his eyes, and finally shook his head. "We're all tired after the fighting. We should set up camp here and get some rest. Once we have recovered our strength, we will find a way through this door. All in agreement?"

None made any attempt to disagree and that was all that mattered for now. He moved back to where the others waited for him.

"It would be best to set up a night watch," he whispered as he removed his weapons from his back. "Just in case."

"Agreed." Kondel growled low in his throat as he glared at those who'd abandoned them.

CHAPTER NINETEEN

There was no way to tell the time underground, but there was no denying that every man and woman who had survived needed time to rest. That added to the fact that they were in a place where they both had no way to move forward and faced no threats meant that the groups separated and began to set up small camps.

The knights even started a fire over which to cook food, although the rest were forced to rely on torchlight and what cold rations they had on hand.

Skharr dug into his stores for dried meats and fruits, as well as some waybread and a skin of water. The food had been purchased before he left the town and was still reasonably fresh. After the day they'd had, he wouldn't be selective about the food that would sustain him.

He had never been much of a connoisseur to begin with.

"I'll take first watch," Kondel muttered. "Not feeling quite like sleeping myself, and if anything—or anyone—has a mind to do us harm while we rest, I would be more than glad to level the scum-swilling bastards."

"You do mean the monsters we have faced in this dungeon, yes?"

"Of course. Among which are those godsbedamned fucking knights with the campfire." The dwarf shook his head. "How were they able to carry firewood in here anyway?"

Skharr had wondered the same thing but he wouldn't lose any sleep over it. There were too many things to worry about and he chose not to waste time on how the rest were able to carry all the creature comforts that they appeared to require.

Weary now, he removed his armor and left only the gambeson on, and leaned against one of the walls to watch the knights as they began to sing around their campfire. At least none of them had brought any musical instruments, he thought with a smirk. From what he knew about them, what time they didn't spend fighting or practicing was spent training in a variety of arts, including music.

"An annoying group of self-serving bastards, aren't they?"

He looked up and almost jumped at the unfamiliar voice. No, not unfamiliar, he realized. Merely one he hadn't expected to hear in the dungeon.

An old man stood beside him with a donkey close behind. His mostly white beard reached below his chest and he had a grizzled look about him.

"You look surprised to see me," the unexpected visitor said as Skharr simply stared at him. "I would have thought that I would be welcome, given that I spared you from having to tend a farm for the rest of your days and gave you a dungeon contract that made you a rich man."

"You did fail to mention the Lich that slumbered inside."

"How was I to know what was inside? All I had was a contract scroll, which I gave to you."

"In exchange for my farm."

"We both know you would never have enjoyed your time there. At least not half as much as you enjoy fighting, killing, and making the lives of others miserable. That is what you have always been, Skharr."

The old man was right, and he had little else to say as the ancient settled next to him.

"What are you doing here?" he asked after a few moments of silence.

"Oh, do you not like it? I confess, these dark hallways are a little dreary to my mind. Let us go somewhere you are more comfortable. Somewhere familiar, I think."

He closed his eyes as the world around him blurred and suddenly, they were in the farmhouse—the one he had built himself. A fire crackled in the fireplace and a boar roasted over it, already crisped to perfection.

Suddenly, a few things became clear and also explained why none of the other mercenaries had seen the odd visitor approach.

"I'm dreaming."

"Congratulations. It took you less time than most to reach that conclusion." The old man smirked and reached out to turn the boar over the fire. "I assumed you wouldn't mind a quick conversation. Most who enter the tower are not aware of what they are entering. All they can see is the reward in front of them and all else is blurred in their minds. It would be admirable but in the end, it kills every last one of them. Well, almost every last one of them. Janus is quite amused by those who approach his temple, looking to prove themselves for his entertainment."

"What do you mean?"

"Oh, well, I suppose he might have provided any number of reasons when he built it for the first time, but we always knew that he built it as a maze to watch the little rats run through."

"Lord High God Janus?"

"The very same."

"He's a fucking ass."

The old man laughed and nodded. "Aye, I suppose that is as good a description for my brother as I've ever heard. Succinct, to the point, and accurate—although I've heard it rendered as well with more…poetic language."

Skharr shook his head and tried to process what he had been told. "If…if he is your brother, that would make you…Lord High God Theros?"

"That is what some have called me, but you may call me Theros, young barbarian. It's only the ass who demands the title of Lord High God. Arrogant prick."

The barbarian frowned and shook his head again. "I am most definitely dreaming."

"Yes, you are, but this is no less real than any moment you have spent awake. I must say that I have not spent much time in my brother's domain and he dislikes it when I do venture in, which means I cannot remain long. However, as you have joined my people, I can help you, though only a little. You must watch your dreams in this tower. Like this one, they are as real as your waking moments. Honestly, if I were all of you, I would simply avoid sleeping altogether."

"You mean you are not the only one who can visit dreams in this fucking place?"

"Indeed. Although the others are considerably less considerate about their presence."

"So…we should avoid sleeping for the rest of our time here?"

The old man nodded and stroked his beard pensively. "Yes, although it will be a challenge. The spells here would make it difficult for you to remain awake. You must fight that feeling or you may never wake again. I may not be able to be there to save you again."

"Me?" he asked and suddenly felt a spike of fear coursing through his body. "What about the others?"

"I cannot be in all places at all times, much less all dreams at all times. I leave the safety of your fellow mercenaries to you. You should be warned that you should partake in no wine, women, or song while in the tower, at least none that you didn't bring with you. And I believe that is all the warning I can give you. It is best to wake up now, yes?"

"But how—"

Skharr bolted to his feet, sucked in a deep breath, and looked around as he tried to make sense of his surroundings.

The darkness, a few torches, and a fading fire told him he was in the hallway again. And awake, or so he hoped at least.

He looked around the room they were in for any sign of the dangers Theros had warned him about. It was difficult to believe that the old man who had bought his farm was a deity in reality, but there was no time to question it now.

Even if there were the distinct possibility that the man was lying. Or maybe it had simply been one of the dreams he was supposed to look out for.

"Wake up!" Skharr roared into the silence. "Wake up now! We are in danger!"

"What? What's happening?" Kondel spluttered, pushed hastily to his feet, and reached for his ax. He had clearly not taken to his duty of keeping watch well, but he was quick to respond.

As were some of the others. They looked around to find the source of the danger or failing that, the loud noise.

The barbarian dropped to one knee beside the two who remained of their party and who had failed to wake. Either they were heavy sleepers or he was already too late.

The woman snorted and shook herself from what appeared to be a deeper sleep than most of the others.

"What's happening?" she asked and stared at him.

He turned to the last of their little group, who was still sleeping—or at least appeared to be. A shadow hovered over him, and the barbarian immediately drew his dagger as the darkness began to move. He could almost see it and hear the dream that played in the man's mind, fed to him by the creature on top of him.

It felt his presence and his intent as well, and he narrowed his eyes as it rose and breathed in the essence of the man who still lay motionless.

The barbarian gaped as his teammate desiccated slowly and he took a step back. The man was already dead. There was nothing he could do at this point except watch in horror as the last trace of life was drained from him.

The being stood and assumed a form that required a few seconds to coalesce. It was like it sifted through his memories and in the next moment, he stared into Tamisen's eyes. The replica of the woman was dressed as she had been when he last saw her—which was in nothing at all.

Before he could react, the image shifted almost as quickly as it had materialized. It transformed into Svana but wavered, shifted, and changed again into a woman with long, jet-black hair that tumbled over her shoulders. Her bright blue eyes, dusky skin, and brilliant smile appeared to brighten the whole hallway. She was fairly short and wore a black dress and a silver necklace with a sparrow medallion.

Skharr shook his head and a small smirk settled on his features. "You truly are fucking useless at this. And besides, you should never make a man like me angry."

The wraith changed forms again but this time, it was no figure from his past. Instead, it manifested in its true form. The creature was almost skeletal and seemed to float and sway like it was attached to the ceiling by a rope.

"You're as ugly as the pus-filled piles on a goblin's ass," he said. "Little wonder you try to appear as someone else." He twirled the hammer in his hand as he lunged forward to attack and the weapon struck forcefully to crush the creature's skull. It shrieked and fell back with its entire head caved in, but it was still alive.

More of them rose from the bodies of those they had killed as if the screech of the first one was enough to bring the others to arms.

The group members who had been woken gathered together, ready for a fight, and made sure that the barbarian was not alone.

The beasts appeared to not have much fighting power, and they fell after only a handful of blows that destroyed the corporeal forms they had taken and turned them to dust in moments.

It wasn't long before the sounds of fighting stopped and they all looked around to take stock of what had happened.

Only twelve of them remained standing, although Skharr noted that all five of the knights were still on their feet. The others were remnants of the groups, including Kondel's.

"What in the seven hells were those ugly fuckers?" the dwarf demanded belligerently.

"Wraiths of some kind," Skharr answered quickly. "They fed on the dreams of those who fell asleep and killed them before they could wake. And I don't think they were killed, not really."

"What?" one of the knights asked. "We crushed them!"

"Aye, but their form was never physical. We drove them off but they will return if we sleep again while in this tower. I will avoid rest, and if any of you have your wits, you will do the same."

Kondel nodded in agreement, although the others did not appear as convinced. Remaining there was no longer an option, however, so they began to gather their supplies in preparation to continue their quest.

They still had no way forward, but none were willing to risk remaining and falling asleep again.

CHAPTER TWENTY

S kharr waited in silence as Kondel and the other survivor of their group paused and knelt over their fallen man. Others did the same, although he knew they would most likely resume fighting amongst themselves before too long.

Out of almost three hundred, only twelve were left. If Theros had been who he claimed to be and had not lied to him, Janus truly was a troll-sized stinking ass. Hundreds had been killed and they weren't close to the end yet.

"More last rites?" he asked as his friend stood.

"Aye." The dwarf nodded. "Always promises that we'll repay their families for their services once we leave here, but... I fear the certainty that we will not leave this tower. Not alive and not dead."

He didn't intend to say it, but he felt the same fear creeping in. If gods were involved, he was no match. All he could hope to do was leave alive, and the odds against that increased by the second.

"How do you think we can continue?" Kondel asked once they had finished wrapping the dead in their cloaks.

"There is only one way—forward. That door is the way."

"But there is no way through it."

"There has to be."

The barbarian shrugged and walked toward it. Despite the heavy stone construction of it, common sense said it was made to be moved—that there was some way to open it and a way through.

When he approached it, however, something had changed. Markings were now visible on it. As with the first gate, the writing included dozens of languages and appeared to have been carved into the stone. He could even see the dusting on the ground in front of him like an invisible hand had written the words only moments before.

This time, he found the one in plain common first. *Only seven may enter.*

"Well, there's nothing to misunderstand about that," he whispered and drew away from the door.

The others had also noticed that the door had changed and rushed to see what it said—all but the dwarf, whose gaze remained fixed on Skharr.

"What does it say?"

"Only seven may enter. This means that five of us have gone as far as we shall in this hellhole."

His companion nodded and turned toward the door as the men and woman who stood there read the words that would spell their doom and responded with loud protests.

The five knights had already moved closer to discuss the possibilities of what they were about to do. The rest began to gather together. Kondel's group of three, which included Skharr, was the only one large enough to fight the knights, but a few alliances would have to be made. The warrior doubted that he would be able to kill all five on his own.

Finally, the men in armor broke ranks, pulled their helms on, and readied their weapons. In moments, they were prepared to engage in battle, although they paused and assessed the other mercenaries.

"You two!" the leader shouted and pointed at Skharr and Kondel. "Barbarian and the dwarf. You are the only competent fighters outside the five of us. We'll allow you to fight alongside us and help us rid ourselves of the others before we can pass through. It seems only fair."

He looked at the man, narrowed his eyes, and approached him. "What are you saying?"

"Only seven of us can pass through those doors." He pointed at the barrier, then at the two of them again. "If you wish to live, you'll be allowed to join us in the next chamber, although we cannot promise your safety once we are on the other side."

Skharr paused, then took a step forward, and he could see the shocked and angry look in Kondel's eyes when he thought he was abandoning the rest of them.

"I have a counteroffer," he stated coldly and met the knight's gaze unwaveringly. "Instead, why don't you go ahead and strip off your armor, weapons, and clothes and proceed to fuck your-selves? Your goblin-spawned whore mothers would be ashamed of the bitch children that issued from their wombs, more so than of the dribbles of diseases that got them pregnant in the first place. And if you think I would spare your lives and take theirs"—he gestured to the six standing behind him—"you are even more addle-brained than I thought, and that is quite an achievement."

Kondel laughed and strode forward to take his place at his friend's side. "In case you turd-eating maggots missed it, the barbarian says no and so do I."

"Very well." The leader scowled and brandished his sword. "I see we will have to cleanse you from the ranks in the name of the Emperor. Thereafter, we shall decide whether any of the others are worthy enough to continue with us or not."

The barbarian took his shield casually from his back and held his spear in the other hand. The knight had one also, and the other four moved with him to quickly create a shield wall for them to stand behind.

He turned to the other mercenaries. "We fight together and we will survive this. Stab each other in the back, and you will die. You choose."

Kondel banged his shield with his ax. "Yaragrim!"

There was no indication as to what that meant, but the sentiment was clear. Skharr grasped his spear firmly and advanced on the center of the line, unsure if the other five behind him would join the fight or not.

In the end, it didn't matter. He would do what was required, with or without them.

The warrior thrust the spear forward with all the power he had in him, and it pounded into one of the shields. The man who held it staggered back a step and the two on each side advanced and swung their swords to try to cut the head off the spear and or catch their opponent.

The spear survived, but he took a step back and blocked one of the strikes with his shield.

They were well-trained and experienced and knew how to use their numbers to their advantage.

Thankfully, they were not the only ones, and Kondel had already targeted the one who was a little slow to retreat behind the shield wall. He swung his ax low at a weak point in their armor and severed his adversary's leg in a clean stroke.

The man screamed, and Skharr stepped in as the dwarf raised his weapon to deliver the killing strike.

The barbarian intercepted a strike aimed at the dwarf's exposed throat with his shield, but the shield held by the knight beside his target was thrust in the way of his spear when he tried to counterattack.

When they saw one of the emperor's men fall, the others in the group rallied, shouted battle cries, and surged forward. Unlike the knights, they displayed no coordination or real training in their movements, and one of them fell back almost immediately when a sword stabbed him in the chest.

"Idiots," Skharr snapped and lowered his shield to block another strike aimed at his throat. Kondel no longer needed his aid, so he drew his hammer and swung it in a high arc with all the power he had.

He was almost surprised when a crack appeared in the shield he struck, and the man who held it staggered with a cry of pain and clutched his broken arm.

Another lunged from the side to attack the barbarian and forced him to sidestep to avoid a slash that would have easily removed his head. "Piss-swilling goblin-fucker," he bellowed, reversed his hammer, and brought it up between the man's legs.

No cry of pain followed, only a whine as his opponent exhaled forcefully. His eyes bulged as he dropped to his knees.

His suffering was short-lived, however, as his head was removed by a clean stroke. Kondel stood behind the corpse, his ax smeared with blood and a broad grin on his face.

"I would love to see your work against a tree one day," Skharr told him.

"Not likely. I never liked working in the woods and out in the open, although as a smith, I did occasionally have to hew my own wood."

The man with the broken arm was dispatched quickly by three who attacked him together, although one of them fell and clutched his throat as blood spurted between his fingers.

The barbarian turned slowly to take stock of their situation. Only two knights remained, and they retreated hastily when they realized they were outnumbered. Before he could initiate another attack, a gong sounded inside the room and drew their attention to the gate, which cracked loudly and began to swing open.

"Kill them anyway." One of the surviving mercenaries spat in evident disgust. "The self-fucking bastards will stab us in the back at the first chance they get!"

Skharr couldn't disagree but he shook his head. "Fight them if you choose to do so. I will proceed."

He hooked the hammer into his belt, collected his spear from where it had fallen, and glanced over his shoulder to confirm that Kondel had decided to join him and move deeper into the dungeon.

"You don't think those fuckers will try to kill you the moment they have a chance?" the dwarf asked as they moved toward the door.

"I think that they will be more concerned with...other priorities," he whispered and paused to peer into the room that had opened for them.

Windows were present and allowed light from the outside in to fully illuminate the chamber. Warily, he stepped inside.

The space appeared to contain a true hoard—the kind dragons were said to possess. Piles upon piles of gold in the form of bricks and coins, jewelry, and hundreds of other items of wealth were stored haphazardly like it had been accumulated by someone who had no interest in keeping track of it.

That did seem like the act of a god—one who had no real concern about what reward his rats would receive if they managed to reach the end of his maze.

On closer inspection, aside from the jewels mixed with the gold, hundreds of weapons, trinkets, and baubles had simply been cast onto the various piles with no regard or care for the value they might possess.

"Well then," Kondel whispered. "It would seem the gods-dammed fucking legends are true. I don't think I could spend this much coin if I lived a hundred lives."

"We wouldn't be able to carry this much coin out if we had a hundred lifetimes," Skharr reminded him.

"Aye, but I can try."

"Is it true what they say about dwarves?" he asked as the others stepped into the room and froze, the same degree of awe he felt etched on their faces.

"They say all kinds of things about dwarves. You curious about our mythologically-sized cocks?"

"What they say is that your kind lean toward something they call gold fever. I simply call it an attack of greed, where you see so much gold that you lose all focus on the rest of the world and attempt to gather more and more until you're buried under it. Sometimes metaphorically and sometimes, very literally."

Kondel laughed. "I would say dwarves aren't the only ones to be attacked by this hunger."

The barbarian had to concede that point at least. "We will need to find what we can carry and take only that. There is no need to over-burden ourselves. Enchanted weapons, trinkets, and charms will be worth fortunes from the right buyers, especially with the knowledge that they were obtained from Ivehnshaw Tower. Jewels will also be more valuable for their size."

"But gold is easier to spend."

"Then fill your purse with it. The rest will need to be left here."

Kondel nodded and they moved to the closest pile. Skharr collected a handful of daggers, strapped them to his belt, and inspected each with the charm on his neck to make sure there was magic to them. One longsword, in particular, caught his eye as it bore the same markings as the dagger the elf had given him.

The handle was shaped in the form of a snake, with the pommel as the head and emeralds for eyes.

He retrieved it quickly, scabbard and all, and slung it over his back.

The others had now set to work to dig into the chests in search of anything of particular value. They opened a massive one that seemed surprisingly heavy with a skull attached to the top with steel nails.

"No," he muttered." No, no, no…"

As the chest opened, another gong shattered the relative silence that had filled the chamber. He spun as the doors began to swing to bar the way from which they had come.

"This cannot end well," he whispered.

CHAPTER TWENTY-ONE

The doors thundered shut behind them with a finality that instilled dread in them all, and Skharr stared at it for a few seconds. Silence fell while he tried to discern what, if anything, would happen next.

"I don't think anything will come through there," Kondel said and nudged him in the ribs. "And we won't return the same way we came, not with the undead waiting for us in the tunnels. There has to be another way out of here."

The barbarian nodded. While he agreed, the fact that the chest had triggered something in the chamber warned him that something larger was afoot, and that was never a good thing.

He couldn't allow himself to think that this part of the tower was any different from the rest of it simply because it was where all the treasure lay.

Suddenly, before he could begin to consider the possibilities, windows opened in the walls above the gate behind them. He looked up quickly and scowled at the apertures that opened outward into the area from which they had come. When nothing emerged through them, he took a step back, hooked his shield onto his back, and retained his spear in hand while he continued to collect those trinkets and charms that emanated magic.

At least one mage he knew in Verenvan would pay a high price for them, and there might be more. Several in the Count's court would no doubt constantly look for something to give themselves an advantage over the others. They would certainly bid and outbid one another to try to keep their fellows from acquiring the items he had selected.

When a piercing screech issued from above them, Skharr adjusted his hold on his spear and glanced up to make sure that nothing swooped in to attack.

A moment later, something did creep through, but it wasn't anything that could fly. His skin crawled at the familiar and unpleasant sight of creatures painfully similar to the hundred-legged monster he'd encountered in the other dungeon. They seemed to dribble down from the windows as the countless limbs rippled to power its descent.

"We aren't alone in here!" he roared, but the others appeared to be deaf to his warning.

Carapaces protected the beasts' bodies, and the countless legs allowed them to move rapidly down the rough walls, although the smaller one lost its purchase on the rock and fell the rest of the way. It writhed on the floor and scattered piles of coins and jewels.

Although a little dazed, it appeared to be uninjured and regained its feet quickly.

The barbarian moved toward the creatures, aware that more of them had entered through the windows that had opened. Numbers seemed irrelevant at that point as those within attack range needed to be eliminated first.

He was surprised to hear footsteps behind him and turned to Kondel, who stepped alongside although his ax and shield were on his back. Instead, he carried a massive, double-winged war ax covered in runes and with the markings of a dragon climbing the haft in gold.

"Found yourself something new, then?"

The dwarf laughed. "This was made by my great-grandfather's hands over seven hundred years ago. It is a family heirloom, thought lost in the wars of the time. I suppose it was brought here by those who built this tower or others who were killed within its walls."

"You will put it to good use."

Skharr retained his spear and advanced on the smaller creature before the others had fully descended the walls. The beast opened its mandibles and reached toward the two of them, but it pulled back when he thrust his spear toward its maw.

It tried to retreat and Kondel advanced and bellowed a battle cry as he swung his newly acquired weapon at its body. The barbarian expected the beast's carapaces to absorb the strike and was ready to defend his friend before the creature could retaliate, but his eyebrows raised in surprise as the ax sliced cleanly through the protective armor and almost cut the beast in half with a single stroke.

The beast uttered a piercing screech and pivoted to retaliate, but the dwarf attacked again. He continued to deliver a flurry of blows until it lay in several pieces. Finally, he stopped, covered in the creature's blood.

"That is a fine weapon," the warrior acknowledged.

"Yaragrim TowersSon was the greatest smith of all time, or so my family says." Kondel laughed and swirled the ax over his head. "The edge is as keen as when it came off his anvil, and the balance is beyond belief. I have never seen or held a weapon like this."

"It's time to introduce it to others." Skharr pointed his spear at two beasts that had reached the bottom and looked for those who had killed their comrade. The dwarf smiled grimly, plainly anxious to test the edge of his ax against the monsters ranged against them.

Winged creatures now swooped from above to join the fight. He recognized them as those that had retreated the night—or day —before. With a scowl, he adjusted his hold on his spear, but the flying beasts seemed to have targeted the other five who still attempted to fill whatever receptacle they could find with as much treasure as they could.

The godsbedammed fools were too distracted to realize that they were being attacked until the creatures swarmed one of them and hoisted him off his feet. His screams echoed through the chamber as the monsters shredded him between them. They worked with ruthless efficiency to tear him limb from limb and his organs slithered out when his stomach split beneath their talons.

The barbarian grimaced but reminded himself that his attention was better focused on the monster that now surged into a scurried assault. He thrust his spear forward in an attempt to injure the beast or at the very least, force it back, but it seemed to simply ignore him. It scuttled forward and its mandible clicked and reached for him as he attacked.

Skharr dove aside, forced to release his spear as he did so.

He moved to grasp his hammer but his hands found the longsword on his back instead.

There was no reason for that. He knew how to handle a sword, of course, but it had never been his specialty. Even so, as it had been with the ax, it felt perfectly balanced in his hands. It seemed to fit like it had been forged with none other in mind.

His attention turned toward the monster that curled to try to find him again, and he stood his ground. The lightness of the weapon intrigued him, and a part of him suddenly wanted to attack the monster instead of following the intelligent course to run away.

The beast charged with its mandibles ready as if it ached to end him. He moved to the side, avoided the assault, and swung the sword upward in a bold arc. It moved effortlessly, and he barely felt the blade slice through his adversary's jaw. The mandibles clattered as they fell.

Silky green blood gushed from where they had been, and he reversed the strike quickly to deliver a powerful blow to the creature's head that carved it neatly in half. Again, it felt as though it required no effort—like he was cutting through air—but the creature was sprawled on the stone floor.

The legs with venomous stingers stretched toward him, and he slashed the blade to sever them cleanly. It took a few more decisive strikes before the monster stopped moving. While it oozed blood and stank, it was finally dead. Skharr looked at the sword in his hand.

The blood dripped off the blade and in seconds, it was as clean as when he had drawn it from the scabbard.

"Useful," he muttered, sheathed it again, as he moved to where his spear had fallen.

Kondel had made similarly quick work of the last creature, and his mind had returned to one of the treasure piles. He currently gathered as much of it as he could, his gaze fixed on his task as one of the flying creatures circled to snatch him. Its talons extended and caught him by the legs.

The dwarf bellowed in surprise as the monster began to elevate. Its talons dug deep into his legs and one into his hip to wound him in its firm grasp as it tried to fly him to the open windows.

"Kondel!" Skharr yelled, yanked an ax from his back, and hurled it almost without thought.

He realized, as it left his fingers, that it was the finest throw he had ever made.

The weapon flew with all the power that had surged through his body. It whistled as it cut through the distance and thunked deep into his target's chest. The beast howled, released the dwarf, and plummeted with a shriek of fury. It took a few more seconds to fall and continued to beat its wings where it lay, but it was already dying despite the instinct within it to fight.

The barbarian rushed toward his friend and cursed volubly when he slipped on the coins that were now scattered everywhere.

"Are you hurt?"

The dwarf glared at him.

Skharr nodded. "Stupid question."

He examined the injuries, took some cloth from his pouch, and wound it quickly around the wounds that were bleeding the most.

"Hurts like a whore's ass," Kondel muttered. "But I'll live."

"We need to leave this place." He tried to staunch the bleeding on the other wounds, his expression grim. "You have as much as you can carry, yes?"

"Aye."

"Because I believe I will have to carry you out as well."

The warrior had found as much as he wanted. He would be a rich man with only the jewels and coins he had filled his pouches with, but he took a moment to push a few into the space where the cloth around his companion's leg had been. It was more than he could spend, especially if he sold all the weapons, charms, and trinkets for good prices.

But there would be no coin in it for him if they didn't escape, and more monsters were coming. He could see them move through the windows, ready to launch another assault.

"Up we go." Skharr groaned as he lifted the dwarf, balanced him on his one working leg, and helped to support him as they moved toward the only door.

A couple of the other adventurers were still alive, but as he approached, the flock of monsters glided through the windows into another airborne attack. One man's hands were filled with as many coins as he could carry and he bolted before three of the creatures cut him down.

The remaining member of Kondel's party was still alive as well, although one of the monsters hovered over her and tried to snatch her with its claws. She slashed at it with a sword but her strikes were panicked and weak and her screams echoed through the chamber to attract more of the winged beasts.

The barbarian tossed the spear in his hand up and caught it in a backhand grasp. He was more comfortable with a spear than a throwing ax and it flew true, punched the monster instantly from the air, and pinned it to the floor.

It was dead, he thought with satisfaction, before it landed. The spear was easily withdrawn and he strapped it to his back to leave his hands free.

He moved to the woman, still supporting Kondel with one arm.

"Can you walk?" he asked.

She looked at her legs that had been savaged by the monster's claws. It had tried to lift her like the other had attempted to do with the dwarf, but her resistance had ended that.

"No," she answered and tears welled in her eyes.

Skharr could see what she was thinking—he had every right to simply leave her there. He could leave Kondel too and collect as much of the treasure as possible. He looked up as a door miraculously appeared on the other side of the room. It swung open, waiting for him to escape with all he could carry with him.

The other man was already dead, so there was perhaps a rule that only allowed three to escape.

But it would close soon. He wasn't sure how he knew it, but like everything else in the damn tower, it would come with a small problem that would not let them go.

In the end, he knew that there was no choice.

"Fill your pockets with as much treasure as you can carry," he ordered her and released Kondel cautiously, who managed to stand on his own. "You too!"

"Why?" she asked.

"So I'm not tempted to leave you in this place."

She seemed surprised but wasted no time with further questions. He used some of his clothes to staunch the bleeding on her legs and filled the empty spaces with whatever treasure that he could cram into them. It would be a heavy weight but he could make it.

Once both the woman and Kondel were finished, he hefted everything he had and balanced it carefully before he slid an arm around each of his companions and lifted them as high as he could.

Two of them made a substantial burden and his body strained as he half-carried, half-dragged them across the room.

More monsters were coming. Those in the air continued to fight over the remains of the others, but a mass had begun to crawl from the windows and advance toward them. He chose not to pause to try to ascertain their number. Even one would guarantee their end if it reached them.

"Come on!" Skharr roared to exhort himself as he pushed forward. He focused on the doors and willed them to stay open for as long as it took to reach them.

Only a moment longer. Keep moving.

Rather than speak the words, he continued to shout with the effort to haul the three of them through the opening until he finally felt the warm touch of the sun on his face and grass under his feet. The doors began to close behind them.

With a gasp, he dropped to the earth and released his companions as he fell. The grass was soft, and he felt like he could lay there for a while. Only a little while, he assured himself.

The woman crawled toward him. "Are...are you..."

He nodded and pushed onto his elbows. "What is your name? I never asked."

She laughed and settled onto the grass beside him. "Rennie. Rennie Tramor."

"It...it was good to meet you, Rennie Tramor."

CHAPTER TWENTY-TWO

His heart still hammered and his fingers cramped from dragging Rennie and Kondel through the last chamber, but he was out in the open again.

The sun shone high above him. It was a few hours before noon, he realized. They had left sometime in the morning, much earlier than it was now, but he knew with certainty that it had not been only hours since they had entered the tower.

It must be the next day or possibly days later.

Every inch of his body ached, but Skharr pushed awkwardly to his feet and grimaced at the added weight of what he had acquired in the tower. He patted himself absently to confirm that it was still there and not a figment of his imagination as he looked around.

People had gathered—he assumed it was the same group that had watched them enter the tower on the first day—but they looked shocked and surprised. He wondered if that was because they had not expected anyone to come out at all.

Or maybe it was because the tower had vanished and they had emerged from what looked like thin air. He let most of the weapons slide from his shoulders. They made standing a chore and he would need to stay on his feet for a while.

"We need healing potions here!" he snapped at those who approached warily. They still wore expressions that suggested they didn't believe they had exited the tower—like they were ghosts of some kind, perhaps.

He couldn't find the strength to blame them and sagged onto his knees again. His entire body felt ready to simply succumb to his exhaustion. That last run had certainly used every last ounce of strength he possessed.

Thankfully, it appeared that the potions were administered to them before the coin was asked for. They would still have to pay the exorbitant prices, but at least there would be no haggling while his two companions slowly bled out.

Kondel was the first to recover and looked around, a little dazed like he had passed out for a few seconds.

"I'm here!" he shouted, pushed to his feet, and staggered a few steps. "I'll kill them all, you fucking watch me, ya bastards!"

"I would appreciate it if you didn't," said the mage who had just applied the healing potion to his wounds.

"Right…right." the dwarf nodded and gaped at the sight of the wide grassland and dozens of people gathered around. "Since Vallassar would be in a mighty hall with mead, meat, and wenches, I assume I am not dead."

"You were close to it," Skharr answered. "But it looks like we escaped barely in time. How do you feel?"

"Godsfucking legs feel like they were trampled by a couple of horses, but that will pass once I walk on them for a while. How about you? You did carry us and all our treasure out."

The barbarian nodded. "I'll need to rest but for the most part, a few scratches and cuts. Nothing life-threatening."

Sure enough, they were charged high prices not only for the potions used but also for the escort to town. A small peloton had already assembled, ready to escort them to Verenvan, and there was no time for them to stop to rest. The convoy would only move through to collect those who wanted to return.

There was only time for Skharr to return to the inn and retrieve Horse before they were summoned again.

"I'm afraid there will be no freedom for you yet, my friend," he grumbled and stowed most of the treasures he had collected inside the saddlebags.

The stallion had no answer for him other than a snort, although he assumed it had something to do with the added weight put on him. They moved out of the stables and joined those who would journey to the city of Verenvan.

He wasn't sure he wanted to return. His mind had now moved to the matter of what would await him once he arrived—those who wanted him dead and had almost succeeded in their assassination attempt.

Perhaps a part of him had hoped that he would die in the tower and save anyone else—including himself—the trouble.

But he would return. The barbarian had been close to death on many occasions, but he had always felt like he had a fighting chance. There was always something that he could do to make a difference in his situation. With the poison, however, all he could do was hope that there would be others there to save him should it happen again.

People would be awaiting their arrival, he realized. After a few days of travel, the walls of Verenvan loomed ahead and a chill rippled up his spine.

"You look uncomfortable," Kondel told him bluntly.

"I am."

"Why?"

"I escaped death in this godsbedamned city. Someone

poisoned me and I barely survived the attempt, but I think they will try again."

"Folk and beasts tried to kill you in the tower and you looked almost comfortable with that fact."

"I am comfortable where I know that I am in danger and I can do what I must to keep myself alive. A battlefield is what I was always trained for."

The dwarf nodded. "We needed to leave quickly, ahead of the news spreading, or bandits would have attacked us at every step. Only the dumb ones, of course. Those with more intelligence will be waiting for us in Verenvan, looking to relieve us of the treasure in a hundred different ways. A few of them might even be legal."

Skharr looked away from the city. There was still time for him and Horse to head into the mountains again. With this much treasure, he would be welcomed by The Clan as a hero.

"You didn't have to drag us out, you know," Kondel whispered and shook his head. "You could have left Rennie and I and taken more treasure for yourself."

"Would it shock you if I said it had crossed my mind?"

"I would know you were a liar if you denied it. Stinking hells, it crossed my mind while you were killing one of those hundred-legged creatures. My greed wormed into my mind and I began to gather as much as I could before that winged fucking goblin-spawn caught me. And you saved me. I felt…well, there was shame, especially as you saved me and then retrieved the ax as well. I don't think I would have forgiven myself if I allowed the priceless heirloom to remain while I left intact. More or less."

There was some comfort to hear that he wasn't the only one who had almost let the greed overwhelm him.

"They will plan a celebration in town," Rennie commented. "They did that for the last two who returned from the tower alive. I suppose we will have to contact the families of those of our party who didn't survive and give them something from the treasure. It will at least allow them to live in some comfort."

Skharr knew nothing of those who had been lost. He had expected to make the run on his own and in the end, had been brought into a fight he was not entirely sure was his.

A vast number of people waited for them outside the city gates and threw flowers along the road for them to walk over. The spectators cheered like the returning mercenaries were conquering heroes, an army returning after a victorious battle.

Everyone seemed to have come out, curious to see and celebrate the three who had survived the tower so many others had died in. The barbarian began to doubt that the other two survivors had forgotten about what happened inside. They had merely chosen to not talk about having to kill their comrades or leave them to be murdered and mutilated.

A young boy moved close to him, a garland of flowers in his hair. He looked like all the other celebrators, but he pushed something quickly into his hand before he was thrust back by the guards who escorted them.

He didn't look at what felt like a piece of parchment in his hand until after the messenger was gone from sight and the people were distracted by the celebration.

It was from Sera, he realized when he recognized the hand-writing.

Danger. Find me, read the first line. The second held an address in the city he assumed was where he was meant to find her.

Casually, he tucked the missive into his pocket and hoped that no one had seen him read it.

No one would try to kill him during the impromptu parade but he also wouldn't be able to sneak away. He would have to return to the Mermaid. His room would still be available to him. Maybe he would do so once the treasures he carried were secured. The bank that stored his gold from the other dungeon would likely be helpful with the rest.

Once that was done, he would find Sera.

While growing up, she had never thought she would spend this much time behind a desk.

Perhaps her sister was right when she chose a simpler life of traveling and escorting merchants across the continent. It wouldn't be a publicly voiced thought but in the end, the woman did have a mind of her own. She refused to be a part of the gentry unless it helped her and even then, she held herself aloof.

"I won't do it," Micah muttered as she studied the papers on her desk. "I will never admit that she was right. Truly, I would never live it down."

"Ma'am?"

Micah looked up. She had almost forgotten that she wasn't alone in the room.

"How can I help you, Denir?"

"A message was delivered." He placed a piece of parchment on the table. There was no seal and nothing to hide the contents of the message from anyone's gaze. She took it and narrowed her eyes when she recognized the handwriting.

This is my business. Stay out of it. Your only warning.

A stamp in black ink in lieu of a signature depicted a raven carrying a sheaf of wheat. A portent of death, she thought with a chill, and not one sent lightly—at any time or by any person.

"I guess Sera is tapping into her darker nature again." She snorted but moved her hand instantly to find the place where her sister had injured her. "That should be all kinds of lovely."

"Should I pay the messenger?" Denir asked.

"Yes, and send him on his way. There is no need for a return message."

"Of course, Dame Ferat." He bowed and left her alone in the

room, where she sat for a long while and simply stared at the message.

"I thought the barbarian wouldn't see the next planting," she whispered, knowing for the moment that no one else could hear it. "There are times when I am not pleased that I cannot be right all the time."

CHAPTER TWENTY-THREE

A t long last, the weather had begun to cool.

She couldn't imagine that the winter months would change things much, not this far from the winter poles. Sometimes, though, the winds blew in the right direction over the seas and they enjoyed balmy weather instead of the overwhelming, sweltering heat they had endured during the past months.

Svana still did not appreciate the oppressive heat that lingered. Long, flowing silks helped, but she wished she could move south to the Imperial City, where they would enjoy the first snows by this time of the year.

But there would be no move for her, not yet. Her wishes notwithstanding, she would have to tolerate the oppressive weather until the wedding.

She waved her attendants away once they had finished with her hair as she preferred to don her jewelry without help. The final touch to complete the portrait she portrayed to the world would always be from her hands, free of the influence of those who helped her.

Her gaze focused on the silver mirror in front of her, she began to attach the silver pendants to her ears. Something moved behind her, however, and her gaze shifted to it in alarm as she froze.

A scream erupted from her lips as she turned to the shadow that stood behind her. Although massive, she had almost not seen it but for the flash of movement caught by her looking glass.

Stories of monsters that came from mirrors were the kind she would never forget, no matter how many years it had been since her nannies had told them to her.

But her visitor was not a monster from those childhood stories.

Perhaps she could say not yet. From what she heard about Skharr, his reputation had grown to the point where folk would talk about him for years to come, likely in the form of tales told to their children.

For now, however, he stood before her in the flesh. His long brown hair was tied back with a simple leather strap and a beard shadowed his powerful jawline. While his clothes were simple, they seemed to accentuate every inch of him and reminded her of what lay beneath.

But his eyes were what caught her immediate attention. They gleamed a clear, deep brown, with a scar over one eyebrow that had seemed to add to the overall menace of the glare he directed at her.

It sent a chill down her spine that was not entirely an unpleasant feeling.

"It is good to see you again, Skharr," she whispered hoarsely and tried to remain in control of the situation. Admittedly, it was difficult when a massive man stood in her chamber and all she wanted to do was rip his clothes off him.

It was allowed, she thought hungrily. She could replace them.

"Did you know?"

She stared at him in bemusement. It seemed she had allowed her mind to wander. Had he been speaking?

"Did I know what?"

"Did you know that your husband-to-be attempted to murder me?"

She took a step forward, and her gaze hardened. "What did Tulius do?"

"He hired an assassin—one who attempted to poison me and very nearly succeeded. As well as a couple more wildly desperate attempts before I left the city."

The heat built in her body and her ears felt hot. Although she and Sera had briefly discussed the possibility, hearing it from the barbarian made her fingers fidget for something with which to stab her husband-to-be in the neck.

"Godsdamn bastard. What did he think he was trying to do? Impress me with his ability to pay people?"

"I assume he was looking to restore his honor after I beat it out of him at your behest."

"That...moron!" she snapped and spun toward her mirror to angrily don the various pieces of jewelry at a faster pace. "When I get my hands on him..."

She paused and a smile crept over her face. The rage dissipated and a calm settled over her as a variety of the pieces of her dilemma drew together.

He noticed the change immediately. "What is on your mind right now?"

"How did you get into my villa? Without anyone seeing you?"

"Darkness has always been my ally. I've climbed snow-covered rocks in the dark since I was old enough to walk. Your villa would have been considered a relaxing excursion at home by comparison."

Svana smirked. "You should know something I assume you do not, as the imperial marriage conventions are fairly complex when the gentry are concerned. In marriage, Tulius and I will be considered a single entity, legally speaking. If he were to die on the day of our wedding, I would be his most immediate family. All his lands, his title, and his positions would fall to me, as well as the duty to avenge a fallen member—or forgive if my judgment saw fit to do so."

"What are you saying?"

"I am merely thinking of a possibility where you would have your revenge and I would rid myself of a husband who would stab my support in the back. He might decide my back is in need of a dagger too eventually. Better still, I would be in a position to absolve you of any guilt and myself of the need to avenge my dead husband."

"Poison," Skharr corrected. "Poison your support."

"I'll simply say kill. If it wasn't a man like you, he would have tried to have someone stab you in the back in the dark. As things stand…" She paused to rake her gaze over his frame. "The little insect would have to acquire a stepping ladder to climb high enough to stab with something that would kill you."

He laughed and shook his head. "How will I get in? I assume Tulius will have guards on the walls."

She turned again, tilted her head, and leaned against the table. "How would you get in if you did not have my help?"

"Over the walls."

That brought a smile to her lips. "You know, I thought you would say that. How very direct of you and quite the barbaric approach, but I am afraid it will not be one we can take."

"You have something in mind?"

A nod and a small smirk followed the question. "Indeed. How good is your tongue?"

Skharr did not answer and narrowed his eyes.

"You will ride with me in my carriage."

"Won't I be discovered rather quickly?"

"Not if you are under my dress. It has very large panniers that would hide you completely from view."

"Pan…what?"

"The skirt." She gestured out from her waist with both hands. "The panniers and hoops keep it spread at the bottom. I imagine I could hide a handful of men—or one very large one—between my legs in the carriage."

He coughed and looked away.

It prompted a laugh from her. "Blushing on you is an interesting new feature. I find I rather like it."

The barbarian shook his head but he had nothing else to say on the matter.

"I suppose it means that we are in agreement regarding our plans, then." She approached him and stood on her tiptoes to leave a light kiss on his collarbone. It was as high on him as she could reach and anything more would leave her with too much temptation. This wasn't the time. "Now go away. I need to finish getting dressed."

Tulius did not know how to do anything subtly. He possessed not a single understated bone in his body, and everything about the wedding showed that.

The man insisted on being the guiding eye over every inch of his nuptials, and no expense was spared. Even the streets would be strewn with white rose petals en route to the temple where they would make their vows.

Guards were positioned throughout the city to show the importance accorded the safety of not only those to be married but also of the guests. Dozens of chefs worked tirelessly to deliver food to hundreds of servants, who made sure that every guest in the temple had their fill of food and drink.

She could see the extravagance that awaited her as the carriage slowed in front of the temple, where armed and armored guards stood steadfast and ready for her arrival.

A bold fanfare played as the door of the conveyance was opened, and trumpets blared while a whole flock of doves was released as she stepped out. She waved with a brilliant smile to the crowd of guests who waited to offer the couple their best wishes.

The guards were there to greet her first, however, and one of them stopped her advance into the crowd as the other checked the carriage she had just left.

"Will you not check under my dress as well?" Svana asked as the men drew away from the vehicle once they found it empty. "There is sufficient space under there too."

"Not for all the gold in the world, my lady," the guard responded and tried to keep his expression neutral. "Please, carry on."

She smiled and bowed gently before she turned to greet all those who wanted to wish her well.

It might have been a little too cheeky of her, but she couldn't resist the temptation as she moved forward. She hadn't been lying when she said the dress had more than enough space to hide multiple men or a very large one, and she had proven it by fitting Skharr inside. It was perfectly understandable that he was not comfortable with his confinement, and the knowledge of that prompted her to use the opportunity to tease him a little.

Everyone who spoke to her expected a few words in return, and she did her best to hear and respond to all of them, although some were missed in the crush.

Her progress—the novelty of which soon began to pall— was made all the more difficult when the barbarian's hands settled on her thighs. She assumed it was for balance—and was a good thing as neither of them wanted to explain should he suddenly roll out from under her gown—but it was certainly distracting and even more so when they ventured higher.

She thought she would not reach the chamber reserved for the bride-to-be without one or both of them giving their secret away. Her breathing was a little more rapid and her thoughts were not those appropriate for a woman about to be sworn into marriage.

When they finally arrived, she held her hand up to her ladies in waiting.

"I will need the room to myself for a few moments." She managed to restrain her gasp until they had closed the door behind them before she patted the skirt of her dress and lifted it.

The hem raised barely enough for him to crawl out from under it.

"Was all that necessary?" she asked as he brushed his clothes.

"Not at all," he answered nonchalantly, although she could see a twinkle in his eye. "Now, how should I leave here?"

"There is a side door." She pointed to it. "A servant's entrance. It will lead you downstairs and into what I assume are the kitchens, and you will be able to join the festivities from there. No questions will be asked. You are somewhat well-known in the city, and your presence will not be considered curious—although I would suggest that you avoid the attention of Tulius for as long as possible."

Skharr nodded and drew a deep breath.

"Are you nervous?" she asked.

"Are you not?"

"Of course, but I am somewhat comforted by the fact that I am not the only one. Now, let me take my leave until the opportune moment."

CHAPTER TWENTY-FOUR

The temple was too large, a place that celebrated the kind of posturing Micah could never understand. She did see the appeal, of course. Men like Tulius needed to aggrandize themselves at every opportunity.

It was second nature to those in that position. Men and women needed to make themselves appear more powerful through lavish displays of spending.

While she did understand it from an outside perspective, she still couldn't comprehend it at her core. To her, grandeur came from actions, not peacocking.

She sipped from a crystal glass filled with the honeyed wine that she had requested and studied the others while avoiding the gazes that were cast at her. It wasn't a boast to know that she looked beautiful in the purple dress with a small pin with her father's sigil on it.

Those who saw it assumed she was of one of the smaller houses associated with the emperor's and only invited to the wedding as a nod to the man himself, who was not in attendance personally.

The count was, as he and Tulius were great friends and it

would have been a great insult for the man not to attend. Still, she had heard from the staff of both houses that they had been estranged through a dispute over a woman.

While unsure of which woman had caused the rift, she did know it was not the woman Tulius would marry.

A hair slid from the elegant bun she'd had people spend hours creating and a sense of annoyance began to fill her. She did not like to attend ceremonies like this and would have preferred to not be involved in any of it. Unfortunately, the invitation was not one that could have been avoided and there was too much to learn from it to squander the opportunity.

Another person who disliked such events was her sister, and she narrowed her eyes as her gaze settled on the woman. Her brown hair hung in a simple yet elegant braid down her back but the rich black of her dress was more than a little eye-catching, especially with the woman's sword hanging from her hip. Sera had spent years being trained by the blademasters, whose tradition insisted that they be armed at all times.

As such, unlike any other person present aside from the guards, she was allowed to be armed while in attendance. Micah could only assume there had been a lively discussion about it with the guards before her entry, but the guild captain always had her way eventually.

Despite her common sense that warned her not to do so, she approached her.

"Good morning, sister of mine," she said softly in greeting.

To her credit, Sera looked genuinely happy to see her.

"Micah!" She dropped all decorum and hugged her enthusiastically. "I'm surprised you're here."

"Pleasantly?"

"Of course. Why wouldn't it be a pleasant surprise?"

She shrugged. "Hints scattered here and there. Although you do look...annoyingly breathtaking."

"You do as well."

"I am surprised to see you here. I know you well enough to know that you hate being involved in these kinds of events."

Sera looked around before she spoke in a lower tone. "Honestly, I do hate being here. The wine and food are good but the company is a little difficult to tolerate."

Micah almost snorted the sip of wine she had taken while listening. "Yes, well, when the count's favorite invites you, you had better have a good reason not to be in attendance."

"And I always did have the reason of working out of the city. Unfortunately, that was not enough to save me."

"Oh." Micah frowned as she looked away. "I have seen someone I have to talk to, but let's meet later and share some mead. Hopefully in private."

"You'll find me here, hating everyone including myself."

A smile played on Micah's face as she moved away, but it vanished the moment she was out of sight. Of course, she had no one she wanted to talk to and couldn't think of a single reason to hold a conversation with anyone in the temple aside from the staff. Well, perhaps a few guards who were interested in earning a few extra coins for their efforts on her behalf.

But that would have to wait or perhaps not happen at all. She scanned the crowd casually and tried to find a giant of a man who would most certainly stand out.

Sera was right. She always managed to find an excuse to avoid situations like a wedding and she was too good at it to have made the simple mistake of forgetting to find someone who needed an escort out of the city.

It left only one explanation. Her sister was there for a reason and she knew that reason was the death of Tulius—and perhaps hers as well.

There was no sign of Skharr in the greeting room of the temple but she didn't expect there to be. The barbarian would be far too noticeable there, not a good idea for a man who had recently made an enemy of the groom. She doubted that he would have already arrived at the wedding but was sure he would make an appearance.

He was not an unintelligent man by any means, but he lacked subtlety, exactly like Tulius. Unlike the noble, he had never needed it. A warrior born, bred, and forged through fire would simply break through the lines of guards with a flaming sword in one hand an ax in the other.

Micah stepped out of the temple and her gaze drifted over the guards stationed around the building. She had heard many tales about his exploits, but he would have to be a mighty warrior indeed if he wanted to break through those lines.

Perhaps not, she mused thoughtfully. He would try to sneak in, probably over the walls. There was no need for guards to be placed around the entire perimeter, although a few patrols would circle the property. If he came over the walls, there was a good chance that he would not be found. That aside, the temple had too many entrances for each to be guarded separately. He would find a way.

On the bright side, she now had a reason to abandon the proceedings altogether.

She strolled to one of the many entrances, slipped out of sight, and removed the pieces of her dress to reveal a light, delicate suit that was similar enough to what the servants wore to avoid raised eyebrows. The light armor was a master of ingenuity as well as being dexterous enough for her to fight in.

Her hair was next and tumbled from the bun she had spent so many hours perfecting. She let it fall in a braid similar to her sister's once she'd retrieved a small dagger that had been hidden inside and that she slid quickly into her belt.

"Oh, you are certainly here looking for a fight, sister of mine."

A fight was the last thing on Sera's list of preferred entertainments.

She looked around the room and her hand drifted toward the sword at her hip. It had taken considerable argument to be allowed to carry it into the temple with her, but the guards eventually relented as they didn't want to cause a scene. A blademaster was only to be parted from his or her weapon after death, a rule that had been ingrained in her from the moment she had arrived in the mountains to begin her training.

More than a few gazes had settled on the weapon, but no one seemed inclined to question it. They recognized her pendant and it was likely that more than a few of them had at least one bodyguard who wore the same.

Skharr had told her that he would be present for the wedding, but she doubted that he would have received an invitation. A hero who had recently survived Ivehnshaw Tower might have been included, but not with the history he had with Tulius—and Svana for that matter.

It was a delicate situation and he hadn't told her how he would gain entry. Nor had she asked questions. She had learned to not push the man for this kind of detail, especially since she didn't need to be involved. It was enough to know what his presence there would mean, and all she had to do was wait for it to happen and help him survive it.

"So very, very you," she whispered into her goblet. "Killing a man on his wedding day. Who says barbarians can't be poetic?"

"Lords and Ladies here present!" a herald announced from a dais. "Please take your seats in the Holy Sanctuary of the Temple of the Lord High God Janus. The ceremony is about to begin."

Sera followed the others into the massive holy sanctuary that would easily accommodate the crowds assembled on dozens of wooden pews. She was cautious enough to find a seat at the end of one on the aisle and balanced her sword carefully against her leg so it couldn't fall and interrupt the procession that was about to start once all the guests were seated.

Music began and silenced the crowd as the various parties began to walk through. Tulius was first and advanced with a small entourage of the powerful and influential men in Verenvan as his seconds. Others followed, but most of the guests waited impatiently for the bride.

Svana was positively radiant when she entered the sanctuary. The woman was already a vision in her own right but her gown was crafted to make her look like an angel and the overlay trailed behind her like wings. Her handmaidens carried her veil behind her to enforce the sense of delicate beauty that surrounded her.

She beamed at the entire group of people, a woman on her wedding day, but her gaze seemed to search out someone in particular. It settled on the guild captain and the woman gave her a subtle nod before she turned her focus toward the front of the temple.

So Skharr was already there. The man had found a way in after all.

Sera couldn't help a smile as she settled again. It would be an interesting wedding after all.

CHAPTER TWENTY-FIVE

"**B**y the power vested in me, by the Lord High God Janus, I pronounce you husband and wife. Your vows are spoken. Now fulfill them to honor each other."

The priest stepped away from the couple. His part in the ceremony was over, and all that was left for them was to make their vows to each other. This was the legal part of the ceremony that would bind them to each other now that they were bound in the eyes of the gods.

It was a tedious process and one that felt like it would never end.

Tulius stepped in front of Svana and took her hands in his. It looked like a moment of strong emotion between them.

"I swear," he said and his voice carried easily through the sanctuary, "that you will always find safety and warmth in my protection and that of my estate, my lands, and my title. They are all yours. My honor too is merged with yours as one."

She smiled and squeezed his hands gently. "I swear that you will always find the warmth of my body, my estate, my ministrations, and my wisdom to guide you to overcome any challenges you might find in front of you."

They both turned to the crowd and raised their joined hands for others to see them bound together.

Those watching stood as one and clapped and roared loudly to celebrate the union. The music began to play as they turned to face each other again.

The priest stepped forward once more. "The lady and lord, now bound in the holiest of alliances, will offer to one another a taste of what they have vowed to share with the other."

"As my offering," Tulius stated, "you will find a connection to my house. Three of my servants." He motioned for them to come forward from where they had remained out of sight of where the ceremony was proceeding. "They are the hardest-working, and you will find that they will alter our villas to any view you would wish to see. Their skills border on the magical, so every sight that greets your eyes is one that fills your heart with joy."

It was a poetic way to put it, a symbolic gesture that his house was now hers as well.

Svana remained silent for a few moments. Traditionally, she would offer him her body, the action usually represented by a kiss, and he had already begun to lean forward in expectation.

She did not approach him in turn, however. An odd smile touched her lips and instead, she turned to face the crowd, who remained standing while they waited for her response.

"Lord Tulius is a fine man," she said and spoke clearly so everyone present could hear her, helped by the silence that fell over the sanctuary. "A fine man with many fine qualities. He is intelligent, wise, and strong in so many ways. And in one matter he stands above other men, which is why so many in this room favor him."

"What are you doing?" her new husband whispered and tried to grasp her arm.

With a bright smile, she avoided his hand. "That quality is, in fact, that I have never known Lord Tulius to ever let anything false be said about him. As such, my offering is this. He has faced a problem that must be resolved. A man has claimed to have beaten my husband, although he claimed that he has not. This injustice cannot stand. My offering is that the man who has made such libelous claims should present himself before my lord so he can publicly refute those who would so sully his name!"

The woman was enjoying her role of entertaining the crowd, and she knew she had them eating from the palm of her hand.

She turned to Tulius with that same gleam in her eyes. "Let us begin this marriage with you finishing this one thread hanging over the honor you offered me."

The massive red drapes that were hung over the ceremony were covered in dust and were all kinds of hellish to hide in, but Skharr had remained as still as he could and awaited her word. He moved them aside and stepped onto the podium where they stood.

He had to admit that it was more than a little gratifying to see Tulius' face, especially as it paled immediately when he saw the giant of a barbarian suddenly appear in what was supposed to be his moment of triumph.

"No," he whispered. "Not you."

"Oh, yes," he replied with a grin. "Me."

The man looked at his wife and realized that she had made a fool of him in front of the entire nobility of Verenvan.

"Guards!" he shouted. "We have an intruder! Take him! Now!"

He almost fell when a group of three guards charged forward from where they had stood at the edges of the podium, surprise as clear on their faces as it had been on his.

Furious, he turned his attention to Svana. "You whore! You will pay for this!" He reached into his vambrace and drew a small dagger, and she inched away from him, her eyes wide.

But before he could get within striking distance, the sound of a sword being drawn echoed through the temple and the blade slid between the man and his wife.

"You will contain yourself, my lord," Sera said coldly and lifted the blade to his throat.

"You—"

"You will face the threat to your honor as a man." She pressed the blade a little tighter against his skin. "Or die like a dog. You choose."

The dagger clattered to his feet and he turned to see that the guards still hadn't engaged Skharr.

"What are you waiting for?" he roared but remained very still as the blademaster's sword still pressed a little too close for his comfort. "Kill him!"

The guards were all too willing to comply. The barbarian stood his ground, rolled his neck, and drew a deep breath as their pikes were lowered to point at him.

"Been a while since I've had a proper brawl." He rumbled a laugh that settled into a grin. "I did have a dwarf with me the last time, a good fighter, but I suppose you three will have to do."

One of the pikes was thrust toward him, and he swayed to the side and smirked as it slid past where his chest had been less than a moment before.

He snaked his hands out, grasped the haft with both hands, and strained with all the power in him.

With grim determination, the guard maintained his hold on it but his balance was lost and he was dragged to the floor. He finally released the weapon when Skharr wrenched it from his grasp and a powerful kick made sure he would not rise again for the rest of the fight.

The barbarian spun the pike and used the haft to block the thrust from the guard on his left and the blade to block another from the man on his right. He pushed both of them back a step with a wild swing of the weapon.

His range was better than theirs, which certainly counted in his favor.

But his intention was to kill only one man and it wasn't either of the guards. After a moment of thought, he snapped the pike cleanly over his knee.

He tossed the part with the blade aside and kept the haft.

The guards were unsure of what he might have planned but knew what their orders were. They immediately began to move forward and attack.

Skharr parried with the broken pike and tangled the weapons as he locked them in place. He swung to strike the man on his right across the head.

While he wasn't knocked unconscious, he was dazed and released his weapon as he stumbled back as if he struggled to remain on his feet.

The second man released the pike and instead, reached for his sword. The warrior discarded the superfluous weapon and used the broken haft instead to hook the right leg out from under his opponent, who fell onto his back. He lunged immediately and used his rough weapon to knock him unconscious, then made sure he would stay down before he turned his attention to the last man.

By now, the guard had fallen to his knees and swayed gently.

"You'll want to remain where you are, yes?" Skharr asked.

His eyes glazed, the man nodded slowly before he leaned forward onto his hands and vomited onto the marble podium.

That appeared to shock the crowd more than anything else they had seen, and a collective gasp rippled through their ranks.

"Fucking nobles," Skharr muttered under his breath as he approached Tulius, who had retreated from Sera's sword.

The lord realized there was now nothing to save him and he backed away hastily. "I am not the one who poisoned you! You... are looking for a woman. Yes, a woman did the job and she is here today. I saw her. She is..."

He looked into the crowd and the barbarian simply waited. Those present exchanged glances as if to determine who the poisoner was, but even Tulius could see she was no longer present.

The warrior shrugged. "If there is one thing I've learned, it is that if a man is killed, vengeance is not to melt down the sword that was used. You kill the man wielding the sword."

The noble thrust desperately at Skharr with his dagger, but his hand was caught at the wrist and his opponent tightened his hold until he could feel bones grinding on bones.

Finally, he dropped the dagger with a pained cry and tried to run. The barbarian yanked him back and immediately gripped the lord's head with one hand high up at the back and the other along the jaw.

A savage twist resulted in a crack that was heard throughout the sanctuary. No gasp or other sound could be heard as the lord fell to his knees first, then toppled.

The silence remained for a long moment, although a handful of nobles rose from their seats, likely to call more guards to help.

Svana stepped forward quickly to address the group.

"My lords and ladies, please do not be alarmed. This was an honorable disagreement between two nobles of our realm, and Tulius has admitted that he acted in a dishonorable fashion. As such, I will discharge all grievances owed to my house by Skharr DeathEater, the Barbarian of Verenvan!"

Everyone seemed confused and Skharr watched the woman curiously as well. Even so, they were unwilling to argue against the wishes of the bride and began to clap. It started slowly at first but picked up momentum until cheers joined the applause.

"Nobles," Skharr mumbled under his breath and turned to Sera beside him.

"I heard that," she whispered and sheathed her sword.

"I did say it aloud."

"We need to leave. No telling what will happen next. You'll escort me out."

She took his arm firmly and stepped into the same aisle that

Svana had started to walk down to more cheers from the crowd.

"So when she said 'my house...'"

The woman nodded. "She united the houses through the marriage, and with Tulius dead, she is the sole head of it, yes."

He nodded. That wasn't particularly difficult to grasp, fortunately.

One of the doves released from the ceremony was disturbed when the doors opened again. It had returned to collect some of the scraps that had fallen while the guests had been in the area, but when they approached, it took flight again quickly.

It climbed upward toward the elevated sections of the temple, where hanging banners were held in place by sturdy, marble structures jutting from the architecture of the building itself.

After a few minutes of fluttering around, it finally decided to perch on one of these and wait for the humans to leave again so it could eat uninterrupted.

Despite its beady-eyed focus on the scene below, it was startled when a shadow moved from the temple and flew off to find another perch to watch and wait from.

The shadow moved again, this time a little closer to the sunlight, and stared at the procession that now began to exit the temple.

Svana was at the head of it with no handsome lord beside her. Directly behind the woman, her sister looked up and said something to a man who stood head and shoulders taller than her and who was dressed in simple garb.

Sera laughed at something he said and they escorted the radiant Lady Svana to her carriage while the guests continued to mingle.

"Shit." Micah hissed and drew into the shadows cast by the temple.

CHAPTER TWENTY-SIX

There were no other humans around, fortunately.

Not that Skharr cared that other people heard him talking to Horse, but it was something to note. There were those who believed speaking to horses was below them for some reason.

The stallion had been treated to a barrel of apples by the looks of it and showed no sign that he might be considering saving some for later.

"You'll be a fat horse by the time they let you out," the barbarian told him and patted his neck.

Horse snorted, shook his mane, and leaned closer to nudge him in the shoulder.

"I suppose this is as good a home as any horse would ever hope for, even the old ones."

He paused at the sound of footsteps approaching the stables.

"She wants to stud you," he continued and spoke loudly enough for the person to hear. "She has a farm outside the city, by all accounts. It seems almost impossible when you think about it—a simple guild captain is, in fact, a noblewoman of some high standing and not only that but is in possession of a house of her own in the city, as well as an estate beyond the walls that raises horses. That aside, any horse would be forgiven for thinking it is an enjoyable way to live until he realizes how much work it would be."

"I've always loved horses," Sera commented as she stepped inside with them. "Even as a girl, I would approach them without fear. I almost had my fingers bitten off when I stuck my stubby little fingers up a stallion's nose. My mother was very displeased by that. I never blamed the horse, of course. I was an inquisitive child."

Skharr laughed. "I can't say I've ever done that myself, but I did get curious about what one's balls were. I wandered in and took hold of one and was knocked over when the horse ran the other way. While I avoided being trampled, I was cut on my head when I fell on a stone."

"You're joking."

The barbarian shook his head and lifted some of his hair to show a long, white streak. "A scar and a lesson. Never grab a horse by the balls."

It was her turn to laugh. "You would think that lesson could be learned in a less painful manner."

"Sometimes, a child needs to do something stupid to learn that doing stupid things can be dangerous."

Sera smiled and nodded and circled to place her hand on Horse's neck. "Well then, Horse, I made the offer to have you stud at my farm for as long as you want to be there. Skharr said you've accepted the offer, and I trust him. I also trust you. I know that most horses can't speak to folk the way you do to him, and I hoped there might be some element to it that could be seen in a new line of horses of which you'll be the sire."

The stallion snorted and Skharr smirked and shook his head.

She looked at him and scowled. "Would it be idiotic of me to ask what he said?"

"He thinks all horses are as smart as he is. The breeding

should be restricted to finding humans willing to listen to their horses."

"Is that you speaking or Horse?"

"I think we agree on the matter. Would you give us a moment?"

"Of course."

She left the stable and he remained where he was until her footsteps could no longer be heard.

Once she was gone, he stood and moved in front of his old friend.

"You know I'll never forget you," he whispered and pressed his head against the beast's, who leaned closer. "Maybe one day, I'll find you at the farm and I'll drink while you eat all the apples you like while we talk about old tales and all our adventures. You'll have sired dozens of colts, and I'll tell them about all the crazy adventures their father got himself into."

Horse snorted.

"Fine, the adventures I got you into and you dragged me out of."

Skharr closed his eyes as tears welled. His attempt to hold them back failed and they dripped wetly on the stallion's forehead.

"I don't know what else to say. I never wanted to say goodbye to you and assumed these would be the last adventures of my life. I might have done things to make sure that was the case. But you will always be my brother."

Horse nudged him gently and forced him back a step, and he laughed.

"I am being maudlin. I apologize. You know, Ingaret will work on the same farm. She doesn't like the city and not without good reason, so she'll be there. You'll have someone to talk to when I'm away."

He patted the beast on the neck before he moved out of the

stable again and brushed the tears that had escaped roughly on his sleeve as he stepped out and turned toward the house.

Sera was waiting for him outside, seated on a barrel with a curious smile playing across her lips.

As he tried to move away, she jumped off and followed him. "You know, I've thought about why you consider Horse your brother, but I am not sure I can ever wrap my mind around it."

"You love horses."

"Yes."

"Can you respect them? As you might a family member?"

She nodded slowly.

"Then you can wrap your mind around it."

A moment of reflection meant that he could continue to move and she hurried to catch up.

"You will give Ingaret a new home at your farm, yes?"

"She said she preferred to not be in the city. It has too many unpleasant memories so I offered her an alternative."

"Horse likes her. They'll be happy to have each other."

"I like to think so."

The woman under discussion exited the house as they reached the door. Ingaret smiled, put the bucket in her hands down, and wound her arms around his waist.

The barbarian was surprised but he returned the embrace gently.

"I never thought it would take a barbarian's heart to heal me," she whispered into his chest. "Then again, I never thought I would be healed."

He held her at arm's length. "It's not the size of the man that matters, but what he cares about in his heart. In fact, the same could be applied to you. Your desire to heal and move beyond your past did more than I ever could."

"Just accept a fucking thank you." Sera snorted and punched him gently on the shoulder before she turned to Ingaret. "Remember to heal well and that not all men are worthless shits."

The woman laughed and picked her bucket up. "I am needed in the kitchens. I'll see you soon, yes?"

Skharr nodded, reluctant to give an answer he would have to commit to one way or another.

As she moved away, the guild captain still looked like she had heard the most hilarious joke ever. "You know, you don't have to leave. You will always be welcome here."

He shrugged as they continued inside the house, where he still needed to collect most of his possessions that had been left behind. "I try to never overstay my welcome in any one place. You might not believe it, but it has ended in mobs driving me from their town in the past. I have learned my lesson."

"I suppose that is fair enough, but you should know that I didn't only do what I did because I owed you my life and that of my men."

"I know," he said with another noncommittal shrug. "But even so, it might be time for me to move. I feel as though I have gathered enough attention in this city. I have too many enemies, and I don't want them to know where I am and put you and yours in danger on my account. As for any debt you feel you might have incurred, you may now consider us even, I think."

They stopped as they approached the gate of the courtyard, and Sera tilted her head to study him closely.

"Where will you stay while you are still in Verenvan?"

"I think you'll find me at the Swilling Mermaid should you long for my company."

"I wouldn't hold my breath," she said with a grin. "You know, I have heard that many of the ladies among the gentry have begun to ask for your services as a stud. You don't suppose I should tell them where to find you, should I?"

"If I am not mistaken, they already know they can contact me through the guild. The last one asked for me by name and made quite a scene of it as well. I avoid that kind of entanglement, however. As it is with horses, it can be fun until you realize how much work it will be."

"Well, if you say so."

A few of the servants arrived with the possessions he had left and Skharr scowled as he tried to decide how he could carry it all. He had counted on Horse's help in the past, but he would have no such advantage this time.

Sera stared at the barbarian as he set off toward the street. He still stood out easily in the crowds, mostly because those who saw him were desperate to get out of his way, although a few pointed and wondered.

Was that the Barbarian of Theros? She could almost hear the questions, but she wondered something altogether different.

"It is quite nice, isn't it?" Esta asked as she stepped beside her. "I've learned to appreciate the barbarian for all his many qualities, and his ass is certainly what I will miss the most."

With a laugh, she backhanded the woman on her shoulder. "If you think he didn't know you were staring, you are in for a surprise. But you are right, it is quite nice."

"Let him know. If the truth be told, it makes it all the more enjoyable. Although I never thought you would admit that you appreciated a little man-flesh."

"Sure," she conceded and dragged her attention away as Skharr disappeared from view. "But who would settle for only a little, anyway?"

CHAPTER TWENTY-SEVEN

The store was a little smaller than most of the others nearby, although Skharr could see it had room to expand if the owner so chose. It made sense to start small and grow as the need arose.

The mage had recently arrived in the city, although he was surprised to learn that he would remain there and wondered if he might have had something to do with it.

Still, there was nothing to do but approach and see if his face was a welcome sight.

A small bell was struck as he entered, although when he looked up and around the door, he could see no sign of one. A few charms could explain the noise, as well as a few other alterations in the room he now entered. The temperature dropped drastically from the muggy heat outside to something a little more tolerable.

The mage looked up at the warning and a hint of shock appeared in his eyes. He turned his attention hastily to the young noble who stood in front of him and placed a small charm in his hands.

"I think you'll find that this will give you all the stamina you might need in any situation. Keep in mind, however, that the charm should be in contact with your skin at all times while you need it."

"And if it does not work?"

"You can return to me and I will rework the charm myself, free of charge. These types of spells and runes will never be reduced to a simple recipe, so we will need to find what works best for you. In the end, it might be effective but not as effective as it could be. Even so, come back and tell me and I'll fix it with no additional charge."

"Thank you," the boy said, laughed, and grasped the charm like it was a lifeline. "Thank you so very much."

He suddenly realized someone else was in the store and his excitement faded. His face immediately turned bright red as he spun and rushed to the door.

Skharr couldn't help but give him a small grin as pushed out, likely hoping that no one would see him leaving.

"Stamina problems?" he asked with a raised brow.

The mage chuckled. "Yes, well. We were all youths at some point and we can understand that their passion can sometimes be all too brief. All I can do is help to keep him on task, even if his passion is expended. I hear from him that a few ladies would appreciate his continued efforts."

The barbarian shook his head. "When I had those problems, there was no magic present that could help me. I suppose it is a good thing, although it does feel like cheating."

"The way I see it, the young man will learn more the longer he has to enjoy himself." The store owner drew a deep breath. "But enough conversations about the issues of youths. I am genuinely surprised to see you again given that when last we spoke, you had a mind to tackle an almost impossible dungeon. I am glad you were able to pull yourself out of that alive, although I suppose I should begin to expect the impossible from you."

Skharr shook his head. "I have no intention to let anyone

expect anything from me. No expectations mean no one will ever be disappointed."

"If you say so. How did the charm I gave you work?"

He pulled it from under his shirt. "Better than I ever thought it would. In fact, I think I feel more vital now than I have in years."

"Would you mind if I look at it? I was hoping to see how it worked and I'll also be able to determine if it is working as efficiently as possible."

The barbarian removed it and placed it on the counter, and the mage stepped behind it, retrieved a few different glasses, and began to inspect it.

"I don't suppose you found any items in that dungeon that you would be willing to part with?" he asked as he continued to study the charm.

"That is the reason why I am here. There were more than a few in the godsbedammed fucking tower, and I took as many as I could while we fought our way out. In the end, I think I took more charms, trinkets, and weapons than gold and jewels. I hoped they would pay out more than the simple riches would."

The man nodded. "I can understand that. A small charm worth thirty gold pieces is easier to carry than thirty gold pieces, I suppose."

"Oh, trust me, mage, they are worth far more than thirty gold pieces. I may not know much about magic, but I do know that anything found in that hell-spawned dungeon will be worth a great deal more than almost anything else." He put the charms on the counter for the mage to examine.

"You have grown wiser." His companion chuckled. "However, even with that, I suppose I have to tell you that you are the best thing that has happened to me in the last ten years. What do you think would be a proper price for what you have brought me?"

His charm was handed back to him, and Skharr was quick to hang it around his neck again. "I would say each one will be worth hundreds to those collectors and mages who want to study what was brought out of there. But given what I owe you for this charm you have given me, I would be willing to part with all five of them for three hundred gold pieces."

"Three hundred?" The man laughed and shook his head. "I could go as high as two hundred and fifty, but no higher."

"Unfortunate. I was willing to drop my price down to two hundred and seventy-five gold pieces."

That drew another laugh from the proprietor. "Well then, I'll settle for two hundred and seventy-five, simply because we are friends. If you'll wait a moment, I will collect the coin."

Skharr nodded as the mage hurried into the back of his shop and returned a few moments later to place a small chest on the counter.

"Always a pleasure doing business with you, mage."

"You do not wish to count it?"

He shook his head. "I doubt there is a need. It will be deposited in a bank, where they will count it, and if there is a discrepancy… Well, I know where to find you now. "

The mage grinned. "Yes, well. I would not wish to incur your wrath, given that I know how potent it can be."

The barbarian hefted the chest and nodded at the weight of it. "Besides, I have other magical items I might wish to sell once I've examined them to see what I want to keep for myself." He paused and fixed the man with a curious look. "What happened ten years ago?"

"Hmm?"

"You said I was the best thing to happen to you in ten years. What happened in those ten years?"

"My wife left me for a cleric who had a rod up his ass, and the two have been miserable with each other ever since."

The looks he received from the other mercenaries were more than a little discomforting.

Skharr noted a few who stared at him with something akin to adoration, while grudging respect could be seen in others. More, however, glared with what he knew was envy and each one felt that if he could come out of the tower with two others, they could do it as well.

They failed to take into account that it was three out of hundreds, and as it turned out, they were the lucky ones. The reality was that there had been every chance that not a single one of them would reach the end of it.

He doubted he would have survived had it not been for the friendly and timely intervention of a certain deity.

Pennar clapped briskly when he saw him and waved him closer with bellows of laughter.

"I knew you would return, laddie!" the man roared, stepped out from his stall, and embraced him. A little uncomfortably, he returned it.

"Glad to hear of the faith you had in me," he admitted when the guildmaster finally released him. "I suppose someone had to. My faith faltered a few times while I was there."

"Not unheard of, but you came out in the end and when the bards want to make songs about your exploits, you will have to avoid any talk like that. Songs are always sung about heroes who never doubted themselves."

While all of that might or might not be true, he wasn't there to debate the matter.

"I am afraid I came here on business. A certain amount is owed to the guild for my contract and I would see it filled without delay."

Pennar nodded. "The guild is certainly glad that you chose them over the Lord High God Janus."

"The Lord High God—"

"Janus is an ass, yes. I've heard your opinions on it. And one would think that he would strike you down for your insolence, although it does not appear to have occurred."

The barbarian looked at the group that had begun to gather around them. Most still had business to attend to, but they had paused to catch a glimpse of him. He wasn't sure he liked the idea that he was a famed figure in the city. It attracted attention, something that eventually soured every time no matter how positive it started.

Without further comment, the guildmaster donned his pince-nez, studied a few scrolls on the table in front of him, and pushed one toward him. "All told, the guild does not demand an additional percentage of your earnings and in this case, I suppose you are thankful for that. The agreed fee came to thirty gold pieces and five silvers."

Skharr had remembered the amount from his last dungeon's earnings, and he took a pouch from where it was hidden inside his cloak. Heavy though it was, he hadn't wanted to risk it being picked by a thief on his way to the guild.

Pennar nodded and poured the coins out on the counter. His eyebrows raised when he counted the coins past forty.

"Feeling a mite generous, are we?"

"I felt I owed the Lord High God Theros for my good fortune. That which is not taken by his guild should be put toward his temple."

"Aye, that will be appreciated indeed."

Skharr bowed his head slightly and tried to ignore a few whispers from around him. Pious was a word he heard from most of them, but he simply kept his head low as he watched the man collect the coins again.

"I don't think I've ever heard of a barbarian from the west feeling particularly devout," the guildmaster admitted. "I thought your people didn't believe in gods of any kind and remembered only heroes, both living and dead."

"Maybe out west. It would appear that the gods have some

sway here or at least more than they do in my homeland. I would say that if there was ever a place or a time to pay them their dues, it would be here and now."

Pennar nodded. "I merely can't remember the last time I've ever heard the words 'barbarian' and 'devout' in the same sentence. It most certainly does not roll easily off the tongue."

"No, it does not," he admitted with a small smirk and patted the man's shoulder. "It was good to see you again. If you need me, I will be at the Mermaid."

"I doubt you will need to work for the next couple of years, not if you don't want to."

He shrugged. "Maybe I enjoy the work."

CHAPTER TWENTY-EIGHT

Skharr knew he had to return the weapons he had been loaned by the dwarves. He was loath to see them go but it was a necessity and it was what was owed. They'd had no compulsion to lend them to him in the first place, and he wouldn't deny that he would most likely have not survived if he'd relied on the equipment he had.

But he had grown attached to what they had given him, despite the fact that they almost certainly wouldn't let him keep them or even sell them to him.

Throk AnvilForge had been right. Any collector worth his salt and with more coin than he could spend would want to possess the weapons and armor carried by one of the few who survived Ivehnshaw Tower.

A little reluctantly, he stepped into the forge, where the young dwarf who manned the front of the shop recognized him immediately.

"You'd like to see my father, I suppose?"

He nodded. "Aye, if it's not too much to ask. I am here to return these fine items and see about the progress made on the weapon I ordered."

"Follow me, then. Mind your head."

The barbarian did as he was told and wandered behind the youth into the back of the forge. The familiar harsh heat greeted him, as well as the sound of dozens of hammers on metal.

"Keep your eyes on your work, you filthy maggot spawn!" a familiar voice shouted from deep inside. "If I need to check every piece going from the hammers to the flames, we won't be worthy to shape plowshares!"

"I guess I cannot disagree with that," Skharr said as he approached Throk with a small grin.

The dwarf's foul temper vanished almost immediately as he caught a glimpse of the massive barbarian. "If it isn't the fucking hero returned with his spoils. It's good to see you again, laddie! Alive and unharmed, no less."

"Alive, anyway."

The smith chuckled, which appeared to startle those he had been berating and he glared at them. "Did I say you could take your eyes off your fucking work? Perhaps I'll take a few burning coals and put them in the sockets. It might be that will help you to see better."

"But you...you laughed, sir."

Throk scowled deeply but he finally nodded. "Aye, I'll let this slip happen once and you are rightfully surprised. But now that you know it happens, I won't let you muck things up again without consequences. Get back to it, lads! I won't pay for idle hands."

The rest of the workers hurried to obey and resumed their rhythm as the proprietor gestured for his visitor to follow him into his office.

"You know, I did come out with another dwarf in tow," the barbarian told him once they were in the privacy and relative silence of the small space. "Kondel TowersSon—a tough bastard and an expert with that ax of his. He retrieved a fine weapon too, one he said was forged by one of his ancestors."

"Yaragrim TowersSon's battle-ax?"

He nodded.

"Well, then." Throk looked impressed. "Now that is reason to celebrate. That weapon has not been seen by living eyes in…well, about seven hundred and forty-seven years come next spring. You don't think he'll be willing to sell it to me, do you?"

Skharr shook his head.

"I did not think so but I'll make the offer anyway. Something ridiculous enough to make him at least think about it. But as for you…well, you must come to our clan home here, all made from stone brought from our mountains. None in this city get in or out without invitation, and I might even claim that it's a safer place than the keep of this fucking godsforsaken pox-riddled city."

"You think the guard would give you trouble over that?"

The dwarf snorted. "They can't come in either. They made us pay for the land we bought above, but none thought to charge for the land below. As long as they know of what happens there, they don't mind our digging. And all the better, we need not worry them about any of the creatures that sleep there."

"Do those creatures exist?"

"Not in these parts. At least, none that we've seen and we all know the signs. Wyrms and the like make their presence known. But there is no need to speak of that. Two days hence, there will be a feast, the likes of which will not be seen beyond the dwarven halls in the mountains. You will be in attendance, and we will speak more at that time."

"How could I refuse?" Skharr nodded and finally lifted the wrapping that contained the armor and weapons he had been loaned, with the spear protruding although the head was covered. "I don't think I could have escaped from that tower without these weapons. They were well-used and appreciated."

"We will always put our faith in DeathEaters." Throk collected the weapons and armor, examined them quickly, and inspected any possible damage done to them. "And as you have proven, that faith is very rarely misplaced. The originals will go for a high price on the market, of course, but replicas can be made, and I'll see to it that you have the first. You, laddie, will make me a rich dwarf."

"You are the AnvilForged, Throk," Skharr rumbled. "We DeathEaters know how rich your clan is."

The dwarf smirked. "Richer, then. Does that satisfy you?"

They shared a chuckle as he turned toward the door and the master smith followed him.

"I look forward to seeing you two days hence," he said and shook the dwarf's hand.

"Aye, laddie." Throk took a deep breath. "Already destroying dungeons and killing royalty. What will this barbarian be up to next?"

"I try not to plan that far ahead in my life. Tends to make things more enjoyable."

The Mermaid was familiar and comfortable and there was an odd feeling of home, especially for those who were a long way from their real homes. It was a viable decision by the owners, given how many traveled far to stay in the city. Sailors and mercenaries, for the most part, would find their place there.

Skharr knew he fell in the latter category, and it was an interesting thought to say the least. There had been no home for him for decades now, and his connection to one place after so long felt unfamiliar.

Even the innkeeper greeted him like an old friend and made sure a hot platter of freshly prepared food was set on his table despite his arrival a few hours after the midday meal rush had passed. He settled the barbarian to the side of the common room so he could eat in peace.

It was possibly due to the fact that he was the talk of the town in one way or another, which meant he would feel all the more that he was an outsider—an oddity that would lose its appeal in short order.

He would have to move on soon. It was best to let these people think about him in his absence.

A few gazes lingered on him, but now that most of the crowd had moved on to their work, the establishment was emptier. Those who remained wanted their peace and quiet and were willing to extend others the same courtesy.

The warrior narrowed his eyes when the calm was interrupted in an abrupt fashion. Everyone looked at the doors of the inn when they were thrust open and a young lad rushed in, looked around the room, and finally located the innkeeper. A few words were exchanged before the proprietor pointed toward his corner of the room.

The boy rushed to where he was seated.

"Good afternoon, sir," he gasped, clearly out of breath.

"I'll assume the guild sent you?"

"Aye, but it was at the behest of Captain Ferat. She asked me to inform you that she will leave the city with a caravan in need of protection in five days and asks if you would be willing to be a part of that escort."

"Five days, you say?" Skharr asked, and the boy nodded. "A large caravan, not a convoy?"

"Those were her words, sir."

Before he could answer, he was interrupted when the doors of the inn shuddered on their hinges as a group of five entered, stamped their boots, and laughed loudly, drawing scowls of displeasure from the patrons.

"The barbarian I spoke of tried to run away," a familiar voice said loudly above the laughter of his comrades. "He ran into the rest of my group, and I swear to you, he looked like he preferred to engage the other six rather than me."

Skharr knew the voice and the face and allowed a smile to supplant his irritation. This particular thief never failed to bring amusement.

"Tell Captain Ferat I'll join her party." He fixed his gaze on the five newcomers who immediately moved to one of the tables. "I'll need to know what supplies to bring, so ask her to send me a list at least a day before."

"Aye, sir."

"Now leave. It will not be safe for a child in the coming minutes."

The boy did as he was told and ran out of the inn as quickly as his feet could carry him. Skharr stood slowly from his table and walked to where the innkeeper watched the new arrivals warily.

He placed a ruby on the counter in front of the man and pushed it across to make sure he knew the gemstone was for him.

"For the damages," he said quietly. "A fight is about to break out."

Felix looked longingly at the clear red stone but shook his head. "I'll tell you what I'll do, barbarian. If you manage to toss those troublemakers from my establishment, I'll not charge you for your next meal. Once it is all said and done, I'll charge you for anything you happen to break. How does that sound?"

The barbarian turned to focus on the group that still hadn't seen him. He had a feeling they would be well on their way to the door if they realized they had intruded on him again.

"Hellsfire and devil turds, I'd break their bones for free. But if you'll make a meal of it, I'll be sure to keep most of the mess beyond the walls of the Mermaid."

"I'd appreciate it."

Skharr rolled his neck and drew a deep breath as he turned

and walked slowly toward the group. It had been a little too long since he'd been in a fucking ball-busting, jaw-breaking, nose-crushing brawl. He doubted the pilgrims-turned-thieves would provide a proper fight, but in the absence of one, they would do.

They would do just fine.

AUTHOR NOTES - MICHAEL ANDERLE
NOVEMBER 13, 2020

Thank you for reading this second book of *Skharr DeathEater* and the *Author Notes* here in the back.

Since I wrote last time, I've acquired a signed Boris Vallejo print and a signed and numbered 8" tall bronze Red Sonja™ casting.

Mind you, I'm pretty sure based on the quality and the price I paid for the figurine that by "bronze," they mean someone spat bronze on the outside, not that it was cast in bronze. That's a shame, really. It's a nice item.

I'm also fairly sure (for those who know what Red Sonja normally wears) that I shouldn't get anything taller and more robust. My wife thought the small model at about 8" was cute. I'm not trying for anything taller.

I enjoy my life.

I'm excited to share that we ARE going to at least five books in the series (I expect more, but I can confirm five books because we have five covers.)

Hopefully, you the fans love the series enough to support it with reviews and passing along to friends that it exists and you enjoyed it.

In these first two stories, Skharr stayed around this city. In the next story (*The Defender*) he will range far afield and get into trouble. At the end of that story, we get a tantalizing taste of what Skharr was before we met him in book one. Then, in book 04 (in production now, presently titled *GodKiller*) we meet a female paladin on a sabbatical.

It's fun times, I *promise*.

Well, it's fun for us the readers. I'm not really sure Theros is very happy that Skharr might be messing with the deity's Paladin, but that situation will handle itself.

In time.

Like, maybe book 05?

I look forward to chatting with you again in the next Skharr DeathEater™ Adventure!

Regards,
Michael

(P.S. – High Lord God Janus is an *ass!*)

CONNECT WITH THE AUTHOR

Connect with Michael Anderle

Website: http://lmbpn.com

Email List: http://lmbpn.com/email/

Social Media:

https://www.facebook.com/LMBPNPublishing

https://twitter.com/MichaelAnderle

https://www.instagram.com/lmbpn_publishing/

https://www.bookbub.com/authors/michael-anderle

Made in United States
North Haven, CT
29 May 2022

19646688R00157